'Tom Carlisle combines his gothic elements — the cursed landowning family, the uncanny pact, the lurking primal presence, the dark side of faery, the hero's reluctant return to his roots — into a potent magical brew often evocative of Machen but grippingly original.'
Ramsey Campbell

'An intriguing debut.'
Priya Sharma, Shirley Jackson and British Fantasy award-winning author of *All the Fabulous Beasts*

'There are worlds beneath worlds in Tom Carlisle's compelling debut novel, which evokes Robert W. Chambers' *The King in Yellow* in its sustained Gothic creepiness and its undercurrent of unspeakable cosmic horror.'
Tim Major, author of *Snakeskins*

'An intriguing folk horror novel, with a Faustian twist and a family drama at its core — right up my street!'
Paul Kane, award-winning and #1 bestselling author of *Sherlock Holmes and the Servants of Hell*, *Before* and *Arcana*

'*Blight* embroiders an intriguing historical setting around a primal fear, to create a lurching nightmare. A splendid addition to the annals of truly nasty folklore.'
E. Saxey, author of *Unquiet*

Blight

Tom Carlisle

TITAN BOOKS

Blight
Print edition ISBN: 9781803360720
E-book edition ISBN: 9781803360737

Published by Titan Books
A division of Titan Publishing Group Ltd.
144 Southwark Street, London SE1 0UP
www.titanbooks.com

First Titan edition: October 2023
10 9 8 7 6 5 4 3 2 1

A CIP catalogue record for this title is available
from the British Library.

Printed and bound by CPI Group (UK) Ltd,
Croydon, CR0 4YY

To Mel –
I finally wrote you that ghost story

"What profit is there in my blood, when I
    go down to the pit?
Shall the dust praise thee?"

PSALM 30:9

1

1883

THE LETTER came to the house he shared with Gabriel. A timid knock at the door, the postboy slipping the envelope through the crack to James. It was from Harringley Manor, he knew that right away: he saw it in the smoothness of the paper, its pointless opulence.

He slipped it into his jacket pocket, hoping Gabriel would stay dozing a little longer. James knew how Gabriel would react if he saw it. He'd tell James to throw it away unopened, might even take it from him – gently, tenderly, but forcefully. Maybe he'd be right.

But Gabriel thought that throwing away your history was easy. For him it was: he didn't have the weight of a family name behind him, the shadow of a great estate over his life. James knew what his father would think if he could see this neat little two-roomed apartment – to him it would seem poky, cluttered, a far cry from the Manor's Tudor grandeur.

This block had been built with high ideals, to provide a superior dwelling for Newcastle's working men so they in turn could work for the good of the city. That was the vision, although James's father wouldn't have seen it that way. He'd have seen a red-brick building full of strivers, upstarts – men just a stone's throw from the Quayside with ideas above their station.

As he passed through the living room James picked up a small and rather tatty yellow grammar book from the end-table by the door, tucking it into his inside pocket. It was a gift for the coffee-seller. Its shabbiness bothered Gabriel: he and James had worked hard to carve out a life for themselves here, but sometimes all this still felt like a façade, a veneer of respectability that could crumble at a single misstep.

James had seen Gabriel's displeasure when he returned from work yesterday holding the book. Gabriel hadn't said anything, but James had bristled at his silent judgement nonetheless: what was the point of reinventing yourself, he wanted to ask, if you couldn't reinvent yourself as someone you liked? But there'd been no point picking that fight again. After all, a life like theirs was built on compromises – and James was well practised at holding his tongue.

Outside the city was stirring – and although the sun was yet to reach their block, there was already a steady stream of men heading up the steep hill towards the city centre. The street was dotted with coffee-sellers brewing up over their braziers, and bakers' boys trying to get close enough to the flames to warm themselves without being obvious. James pulled his jacket tighter around him – it was smart but not especially warm, another concession to looking respectable.

For the past six months he'd bought his coffee from a

boy by the name of William, whose efforts to better himself were painfully obvious. There was nothing casual about him: from his deferential manner to his poorly concealed Geordie accent, and his damp, recently laundered clothes steaming in the heat from the fire, everything screamed of self-consciousness. It was all so familiar to James. Even after seven years here, he still remembered what it had been like as a newcomer, trying to convince the city's businessmen to take him on as a clerk and dreading the darkness of the slums if they refused.

William was already lifting the coffee pot as James approached with two mugs in hand, and today James handed over the grammar book along with his payment. 'Here,' he said. 'Sorry it's not in better condition.'

The boy took the little yellow book, turning it over in his hands and frowning. 'Much obliged, sir,' he mumbled, nodding in gratitude but not meeting James's eye. 'What's it about?'

'Could be just what you need,' said James, himself a little awkward. 'Less exciting than a novel, but a damn sight better for helping you understand how to blend in.'

William met his eye now, his expression quizzical. 'Blend in, sir?' Behind his eyes there was a glimmer of fear, as though he were a frightened animal recognising an unseen predator.

James put a hand on his shoulder. 'It's okay,' he said. 'You're doing well. But—' He closed his eyes, aware of what Gabriel would say if he heard James speaking like this. 'Let me know if I can help in any way. It's a hard thing, what you're doing.'

The boy stuck out his lower lip and nodded. 'Thank you, sir,' he said, thoughtful. 'Thank you very much.' He sniffed, tucked the yellow book into his inside pocket. 'Enjoy your coffee.'

Back home in the firelight, James removed the letter from his pocket. The hand was his brother's.

James,

I'm writing with a heavy burden. Father's not himself, & he hasn't been for some time. His mind isn't what it was. Last year he stepped down as a magistrate, & now he barely leaves the house. He's confused, agitated even.

God only knows I'd hoped never to hear the Tall Man's name again – my hand trembles even to write it – but I'm afraid that, in his old age, Father has returned to those superstitions, & I fear I'm not strong enough to help him back to sanity alone.

Perhaps you buried this stage of your life long ago. I would not blame you for that. But if you retain any love for this family, for your father, I urge you to return as quickly as you're able. I fear that Father may not have long left, & although he may be beyond help, I hope we can yet save his legacy.

Enough. I have made my plea, & I trust it to God. I pray this finds you, & that you see fit to set aside whatever bitterness still dwells in you in pursuit of reconciliation. Send word of your coming when you're able.

I remain your brother,
Edward.

He recognised that tone right away – it was the house speaking, the voice in the back of his head he spent every day trying to bury. Here in Newcastle, people spoke to him plainly, without that peculiar blend of assertiveness and deference; that was why he liked it.

But he heard the fear behind Edward's words too, and knew right away that this was a letter he couldn't bury. Maybe Edward didn't understand what it meant, but James did. If the Tall Man had returned, if his father had truly seen him again, then all his family's efforts had failed – and the void was reaching out into the world once more.

Half an hour later James was shoving clothes into his travelling bag, Gabriel watching from the doorway; no matter how casual Gabriel's posture, he couldn't hide the tension in his jaw and shoulders. 'Don't do this, James,' he said, his careful tone a little strained. 'You're out of that world. Don't put yourself back into it.'

James only glanced up, keen not to meet Gabriel's eye for too long. He couldn't bear that look of concern. 'I have to, Gabriel,' he said. 'Pass me my stick.'

Gabriel held out the gnarled, twisted thing across outstretched palms, as he had the day he'd given it to James. It was still the most beautiful thing James owned. 'You broke with them once,' Gabriel said, holding onto the stick for a second longer than he needed to. 'No sense in trying to mend it now.'

James shook it off. 'They're not bad people,' he said, searching for his shaving brush, his razor. 'Just insular.'

Gabriel scowled. 'You told me you were done with them,' he

said. 'Looks to me like your brother only had to ask and you're on a coach back to Yorkshire.'

James paused and studied Gabriel's face. The familiar contours he loved so much: the harsh line of stubble at Gabriel's jaw, and those resolute, pained eyes, as if the whole world could be conquered with enough effort. It was madness to leave him. And yet. 'That's not fair,' James said eventually. 'My father's in trouble, Gabriel. Real trouble.'

'He broke your leg so badly you couldn't walk for a month. You don't owe him anything.'

'He's still my father.'

Gabriel shook his head. 'You promised me you wouldn't go back, James. You swore.'

'I didn't promise you that,' James said. 'You heard what you wanted to hear.'

He saw Gabriel flinch at that, and he felt dreadful. But he could see Gabriel recalling their conversation too, and realising his error: there was a resigned look in his eyes. 'You know I can't lose you,' Gabriel said finally, holding James's gaze. 'I told you that.' He paused, sighed. 'So help me understand. You've spent the best part of a decade building yourself up from the ground after what your father did to you. After what that place did. Why the hell would you want to go back?'

James ran his hands through his hair, trying to justify the decision to himself as much as to Gabriel. 'He's an honourable man,' he said eventually. 'Fought to keep the mine open for as long as he could. Put himself forward as a magistrate when the seams ran dry. He's spent the past twenty years trying to make sure that village is safe and prosperous.' He sighed. 'He has his flaws. But what he did, he did to protect me and Edward.'

'That's exactly the kind of statement that tells me you shouldn't go back there.'

'Gabriel, I have to go.' He could feel a headache coming on. There was already too much to think about. He didn't need this too. 'I suppose I'd best send him a telegram. Let him know to expect me.'

But Gabriel was still brooding. 'If you were going back to cut his throat—'

'Listen,' James said. 'My father spent years telling Edward and me to beware of the Tall Man. Years.' At that name, James felt a familiar vertiginous terror – as though by speaking of him, he might be summoned here. 'Now my father's gone looking for the Tall Man, although God only knows why. If he's done that, then things are worse up there than I ever imagined.'

'They're not your responsibility anymore.'

'You don't know what it's like growing up in a family like mine,' he said, his voice pained. 'Families like mine have a duty to the land and its people. You're connected to them.' He rolled his eyes, trying to bridge the gap with this man who was so unlike him. 'I don't suppose you'd know what I mean if I called it *noblesse oblige*?'

That almost made Gabriel smile. 'As if you even had to ask.'

'People rely on families like mine. They look up to them. Even now.' He paused, not wanting to catch the look of disdain in Gabriel's eye. 'If my father's in trouble, it's not just him who's affected. You know that.'

They were silent a moment – both thinking of the day, not two weeks ago, when they'd stumbled through a crack in the world and seen the void first-hand. It was coming for them. There was no longer any denying that.

'And what about your duty to me?'

'Don't do that, Gabriel. Please.'

'You say you owe this to them,' said Gabriel, crossing the room to James and putting both hands on his shoulders. 'But your life is here, James. With me. Don't forget that.'

'Never.'

2

B Y T H A T afternoon James was jammed into the corner of a stagecoach, wedged onto a bench with four other men in various stages of disarray: factory workers, judging by their grimy hands, no doubt heading out to Yorkshire to seek work in the clean air.

He felt a deep and lingering tiredness in his bones. Through the window came flickers of a landscape half-remembered. Long, straight roads disappearing into the horizon. A steep valley, with sharp rocks buried in a blanket of heather that was just beginning to bloom. There were houses pinned back against the moor, their doors and windows small, their stones weathered by the years.

On the roadside were the skeletons of sheep, bleached by the sun, their bones angular pictures of agony. Men in rags working the fields. Vast towers of stone James supposed were cairns – he didn't recall them being so imposing. How much loss it must have taken to create such a monument: a village destroyed in a landslide, a whole town taken by pestilence.

The priest used to speak of home as a sanctuary: a place with doors you could shut against the world, a place of rest and refuge. *Man is forever restless until he finds his home in God*, that was how he put it. But the only place James had ever felt that was with Gabriel.

Never here: not in these hills, beneath this bloody sunset.

James's last memory of home was a door in the walls of his adolescent bedroom: a rectangle of pure darkness, the wood panelling set to one side, revealing a tunnel stretching impossibly deep into the guts of the house. He remembered running for it, running with a sense of elation so strong that it could almost have been terror – knowing how close he was to being free of that place—

And then somebody had grabbed him roughly from behind and when he turned, there was his father's red face, and the mahogany cane cracking through the air. The first blow knocked the wind from him, but that was only the beginning of his agony. Harder and harder the blows came – into his shoulders, his sides, his head – until, finally, he found merciful oblivion.

He assumed after that his father had stopped. James spent the next two weeks in bed, reading as best he could through a black eye, but it was six more weeks before he could walk on his right leg – even now it was still slightly crooked, and ached on cold winter nights. He and his father never spoke of that night again: he wondered if the old man even remembered it.

∞

He spent a sleepless night in an inn outside Castleton and awoke stiff and cold, but the coach soon sorted that out. Its windows were steamy before he even got in and after less than an hour there was sweat plastering his hair to his head. All around was the smell of unwashed men. Shit and mud and piss and blood.

Everything he'd brought from the house reminded him of Gabriel. The yellowing pamphlet with its story of a subterranean world, the pages now soft and crumbling. The sketchbooks filled with their angular caricatures of the neighbours. And the stick, of course. That beautiful, twisted thing was the first thing he reached for in the mornings.

If only he'd realised how alone he'd feel without Gabriel by his side. But Gabriel was a hundred miles away now – a lifetime away, at least while the railways stopped at the moors.

James wondered if anyone in Yorkshire would know him when they saw him. His case bore a different name, and the emblem of a different family – he'd bought it for sixpence, in the corner of a public house, on his first week in the city – and these days he had a new voice too. Coarse and abrasive, filled with the flattened vowels and rough slang he'd learned in Newcastle. He'd been using it so long now it felt it had always been his. He had the same old face, though, albeit nicked with scars, and gaunt with hunger and sleeplessness. When he looked in the mirror he couldn't see much resemblance to his father, except a certain sly smile when he got his way. He supposed that meant he looked more like his mother, not that he could remember any of the paintings of her now. Supposedly they weren't a good likeness anyway.

Once more he removed Edward's letter from his pocket, and reread it carefully. He'd been foolish to come back here. Haste and grief had made him sentimental.

But he couldn't forget what lurked beneath the soil. The hum of the void, its monstrous force, drawing the world down into itself. The Tall Man its unlikely warden.

All those years his father thought himself wiser than the Tall Man. Thought he could defy those iron rules, save this place from darkness by his own strength. He'd believed he could teach them a better way. How wrong he'd been.

The view from the coach window should have been charming. The stagecoach rolled over the moors and into the village, its long road bordered on one side by houses and, on the other, falling away to the village green. In places, James could even see the skeletal frames of several massive new structures, each of them a monument to hope – and then, lining the hillside dead ahead of him, were the woods. The sky was clear, the birds singing, and all James could think about was the blood he'd seen shed on this street, the terror he'd felt amongst those trees.

He'd thought he remembered this place, but his memories had been only pencil sketches, their shadows a pale imitation of the greater dark.

When he saw the house at the top of the hill, its silhouette vast and austere against the darkening sky, he felt his skin prickle.

It was just as it had always been; of course it was.

3

WHEN THE coach crested the hill, James saw Edward waiting by the gatehouse, his long coat pulled tight and his arms folded to his chest. He hung back, motionless, while the coachman hauled James's travelling case from the roof in a single swift motion and set it down on the ground. He seemed content to let James bear the weight of his own luggage – but then James supposed he shouldn't have expected to be welcomed home like the prodigal son.

As a boy Edward had been ruddier and more robust than James, a stocky blonde boy who always seemed better fed. Now he too seemed a little worn thin, the hollows in his cheeks deeper than they once were, the skull beneath his skin easier to discern. Age had softened the distinction between them, pulled their faces into a warped mirror image of one another.

Edward was studying James too, taking in his cheap work suit, apparently unsure whether to offer a hand or to try and embrace his brother. He didn't look much like he wanted to do either. Eventually he stepped forward from where he'd been leaning against the wall and gave James a slight, formal nod.

'Thank you for coming,' he said. 'I didn't expect you to arrive so soon.'

'I'm grateful you let me know. I've been away a long time.'

'Yes, you weren't that easy to track down.' Edward sounded prickly, almost offended.

'I wasn't trying to be,' said James, trying to sound conciliatory. He'd not come here to pick a fight. 'I didn't leave home under the best terms.'

'I suppose not. It wasn't the easiest place to grow up.'

The house lay behind Edward, at the end of a long driveway. James couldn't see it, but he could feel it. 'Tell me about Father,' he said, not wanting to let the silence linger too long. 'How is he? What can I do?'

'You remember how he used to warn us about the Tall Man? Told us he was a liar, a curse on this place, that we shouldn't even entertain the thought of him in case he appeared?' Edward was silent, letting the memory hang in the air.

'You think he's changed his tune,' said James eventually. 'He's starting to reconsider.'

Edward nodded. 'For the past three months he's been preoccupied with the Tall Man. Obsessed with how this place has changed since you left, and how he's to blame.' He studied the village below him, little pinpricks of light among the blackness. 'There's a darkness here,' he said, 'I can't deny it. But now he seems to be – seeking it out.'

'What's he seen? What's happened?'

'The servants say he's taken to wandering at night. When they find him, there's mud on his feet, and more than once he's vanished for hours without leaving the slightest trace...' Edward trailed off. 'I thought all of this had stopped when you left us,' he said after a second or two.

'Do you think he's trying to get to the woods? To... him?'

At this Edward glanced around, as though realising where they were for the first time. As he did, a sudden, horrible flicker of memory assailed James: he was sheltering on the edge of the woods in a storm, not more than twelve years old, and a figure was coming towards him through the sheeting rain, tall and thin. He felt a roiling in his guts, a nausea that had to show on his face.

'Let's head on up,' Edward said. 'I expect you're hungry. Most days the coach rattles by here an hour or so earlier than this.' He set off towards the house at pace, leaving James to stump after him.

Everywhere James looked there was decay. What grass he could see was patchy and brown, the trees gnarled and twisted. The long pathway was lined with rotting shrubs; where James recalled bright colours, now there were only wilted leaves at the end of long, drooping stems. He could make out dandelions in the shrubbery, their bright yellow heads bobbing in the breeze, swaying in a hypnotic dance. Ragweed, nettles, a great clamour of weeds snarling over one another. The air was heavy with the smell of rot.

'I don't remember all this being so overgrown,' he said when he caught up with Edward, but Edward seemed not to hear him, so determined was he to get inside. A short way up the driveway, James came to a halt, his leg in agony.

'Edward, wait,' he called, and to James's relief his brother stopped too. His shoulders were slumped in a sigh. 'I can't do this.' Edward still hadn't said anything, and James had the sense he was trying to muster his courage. 'There's more, isn't there?' he said.

Edward turned to face him. 'You remember Janey?'

James searched his memory; so much of what he remembered from his time here was hazy. Eventually it came to him. 'The groundskeeper's daughter? Stocky little thing?'

'The groundskeeper herself, now, actually,' said Edward, raising an eyebrow. 'Her father passed away a few years ago.'

Another flash of memory: finding Edward in the nursery, watching from the floor as a young woman sliced the flesh of her arm from wrist to elbow, her face placid. He swallowed back his nausea. 'Like the – like the governesses?'

'No,' said Edward curtly. 'His heart gave out. He'd been unwell for a while.'

'Thank God,' said James, a little shakily. 'Still – I'm sorry.'

'Don't be,' said Edward. 'It's not as though we were close.'

Of course they weren't. 'The estate's a lot for a young girl to take on,' said James. 'Hardly surprising if it got the better of her.'

'Actually, Janey was excellent,' said Edward, a little affronted. 'Until she got herself pregnant.' Edward left the statement hanging, as though he'd have liked to disown it.

'And the child—' James swallowed hard. 'Did she leave when it was born?'

Edward shook his head, a brisk, irritated gesture. 'The child's gone,' he said, kicking at the dirt. 'And Janey too. She took off a couple of weeks ago, and took the boy with her.'

'Do you think something... happened to him?'

'God knows. Maybe.' He sighed. 'Or maybe she got out. Like you did. Ran away.' They were in view of the house now, its imposing frontage casting an even deeper shadow over them. In the gloom his brother looked haunted, his cheeks gaunt and his face hollow, as though something were eating him from the inside out.

'Is there any chance it was the old man's?' said James, recalling the night he'd stumbled across his father in the village, a local woman on his arm. Until then he'd never realised the old man had desires. 'Was he tupping her?'

Edward winced at his brother's coarseness. 'Listen,' he said. 'I don't mean to sound callous. But this isn't really about Janey either.' He folded his arms, apparently deeply uncomfortable. 'You're an uncle,' he said. 'You'll meet Sophia – my wife – up at the house.' He wouldn't meet James's eye, sounded almost bitter. 'You've a nephew. He's nearly three months old now.'

'My God,' said James, dizzy with sudden emotion. 'I didn't even know you'd married – I mean, congratulations, for heaven's sake – that's wonderful news.'

'Is it?' said Edward. 'Because I'm not so sure.' His voice trembled. 'Do you think the Tall Man will stop if he's got Janey's child?'

So that was what Edward wanted: reassurance. He looked utterly dejected, but James had lived in this house long enough that he knew there was no point in trying to comfort him. 'You want me to tell you he can be stopped,' he said, 'but I'm not sure he can.' He could feel the terror welling up in him again – he'd swallowed it for so long, but never entirely buried it. 'If he's back, Edward – if he wants your son – then you have to get out of this place once and for all. There's no other way.'

'Of course,' said Edward with a resigned nod. 'I was worried that's what you'd say.'

'Is that why you're still here? Duty?'

Edward glanced down in the direction of the village, now no longer visible beneath the thick canopy of trees. 'You know that if we leave this place, it'll be the end of it. God only knows how Father's been keeping it all afloat since the mine closed.' He rubbed his temple. 'Half the people here work on our land. If we abandon them for the city it'll devastate them.'

James felt as though he'd lived through this argument a hundred times. 'And what about your duty to your wife, or your son? Have you thought about how living here will impact them? This place would be bleak enough without the Tall Man.'

Edward's pained expression suggested he'd thought about this more than he'd like. 'What will it look like if we run, James?' He shook his head. 'If we abandon the village?'

'When did you last go down there? I don't know that those villagers think about the Harringleys all that much, if at all.'

'That may well be true,' said Edward with a little nod. 'Still. Our presence here counts.'

'Only if you've got something worth living up to.'

That stung Edward, James could tell. There was a tension at

his jaw now, a defensiveness. 'I can't leave,' he said, running a hand through his thinning hair. 'It'll be the end of this family.'

'Wouldn't that be a relief?'

Edward's anger came without warning. 'No!' he yelled, barely able to look at James. There were years of history behind his words. 'I'm not sure you ever loved this family, James,' he said, staring into the trees. 'As long as you've been alive you've been running away from it.'

'That's not true,' said James, trying to hold his own temper.

'You've been in hiding for seven years,' Edward muttered. 'Looks very much like running away to me.'

James didn't say anything, but instead glanced up towards the house. He couldn't shake the sense that its shadow was tainting their conversation. Now, it felt more like some great factory than a Tudor manor. It was wider and more squat than he remembered it, the three tall chimneys jutting up towards the sky like leafless trees, the windows small and deeply set. It was a strange, brutal, angular thing, quite at odds with the explosion of nature all around it; it sat uncomfortably amongst the trees, as though fearful they might swallow it up.

'Look at this place, Edward,' he said, nodding up towards its towering frontage. 'It's like we're still pretending to be Henry Tudor.'

Edward spoke more quietly now, but his lip still twitched, as though at any second it might twist into a sneer. 'That's always been your problem,' he said bitterly. 'You want to throw away our history. Everything that made this family who we are today.'

'Not throw it away. Just – examine it. Update our traditions, if need be.'

'Those aren't the words of a man who believes in this family.'

'My God,' said James, unable to hide his exasperation, 'would you listen to yourself? A family's not a matter of faith – it's here, no matter whether we believe in it.'

Edward shook his head. 'Enough,' he said firmly. 'Can we at least agree the Harringleys have been good to this place for nearly four hundred years?' He fixed James with a stare, as though challenging him to disagree, but James held his tongue. 'Now Father's threatening our very reputation, and everything we ever stood for. So I'm asking you to help talk Father out of whatever madness he's fallen into. Can you do that?'

James held his hands open in a gesture of helpless supplication. 'I can try.'

Look at how well that ended last time, he heard a voice whisper inside.

4

As a child James spent most of his life in the library, a vast rectangular room tucked away at the back of the house, its walls filled from floor to ceiling with books. Many of them were great scowling tomes on economics or animal husbandry, their pages dense with type and rimed with dust, but a small section of the room had been set aside for the servants, and James immediately gravitated to the more well-worn texts he found there. They were adventure novels, folk romances, knightly tales – some of them, he'd learn later, were classics of the form, but at the time he'd not known good from bad.

At first he simply pored over their pictures, the strange and arcane woodcuts he found among their pages, the maps of unknown lands. But as he learned his letters, the riddles seemed to unfurl themselves, and he found new worlds in which to lose himself. He recalled the day he first read a book by himself, curling up in one of the library's wingback armchairs to read what turned out to be a simple tale of warring peasants, and re-emerging from a kind of trance hours later.

His father thought it was a waste of time: there was a business to learn, and James was neglecting it in pursuit of foolish stories. But James had been down to the village with his father, the two of them dressed up like lords and rattling down the hill in their carriage. He saw the fear beneath the villagers' deference, their barely concealed anger; heard how hollow their thanks were when James's father offered to organise repairs or delay a rent payment by a week. They loathed him, with his fancy clothes and his big house, and by extension they loathed his son too. He wasn't sure if his father was too naive to see their hatred, or if he simply chose to ignore it. Either way, James couldn't bear it.

When his father next sought James out in the library and asked for his company on a trip into town, James told him he'd prefer not to. He remembered his father pausing as though he'd been struck, his voice oddly cold when he spoke again.

'You understand that one day this will be your job,' he said.

'Maybe I'd prefer that it wasn't.'

His father's bitter laughter surprised him. 'That's not a choice you'll get, I'm afraid.'

'Why not?'

'Because families like ours have a duty,' he said, after a moment's consideration. 'Those villagers need us to maintain order. To provide what they cannot provide for themselves. And to teach them how to live well.' He held James's gaze. 'It's a noble life.'

'It doesn't sound like it.'

He saw his father bite the inside of his cheek. 'Well, it's the life you were born to. So you'd better learn to accept it, or you've many miserable years ahead of you.'

Perhaps James might have made his peace with it, had his father not taken Edward along with him that afternoon instead. Edward had always preferred to follow their father around, and from that day he insisted on accompanying the old man when he travelled to the village to collect rents or supervise the harvest. When James asked him what they'd done, Edward's answers were brief – *we arranged men to unblock the stream*, or *we sent Ephraim Miller to jail for a week* – but James was no fool, no matter what his father thought. He knew what it meant to his father to have a willing shadow, the bond those shared carriage rides would forge.

He was surprised to discover how little he cared.

Until he was eight, James hardly considered there was a world beyond the estate. He'd never needed to. The woods were full of mysteries he'd not even begun to exhaust.

Among the trees were the remnants of low stone walls, slippery with moss and overgrown with roots. The bones of some structure long forgotten. Somewhere out in the woods was a spiral staircase descending to a door in the earth, walls cool and clammy to the touch; he knew it because he'd stood for hours at the bottom of the hole, staring up at the aperture of light far above and feeling like the last person alive. He'd never found it again.

One afternoon he discovered a clearing filled with what looked like Grecian ruins, and a group of servants lounging on the grass. There was no fear in their eyes; when they saw him they just smiled, raising silent fingers to their lips.

He was an imaginative child, given to acting out stories he'd read in the estate's library – and he spent one fine day imagining himself going upriver, some great explorer of the world's undiscovered places, so engrossed in the progression of a stream that he'd not noticed the thick roots criss-crossing his path until they sent him flying. When he tried to push himself to his feet, his ankle stubbornly refused to support his weight, leaving James to crawl out of the stream on his hands and knees.

His first thought was dismay – this would never have happened to David Livingstone – but then came panic. Although the servants knew he was out here, they didn't know exactly where, and he was far too deep in the woods for them to hear him calling. They'd surely come looking for him when he was absent from the dinner table, but that could be hours yet – and the thought of still being out here at night, listening to the sounds of movement among the branches, left him faint.

It was that last thought which set him calling for help, even though doing so felt futile. 'Help!' he shouted into the trees, but the only response was a scatter of birds somewhere out of sight. His voice sounded tiny and feeble.

He wasn't sure how long it was before he gave up calling. By the time he did, his throat was hoarse and his mouth dry. The day was drawing on and the late afternoon had robbed the sun of much of its heat – he was already beginning to shiver in his thin shirt.

He couldn't bear the thought of waiting another moment for help. He needed to be moving, towards the house, to safety and shelter. Anyway, his father would be appalled if he found his son sitting by the edge of a stream, calling for help like some defenceless animal.

He leaned against a tree trunk and tried to prop himself upright using the tree as a crutch, but it was no use. Every step he took on his wounded ankle sent a jolt of pain through his entire body, leaving tremors in his wake. He'd never make his way through the woods on foot: he'd have to crawl.

He pulled himself along on all fours for what felt like hours, the wet earth soaking through the elbows of his jacket, his whole torso bitterly cold. Whenever his body cried out in exhaustion or pain, he swallowed it and told himself he couldn't stop; he had to maintain some kind of rhythm, a forward movement. But the woods felt endless, a natural labyrinth, and he had no way to tell if he was even heading in the right direction.

And then, from up ahead, he heard the voice. Leisurely, unhurried, a kind of drawl.

'Looks like you've done yourself a mischief there, young master.'

Before him was a figure lounging against a tree, dressed in rags. In the gloom of the forest James hadn't even noticed him appear; he could have been there some time, watching James stumble towards him.

He was a man in his early fifties, dark brows hiding sharp eyes, and a noble face under shabby stubble. On his back he wore an oversized brown coat, mended several times at the sleeves with little spiderwebs of multi-coloured thread and a huge, floppy hat. There was a faint smile on his lips.

'I say, do you need some help there, young sir?' the man said in that rough accent, when James was finished looking him up and down. Then, without waiting for an answer, he stumped across to James on a leg that looked halfway lame. 'Come on,' he said as he approached. 'Roll up your trouser leg.'

James forced himself to stay strong as the man drew closer. Shuffled himself up against the trunk of a tree so he could push upright, and squared his shoulders like he'd seen his father do. Moments like these were a test, after all: you had to maintain your authority.

'What are you doing here?' James said. 'This is private land.'

The man stopped a few steps away from James. 'Is that so?' he said. There was a new wariness in his tone, as if he was affronted. 'Suppose I must have missed the boundary line.'

'They're clearly marked,' said James, who knew no such thing – he'd not yet made it as far as the estate's bounds – and the man's eyes narrowed.

'You're sure of that, are you, young master?' he said, a little more curtly. 'No chance those fences are overgrown, or tumbledown?'

'I'm not sure my father would care for that excuse,' said James.

'Your father being Mr Harringley, I suppose,' said the man. 'That's right.'

'Aye, I know him well enough,' the man said, with a look of distaste. 'Hard man, your father is.' He rubbed at his nose with a dirty hand and sniffed. 'Well, let's see how grateful he is when I save his son from dying of exposure.'

Not very, James thought, but he kept that to himself.

'I'd like you to lean on me, young master,' said the man. 'I'm going to bend down, and you ought to be able to get your arm around my shoulders. Mighty unwieldy, but it'll do until we make it to where I'm camped.'

'Can't you take me back home?' James said, hardly keen to spend another moment in these woods.

'Later, maybe,' said the man, a little wary. 'It's getting late, and there'll be no moon tonight. There's creatures in these woods I'd prefer not to stumble across in the dark.' He didn't meet James's eye, but knelt, allowing James to hook his arm across a broad back before standing. From this close James was aware of the man's strange, loamy smell: it was rich and musty, with a ferric tang.

On they stumped, a strange pair, the shabby vagrant taking the lead in their hobbling dance. On through the gloom of the forest, finding paths where there appeared to be none, through the narrowest of gaps between trees. Then, after what felt like an eternity and no time at all, James saw a low hill, and in front of it the dim light of a fire.

And then off he went, into the hillside itself, where a set of ragged steps led down into a dark hole. In the firelight James could see it was reinforced with what looked like thin wooden struts, a much more substantial construction than he'd been led to believe.

Despite the agony in his foot, he remained standing, propped up against the spindly trunk of a tree. He wanted to be able to run. If it came to that.

'You live here?' he called after the man, but there was no answer. He left it a moment, but the hole was black and abandoned, no flickering shadows that spoke of movement. 'Sir?' he called again. 'Excuse me?'

There was only the crackling of coals, the rustle of leaves in the early evening breeze.

He should flee. He knew that then. This was not a good place. And yet he was just as lost as he'd been before, if not more so: deeper in the woods, further from the house. He needed this man, no matter how shabby and uncouth he might be. His choice was already made.

James loped around the fire with long, unsteady strides, staying close to the trees in case he needed to grab one for balance. Every step sent a stab of pain through his leg. He felt woozy, disorientated, only halfway awake. It took him several minutes to make it to that rough doorway, and there was still no sign of the vagrant.

'Sir?' he called into the earth. 'Is everything alright down there?'

His voice echoed briefly and then was swallowed by the darkness. The light only penetrated a couple of feet into the tunnel and so he had no sense of how far it stretched, but for reasons he couldn't articulate it felt immense. He imagined underground banqueting halls, throne rooms, churches to some lost earth god – an entire civilisation, living out its life, hidden just below the surface of the world.

If he closed his eyes he could see it. And it was beautiful: ornate and austere and yet warmed with a strange heat. Before he knew it, he'd taken a step into the tunnel, and then another—

And then he walked straight into the vagrant.

'Leg feeling better, then, young master?' he said, with a chuckle, rubbing his sternum good-naturedly where James had collided with him. 'Won't be needing this, then,' he said, holding up a small stone bowl in his left hand. The inside was smeared with some kind of green paste.

'I'm sorry—' James said, filled with sudden anxiety – which wouldn't shift, no matter how often that voice in his head repeated *this is your home, your father's land*. He felt as if he'd transgressed on sacred ground. 'I didn't mean to – I was just wondering where you'd gone—'

'Takes a while to make this,' the man said, waggling the bowl. 'Come back out into the firelight so I can see where to apply it, why don't you?'

James glanced back over his shoulder at the tunnel, filled with a mad desire to see further into it, but he managed to pull himself away and follow the man back to the fire. 'What is it?' he said, setting up against a tree.

'Don't you worry yourself there,' said the man, with a crooked smile. 'It'll do you no harm. It's a simple poultice. Bring down the swelling, numb the pain.' He nodded towards James's ankle. 'Afraid you'll need to roll up your trouser leg, though. Won't do much good for fabric.' He held out the bowl, motioned for James to take it. 'I'll turn away,' he said. 'It's only polite.'

James knelt and removed his shoe, pulled up his trouser leg. Beneath his sock his ankle was the size of a melon, criss-crossed with jagged blood vessels and covered in a dark bruising like a storm at night. It hurt to touch. James took a deep breath and scooped up some of the poultice, then smeared it over the areas that looked worst.

The change was instantaneous – the pain seemed to melt away, to disappear beneath the surface of his consciousness. He was still aware of it – as a dim, throbbing hum somewhere far away – but it could have been happening to another person altogether, in an entirely different world.

'It's incredible,' he murmured, half to himself, and when he glanced up he could see the vagrant smiling. 'Where did you learn to make this?' he said, more loudly.

The man half-turned towards him, his eyes wider now. 'My wife taught me how,' he said. 'It's an old recipe.'

'I'm grateful,' said James, and he meant it. All his fear had melted away along with the pain; he felt only gratitude, and a strange lightness. He tested his ankle gingerly, resting more and more of his weight upon it, astonished that it seemed to support him. 'I could even walk back to the house on my own now,' he said. 'My father need never know you're out here.'

'Ah, I'm not afraid of him,' said the man casually. 'What's the worst he'll do?'

James thought of his father's rages, his unpredictable temper. 'He's very protective of the estate,' he said. 'He might be angry.'

Now the man turned to look at him directly. 'It's a special

place, this,' he said. 'Maybe your father never realised exactly how special.'

James rubbed his ankle, only half listening. 'I can see that,' he said.

'There's a deeper wisdom in the soil here,' said the man, with a new intensity. 'Do you understand what I'm saying, young sir?'

James's bewilderment must have been written across his face, for the fellow's smile widened, and he went on. 'You might never read the name of this village in the history books, but you best believe it's part of this nation's destiny.' He gave a little chuckle, dipped his head, and when he looked up again James was startled to see his eyes were watery. 'If you only knew what people here have given up,' he said, the words catching in his throat. 'The sacrifices they've made.'

James stood up straighter then, more alert, fear prickling across his skin. 'Sacrifices?' he said, trying to sound merely wary rather than afraid. 'What kind of sacrifices?'

The man cocked his head, thoughtful. 'This place takes the best of us,' he said, half to himself. 'Leastways that's what I believe anyway. Explains why it took her.' He looked rueful. 'My daughter.'

The man was quiet then, staring into his fire, lost in his own thoughts. For a minute or two James held back the question he was desperate to ask – the one he believed he already knew the answer to – but the sadness in the fellow's face, the loneliness he'd tried in vain to hide, made it impossible to remain silent.

'And that's why you're out here? Because of her?'

'I didn't understand what it meant,' the man murmured, as though reading James's mind. 'When I gave her away to him.' Another low chuckle. 'Didn't understand the honour it was. All I knew was that she was gone, and not long after my wife went too. Vanishing, day by day, by slow degrees.' He shook his head, glanced back over his shoulder into the darkness of that tunnel. 'I thought maybe I'd see them again.'

When James looked down he realised he was digging his fingernails deep into the flesh of his palm. This man was talking in riddles, every statement he made inviting a new question.

'You said they went away,' James said. 'Went away where?'

'He took them to the pit,' said the man, swallowing hard. 'Gave them to the void.'

'Who?' said James desperately, his curiosity a knot in his guts.

The man sucked on his teeth, thought for a moment. 'He doesn't have a name,' he said eventually. 'Or else he has too many.'

And then two things happened, and he couldn't tell which came first: he opened his mouth to ask another question, and he saw the vagrant wrenched backwards by an unseen force, a startled gasp slipping from his lips.

His father was there, towering and furious, looking stronger and more terrifying than James had ever seen him. He was straddling the vagrant, pinning him down, yelling into his face.

'Stay away from my boy, you hear,' he could make out his

father's words, gruff and menacing. 'I won't let you drag him into this.' He lifted the man up by the lapels and then slammed his back against the hillside so hard he sank down some way. 'Are you listening to me?'

James couldn't tell what, if anything, the fellow said in response. His hat had fallen from his head, his hair was a mass of tangles, but the eyes were just as sharp and mocking. James thought he saw the man glance over in his direction, thought he caught an impossible smile on the fellow's lips.

'Answer me, God damn you,' shouted his father, and the fellow lisped out a reply in as loud a voice as he could manage.

'You're a fool, sir,' he said. 'You thought you could defy him, and taught others to do the same. Just look at this place now.'

His father took a great, shuddering breath, some of the colour draining from his face, and loosened his grip on the vagrant's oversized coat. For the first time James registered the strangeness of the sight: his father, impeccably dressed in smoking jacket and tweed trousers, towering over this vagabond, splattered from head to toe in stinking mud. 'If this place has gone to ruin,' he said, 'it's your lot that are to blame.' His face was twisted into a snarl. 'I gave you the chance to be better.'

The vagrant put his hands around James's father's, and gently prised them off; his father was putting up little resistance now. 'You ought to check your boundary lines,' the vagrant said. 'You'll find this is public land, not your estate. Thought a magistrate would know that.'

'Try taking this to court,' said James's father with a coarse laugh, 'and we'll see how well it ends for you.'

'Perhaps I will,' said the vagrant, brushing thick mud from his coat; it seemed to blend with the folds, so he hardly looked more dishevelled than he had when he first appeared. 'You don't have many friends down there, you know.' He gave a little chuckle. Adjusted his hat, shrugged his shoulders so they better held his coat. James's father was still glaring.

'If you dare show your face on my property again, I'll have the groundsman shoot you,' he said, purple with impotent fury.

The vagrant stared at James's father for several seconds, as if considering, then shook his head faintly. 'You'll do no such thing,' he said, then took a step towards James and bent on his haunches to look him in the eye. 'It was a pleasure to meet you, young master,' he said. 'I'm only sorry it was marred by such – impoliteness.' His eyes darted to James's father, who stood to one side, fists clenching and unclenching at his sides.

Then, with a single brisk turn, he was gone, striding off down the hill towards the village. James had only a moment's peace before his father grabbed him and hauled him over.

'What the bloody hell do you think you're doing?' he snarled. 'You're lucky someone came and found me.'

He supposed he should be glad that somebody had noticed his absence, but mostly he felt a deep sense of humiliation. 'Some days I feel like a prisoner in that house,' he said.

'Don't be ridiculous,' his father said, not looking James in the eye but somewhere else, closer to his collarbone – giving their conversation the air of a monologue. 'You have people at your beck and call every hour of every day and all you want to do is escape them?' He shook his head, eyebrows knitted together in a deep frown. 'I'll never understand you, James.'

James wasn't sure what made him speak up: maybe it was seeing his father bested by the vagrant, the cracking of his façade, but for the first time his father seemed like a man, rather than the golem James had made in his place. 'There's more to the world than this village, you know,' he said. 'I've read about it.'

His father's eyes widened, and he stared at James for several seconds, apparently amazed. 'Don't you understand a thing?' he said in a tone of bewilderment, releasing his son apparently without noticing he'd done so. 'We're here because people like that fellow need us. Need our example, need our charity, need our – our service.' He pressed his hand to his forehead, visibly agitated. 'You've a duty both to this village, and to this family. That's why we're still here now.'

'Well maybe they're better off without us.'

His father stared at him for a second or two more, looking like he'd swallowed a lump of gristle, then spoke through gritted teeth. 'You're a child, James. You don't understand what a privilege it is to live like this.' He paused, running his tongue over his teeth. Took a deep breath. When he spoke again it was with a little more warmth. 'You're lucky to have people who indulge your whims,' he said. 'Many wouldn't.' Perhaps he hoped this thaw would win James round, but James gave him nothing in return.

After what felt like an eternity, his father folded his arms, apparently unsure whether he'd gone too far. 'Come on,' he said then, a little more softly. 'Back to the house now.'

Not for a moment did James consider disobeying.

When they emerged at the house, the light was dimming towards twilight; inside its walls the kitchen staff would be serving dinner, and Ransford would be uncorking a bottle of wine from the cellar.

At the front door, his father paused, fingers drumming against his thigh, his back to James. He took a deep breath and when he turned to address James his voice was weary. 'I need to think of a suitable punishment,' he said. 'There will be consequences for what you've done, you understand?'

James nodded mutely. His father still seemed reluctant to meet his eye, and while he was taking great pains to appear composed there was a twitch in his jaw that belied some deeper emotion. Still James waited, reluctant to move until he was dismissed, lest the anger he'd expected from his father should flicker unexpectedly into life.

After several seconds his father swallowed hard and then his eyes met James's for just a moment. 'I thought I'd lost you,' he said. 'Your mother would have never forgiven me for that.' He sighed. 'I won't let it happen again.'

The mere mention of his mother sent a thrill down James's spine: she was a kind of legend, rarely spoken of, and always with the same stories. This was new. But his father's brief openness didn't last long: he seemed to remember himself, straightening his spine and making a great effort to resume his former bearing. When he looked at James again, it was as though he were a different man.

'We'd better eat something,' he said. 'Go and change your clothes first.'

James knew then there would be no escaping a punishment. Perhaps he could appeal to whatever compassion lurked beneath his father's veneer, whatever had briefly surfaced in the woods, but no good would come of it.

The next thought to enter his mind was a lie: he knew that much. And yet he didn't brush the whispered voice off right away. Instead he let it linger, far longer than he should have, taking root in the darkness of his secret heart as he made his way upstairs:

Maybe I'd have been better off in the woods.

5

AFTER SEVEN years away, stepping into the house felt like something from a dream: that vast, gloomy entrance hall, its oak panelling absorbing the light falling in dusty shafts from the two large windows. The two great staircases curving up like vines on either side of the hallway, each leading up to a set of bedrooms. That warren of rooms on the far side of the ground floor – library, drawing room, billiard room – tucked away behind closed doors. But James was only half here, searching memories he couldn't quite recall.

'This hasn't changed much,' he murmured.

'No,' said Edward. 'Not sure it's changed since Father was a boy.'

It was all so familiar, all of it: the faint smell of mould hanging in the air, the eerie stillness that came upon the hall when the front door closed, the chill in the house even with fires lit throughout and a throng of people filling it. He thought he'd dreamed it all. He half-expected Emily to come barrelling out of a side room, breaking the silence with her hard, cackling laugh – but she was long gone, and the only touch now came from Edward at his elbow.

'Come on up and meet Sophia,' he said. 'Best not to linger here. He'll hear you.'

He followed Edward upstairs, bewildered by memories. Up to the landing, the perfect vantage point to spy on visitors as they entered. 'We're over in the West Wing,' Edward said. 'These days the East Wing is all but shut up. We've no cause to use it.'

Despite himself, James felt a dim sadness for all those rooms now left sheeted and empty. On his right he spotted the guest bedroom, small and cold, in which he recalled having trapped Edward for a whole day before someone heard his cries. Beside it was a bathroom, immaculate but now utterly old-fashioned. And a rickety staircase led up to the roof space, an attic playground of long-neglected items which James had given second life through elaborate stories.

All of this must have shown on James's face, because Edward gave him an indulgent little smile. 'You're not missing much,' he said. 'It's mostly clutter.'

Edward's apartment was the door nearest the stairs – near the heart of the house, where the rooms were at their warmest. Not so long ago James's own rooms had been directly opposite; he remembered them as gloomy and small, their furniture shabby and outsized even then. Next to Edward, on the very edge of the house, was his father's suite: his study, sitting room and bedchamber, all with a view of the woods.

And behind every one of those rooms lay the darkness: that world of hidden corridors that only James knew how to navigate.

After all these years he still kept the tiny iron key in his breast pocket. Just in case.

'Come on in,' said Edward, opening his door with as little noise as he could manage, and James had to shake himself out of his reverie.

Sophia sat at the far end of the room, a small woman with pale skin and wide-set eyes. She looked surprised when they entered unannounced; she leaned over the crib next to her to quiet the child inside, not taking her eyes off James as she did, her expression one of frank curiosity. From inside the cot came faint murmurs, but its high sides were a solid, dark wood, and all James could see was two flailing fists.

Edward made the introduction, as was proper. 'My wife, Sophia.' She muttered something to calm the child and then crossed the room to James, offering him her hand. Her elegant demeanour couldn't entirely hide a harassed look behind her eyes. 'My brother, James. I'm sorry you've not met before.'

James took her hand and kissed it. 'I wish I'd known about your marriage,' he said, trying not to make it sound like a criticism. 'You must think me unfeeling.'

'I'm not sure you understand how hard it was to track you down,' said Edward, with an unsuccessful attempt at sounding jovial. 'You're lucky Sophia was so persistent.'

Sophia's laugh was bright and genuine, wholly unexpected. 'I think Edward was just afraid to invite you here,' she said warmly. 'Thought I'd catch something.'

James couldn't resist sneaking a glance at Edward then, who

at least had the grace to seem a little abashed. He supposed he didn't much deserve Edward's respect.

Sophia missed the look that passed between the brothers – or else chose to ignore it in the interest of unity, James couldn't tell. 'I'm concerned about your father, though,' she went on, her brow furrowed. 'He's in an awful state.'

'Edward told me a little. He's not shown any sign he might harm you? Or the child?' Both Edward and Sophia were silent for a moment then, and James could feel an unspoken tension between the two of them. 'Have you called a doctor?'

They both tried to speak at once. 'Absolutely not,' said Edward firmly, cutting across his wife. 'Father won't stand for that. Says he's a reputation to uphold.'

Sophia spoke more quietly, and she didn't look at Edward when she answered. 'Your father's a danger to himself, and the servants.'

James raised an eyebrow. 'Edward didn't mention that.'

Edward's lips pursed as though he'd tasted something unpleasant. 'It was a minor altercation,' he said a little too loudly, with the air of a small child being told off. 'One of the kitchen staff caught him trying to get out through the front door. He gave them quite a clout with an iron poker.' His gaze flicked to James's cane then, just for a second, his eyes darkening.

'And he keeps talking about the Tall Man,' said Sophia, cutting in again.

James turned to Edward, startled. 'You told Sophia about the Tall Man?'

Edward threw his hands up in apparent dismay: *perhaps he*

feels like he can't win, James thought. 'I could hardly keep it from her,' he said.

'No, I'm impressed.' Maybe there was hope for them both after all.

Sophia's voice was tinged with quiet desperation. 'But they're just stories,' she said, with the air of someone who wanted confirmation. 'Folklore. Every village has them.'

Again James glanced at his brother, but Edward wouldn't meet his eye. James took his silence as permission. 'I'm not sure Edward has told you the full story of why I left,' he said.

'Edward—?' said Sophia, and his brother's irritation was obvious now.

'My God, James,' he said, rubbing at his temple, 'do we have to do this now?'

'No,' said James, holding up his hands in conciliation. 'No – it's a story for another day.'

Sophia's frown deepened. 'I don't like traps,' she said to Edward.

'It's not a trap,' Edward said. 'It's just – ancient history.'

James studied his brother's face, wondering what Edward's game was here. This was all so different from what he'd told James outside. For a fleeting moment he'd thought his brother was going to do away with secrets, let the light into this house, but now he was acting like his father's son all over again.

James spoke before he could think better of it. 'I saw him,' he said. 'The Tall Man. When I was a boy.' He didn't need to look over at Edward to feel his anger.

Sophia glanced from Edward to James, her mouth falling open. 'You saw him? What does that mean?' She put a hand to her mouth. 'What was he like?'

'He's hard to describe,' said James, hearing the weariness in his own voice and hating it. 'It's like he's – made of shadows. And yet somehow he's darker than the shadows – I mean, it's as if the shadows seem to distort around him.' Even trying to speak of him inspired a sort of terror. 'He wears a long top hat, and an old-fashioned tailcoat, and although his eyes are in darkness, you can tell when he's watching you closely. And he's tall. So tall – impossibly tall, taller than anyone you've ever seen – and spindly, like a silver birch tree, only one that's been allowed to rot away to nothing.' James sighed, rubbed his eyes. 'I can't do him justice,' he said. 'No one could. I think he might be as old as the world itself.'

'And you remember this?' said Sophia, staring at him with a kind of awe. 'That is to say, you were old enough when he came to remember seeing him?'

'That's right,' said James, holding Sophia's eye and hoping he might have found an unlikely ally. 'Maybe you've heard he only comes for infants. But that's not always how it is. Or at least, it's not how it was for me. I first saw him when I was twelve.'

She glanced across at Edward, but his head was bowed and he seemed to be barely there. 'Why?' she said in a whisper. 'What did he want with you?'

James rubbed his forehead. The words wouldn't come: these were things that belonged in darkness, upon which he hardly dared shine a light even now. 'It was different for me,' he said. 'I'm a Harringley. I don't think he wanted sacrifice from me, so much as – as service.'

He could see the look of bewilderment on Sophia's face, and he could hardly blame her. All these years later he still wasn't sure he understood it all himself. 'Has Edward told you about the void?' said James, trying to catch his brother's eye, but Edward was staring stolidly out of the window. His face was twisted into a grimace, and he looked as though he were struggling to digest a heavy meal.

'No,' said Sophia, swallowing hard, as though braced for something awful. She made her way back to the child then, laying a hand upon his chest while he slept.

'There's something beneath this place, something terrible. A sort of – reservoir of darkness.' James felt a rising nausea at what he'd seen down there all those years ago. 'Left unchecked, it will leach out into the soil, warping anything it touches into something unrecognisable – something monstrous. And so the Tall Man needs a vessel, someone the void can consume. He calls it a great and noble sacrifice. Perhaps he's right.'

'My God…' said Sophia. She turned to Edward, and there was a quiet fury in her voice. 'My God – you knew all of this—'

Edward answered her with aggression. 'We're still here, aren't we?' he said, gesturing towards his brother. 'James and I? And that's because my father knew about all this – about the Tall Man, about the void.' He glared at Sophia, daring her to challenge him. 'He resolved to stop it. To show people it could be different.'

Sophia's gaze was level, uncowed. 'But he still came for James.' She put a hand to her forehead as though pained. 'No, Edward,' she said. 'If what James is saying is true, then we can't stay here. You can't ask me to do that.'

'You knew what you were marrying into,' said Edward quietly, his eyes narrowed.

'It wasn't this!' said Sophia, aghast.

Edward was shaking his head now, apparently feeling he'd been done a grave injustice. 'You knew my family's ties to this place,' he said, sounding a little breathless. 'Everything we're doing for them. The mill, the cider press, the pottery.' He bit his lip. 'If we leave here, then all of that leaves with us.' He folded his arms. 'Please, Sophia. We owe this to them.'

Sophia stared at him, stunned. 'We owe it to them?' she said, raising her voice for the first time. 'I admire your compassion, Edward. I always have. But you're asking me to put our child's life at risk from this – this demon.'

'No,' said Edward fiercely. 'No, I'm not. Do you think I'd do that to our little boy?'

'How many other people do you think said that?' said James, matching his ferocity.

Edward took a breath then, calming himself with visible effort. He held up his hands in a gesture of surrender, and when he spoke again he sounded almost in control. 'They did what they did out of hopelessness,' he said. 'We're not like that – can't you see that what we're building here makes us stronger than them? We've got a reason to be.' He closed his eyes. 'Our example means something to those people. We can continue my father's work, show them it doesn't have to be like this.'

Sophia turned to James again, a tremor in her voice. 'Is he right?' she said. 'Can this – this Tall Man – be beaten?'

James could see the desperation in Edward's eyes, but he couldn't lie anymore. 'I never found a way,' he said. 'Not that I was trying.' He sighed, thinking back to those years of despair, of blood and rage and constraint. 'I was a boy, true. But the Tall Man scares me, even now.' He turned to Edward. 'Are you sure you want this fight, Edward? After what it did to Father?'

'I'm no fool,' Edward said coldly. 'And I won't be made to feel like one for believing in this family.' His eyes were still on Sophia. 'I'm asking you to trust me,' he said, and despite himself James was impressed by Edward's resolve. 'We can do this – can overcome him – together. Not only for our own sakes, but for everyone down there in the village.'

Sophia glanced back into the crib where her child lay, unable to hide her anxiety. She closed her eyes, her teeth biting into her bottom lip. But just as she began speaking again, she was interrupted by a single, hard knock at the door, followed by an expectant silence.

At the sound, Edward reached into his jacket and withdrew a pocket watch. 'Damn, damn, damn,' he said, his face falling. He turned to Sophia, obviously alarmed. 'I lost track of time,' he said, almost apologetic, 'James's coach was late—'

So it was him. The old man. How things had changed: in the old days his father would never have knocked. Back then he held all the keys, went wherever he chose. God only knew the effort it had cost Edward to cultivate this sanctuary, this secret home.

Edward sprang into action right away, setting up what seemed to be a well-rehearsed tableau. Sophia lifted the child up from the cot and seated herself with him in her arms, Edward at her side, as though presenting her for the first time in company. The child grizzled in its mother's arms, tossing back and forth, its sleep disrupted.

'What should I do?' said James, an unreasoning panic rising in his throat.

'Get out of sight,' hissed Edward, jerking his head towards the corner.

James did as he was told, made his way to the room's back wall, hoping he'd be out of his father's field of view. This was all wrong, wasn't how he'd planned it at all. All those years he'd spent skulking in the dark; he'd hoped to walk back in here with his head held high.

There was still a way out, of course: the house behind the house. The panel in the wall that slid back to reveal one of the house's many priest holes, the easiest way to disappear. Perhaps Edward had all of them blocked up. They'd been James's refuge for so many years.

He stood with his back pressed against the wall and watched as Edward opened the door to his father. He was an old man now, still tall, but craggier and more austere than James recalled. If anything, age made his father appear more solid. He looked carved out of stone.

He strode into the room, his jaw clenched, his nostrils flaring as he surveyed the scene. There was a determination to him that James had forgotten, and when he caught sight of his eldest son in the shadows his jaw hardened further. He let out a low, menacing growl, and turned his head slowly to face Edward.

'I knew it,' he said. 'I knew you were hiding something from me.'

Edward let out a barely suppressed shudder of a sigh. 'You sent for him,' he said. 'Or don't you remember that?'

'I did no such thing,' said their father, glaring back at Edward, 'and you know it.'

'Fine,' said Edward. 'Maybe you didn't ask me outright. But it was clear you wanted to see him, Father. I heard you muttering about him, about making things right. I'm not a fool.' His arms were folded tight across his chest.

'And so you had the bright idea to bring him back here?' the old man said, jerking his head towards James. 'Because it was a bloody stupid thing to do, I'll tell you that.'

'It was Sophia's idea,' said Edward without looking at her. 'She said we had to make this right, help you understand we're on your side.' He closed his eyes, swallowed hard, and when he spoke again his tone was a little more confident. 'To help you understand everything we do for this family,' he said.

'So you told her what I said?' said their father, his eyes fixed on Edward, his face hard.

'She's my wife,' Edward spat back. 'I owe her that much, at least.'

'It was a terrible thing you said about Edward,' Sophia interjected, one hand reached out towards the old man in entreaty. 'But it was coming from a place of hurt—'

'I don't need your judgement,' the old man snarled. 'And I don't appreciate your meddling in things you don't understand.'

Sophia looked as though she'd been slapped, but before she could strike back Edward broke in. 'You said it would have been better if I'd run away, not James,' he said, his voice trembling with anger. 'After all the years I've been here for you, all I've done for this family—' He nodded towards James. 'If he'd stayed around, you'd have killed one another within a year.'

Their father gave a curt, dismissive sniff. 'James and I are more similar than you ever realised,' he said to Edward. His anger seemed to be burning itself out now, the threat of actual violence receding.

James took his opportunity – he wasn't sure how long it would last. 'I heard you were ill,' he said from behind his father. 'I thought perhaps I could help.'

His father glanced back, his expression full of contempt. 'So that's what Edward told you?' he said, the menace not yet gone from his voice.

'You are ill,' Edward shot back. 'Maybe you can't see it, but it's true. You're forgetting things – half the time you can't even remember the conversations we had the day before. Every time we eat dinner you shake like you've got palsy. And you keep skulking round like nobody's noticed that rash on your arms because you're afraid we'll call the doctor.' He took a step towards his father, but was stilled by a hard glare. Edward held up his hands in a gesture of surrender, said wearily: 'I'm worried about you, that's all.'

The old man surveyed his son, his eyes narrowed, his expression flinty, as though trying to determine the nature of the trap he'd been led into. When he spoke again it was to James. 'He's using you,' his father said. 'Needs you here to testify to how reasonable he's being when he packs me off to some asylum and takes control of the house.'

'That's not why I came.'

'Oh no?' said their father, his eyebrows raised. 'Why, then?'

James swallowed hard. Was he truly going to do this? He glanced over at Edward as if asking permission, then checked himself. 'In his letter Edward mentioned – the Tall Man,' James said, the words catching in his throat. 'Edward said you'd been… searching for him. Seeking him out.' He heard the tremor in his voice. 'I wasn't sure I believed him until I saw the state of this place. The state of you. It's enough to make me wonder.' He closed his eyes. 'Tell me it's not true,' he said quietly. 'You wouldn't do that.'

The old man's anger was sudden and fierce, as though it had lain just below the surface for years. 'How can you even imagine I'd seek out that – that thing?' he snarled. 'All those years I spent resisting.' The tremor in his father's voice was all anger. 'All those years I spent telling the villagers there was a better way. Does that count for nothing?'

James could feel his own temper rising, but he swallowed it as best he could. 'So you're accusing Edward of lying?' he shot back. 'Why would he do that?'

'Enough, James,' said Edward, his tone grim. He wore an

expression of weary resolve, as though he'd expected this to happen and yet hated every second of it. 'What good are all these questions? If anything happened, he doesn't remember doing it.'

'I need him to understand,' James said, and he found to his surprise that his hands were trembling. In that moment, his brother seemed every bit as steely and resolute as his father; it was disorientating to see the resemblance. He looked his father in the eye. 'I know what the Tall Man promised this family over the years. A legacy that lasts.' His head was pounding. 'Tell me you weren't swayed by that in your old age. That he didn't finally win you over.'

A lock of wispy white hair had fallen down past his father's face and there was a look of panic in his eye. 'Stop pressing me,' he said through a clenched jaw. 'I've told you I had nothing to do with this. Isn't that enough for you?'

James's anger came on fast, much like his father's. He'd not realised how close to the surface it still was. 'No!' he yelled. 'All those years of locked doors – all those secrets – I don't think you ever told us a thing unless you had to.'

The old man stood up as tall as he could manage, staring James down. 'You've never understood what this family stands for,' he said coldly. 'Not like Edward.'

James hated his father in that moment, hated the lot of them and every brick in this house.

'Don't tell me you can't see the signs,' he said. 'This place belongs to the void.' It was all coming back to him now, this family's perverse logic. 'Is that why you took Janey's little boy?

Better to sacrifice her child than a Harringley one?' James saw
a look of mingled fury and panic cross his father's face at the
accusation, but found he didn't much care anymore. 'It's no
wonder she couldn't bear to stay here.'

His father spoke slowly, with an obvious effort to keep his
temper in check. 'How dare you suggest such a thing.' he said.
His fists were clenched. 'Get out of my house.'

'It's not your house anymore, though, is it? It's his. Or at
least it might as well be.'

The old man's façade was starting to crack now, something
of his father's true feelings coming out. 'I'd never throw this
family's legacy away like that. I'd think you'd know that,' he said,
with a hint of a tremor in his voice.

'Maybe you wouldn't have once,' James said bitterly. 'Now
I'm starting to reconsider.'

James's words had the desired effect. His father let loose his
full anger, his voice a bellow, finger pointed imperiously at the
door. 'I said GO!'

And before he knew it James found himself descending the
stairs, crossing the gloom of the great hall, and heading for the
watery sunlight of the late afternoon. Halfway across the hall he
heard running footsteps behind him. He turned, braced for a
blow, only to see Edward. His brother's hands were outstretched,
apparently in conciliation.

'I hadn't realised how much you hated him,' Edward said,
a little warily.

'I don't hate him.'

'You could have fooled me,' said Edward with a mirthless

laugh.

'He's a good man,' said James, attempting to shake off his anger. 'At least he tries to be.' He shook his head again, dizzy with adrenaline and honesty. 'But he's so desperate to be important, Edward. Can't you see that?' He sighed. 'It's nearly ruined him once. And it's so deeply ingrained in him that it's going to ruin him all over again without his even realising it.'

Edward was silent, preoccupied, and James had the sense that his brother had only heard a fraction of what he'd said, if anything at all. 'Listen,' he said. 'What you said about the Tall Man...' He ran his fingers through his hair, obviously uncomfortable. 'Do you truly believe you saw him?'

James stared at him, horrified. 'You can't honestly think I'm making this up?' he said. 'My God, Edward, after all I've seen—'

Again Edward held his hands up in that same gesture of conciliation, and James saw him glance towards the door, as though afraid his brother might run for it once again. 'I know a lot of people have done a lot of things in his name,' he said. 'But for the longest time I never thought he was a physical being. Just – a helpful myth. A fear given human shape.'

'He's not just a story.'

'I understand, James,' Edward said, calmer than James thought possible. 'I didn't before. I suppose I thought you were unwell, and that this place – everything we saw as children – was the cause.' He sighed. 'I swear to you, this place has changed since you were last here. We're starting to let the light in.'

'What, you're going to be different from all the others?' James said, looking him straight in the eye. 'You're just like Father. Which means you're exactly where the Tall Man wants you.' Edward's composure faltered just slightly when he saw James's concerned expression. 'I need you to hear this,' James said. 'Everyone in this house – your son included – is in terrible danger.'

Edward ran a hand across his chin, where a fuzz of wiry bristles was now dimly visible, and sighed. 'I think Father may be right. It might be best if you stayed in the village tonight.'

'You're sending me away?' said James, stunned.

'Listen. You've said your piece. What more is there to gain by staying?' Edward paused, took a breath, and then spoke a little more calmly. 'Today was a mess. It put Father on the defensive, and you too.' He glanced up towards his rooms, and then lowered his voice further. 'Let's try again in a day or two. When tempers have cooled.'

'And what if that's too late?'

Edward's voice was still quiet, but there was a sharpness in it now. 'I'm not going to sacrifice my only heir to some underground demon,' he said, 'no matter what he promises me.' James could hear his anger rising. 'I can't believe you'd think so little of me. I love that boy.' He reached into his pocket, shaking his head, and withdrew a handful of bank notes. 'Get out of here,' he said, shoving them into James's hand. 'I'll send for you when Father's calmed down.'

Outside the air felt no clearer, the smell of rot heavy on the breeze. His leg bothered him with every step as he made his way down the long driveway, his travelling bag slung over his shoulder.

The village was a couple of hours walk at most. If he hurried, he'd be there in time for lunch.

He thought the rumbling sound was inside his head, the noise of blood rushing, and would have continued to think so had the coach not rattled to a stop just a few metres behind him. At the sound of the driver's call, he turned to see two black horses, a figure in a thick woollen travelling coat, and an old-fashioned coach.

'Could've run you down,' the driver called. 'You're lucky I spotted you.'

James stayed silent, dimly aware of how close he'd come to dying. Every night in the city he'd imagined a dark figure emerging from some stinking alley to cut his throat; he'd never imagined anything so prosaic as being run over.

'You do speak, don't you?' called the driver again, hand tapping nervously at his hip.

James knew he'd have a knife on him somewhere: no sensible driver would go without.

'Yes,' said James, his voice hoarse. He was startled at how dry his throat was, how effortful the words.

The driver cocked his head, watchful, as though wondering what sort of decoy this was, where the attack would come from. After what felt like a long time, he put his hands on his hips, satisfied if not happy. 'Can you pay?' he called.

'I can pay,' said James, reaching into his pocket for Edward's notes. 'I'm not going far.'

'Suppose you'd best get in,' said the driver. 'Before something worse happens to you.'

The road down to the village was a series of long, sweeping curves, and from the moment James sat down he felt like he was in perpetual motion, being jolted from one side of the coach to the other, his cane jabbing the ragged woman who sat beside him. Across from him sat a man – his face deeply lined, his hair prematurely grey, his face like seasoned wood – who could have been anywhere between thirty and sixty. His eyes were small and thoughtful, a deep brown, and from the moment he took his seat James could feel himself being meticulously catalogued.

'You're here for the festivities?' said a gruff voice from next to him after he'd been seated a couple of minutes, and James looked up to find the woman staring. Her rags were faded, and fraying at the edges.

James frowned. 'Festivities?'

The woman stuck out her lip, gave a thoughtful nod. 'Aye,' she said. 'Each year at this time we hold a celebration. To revel in the fact we're still here.'

The fellow opposite snorted. 'That's awfully bleak,' he said.

Glancing over to catch James's eye, the woman rolled her eyes. 'Wouldn't expect a man like you to understand our local customs,' she said to her travelling companion. 'Plenty don't.' Again she glanced at James – then, confident she'd found an ally, nodded over to him. 'He knows, though,' she said. 'You can see it in his eyes.'

James felt uncomfortably exposed. 'I heard stories as a boy,' he mumbled.

'Such as?' said the woman, her eyes widening.

'One of our governesses had a storybook. I remember – "The Crimson Man".'

'Ah, "The Crimson Man".' Her smile was disconcertingly wide. 'One of the greats.'

'Yeah. It made – quite an impact.'

The fellow opposite's eyes were narrowed. He was silently taking in every word, and he couldn't hide his distaste. Noticing him, the woman leaned forward, bowing her head in a parody of deference. 'Do you know this story, sir?' she asked, with a tinge of glee.

'No, I'm not sure I do,' he said warily. 'Please, indulge me.'

The old lady looked at James, as though waiting for permission. He'd forgotten what it was like to have people defer to him. 'Be my guest,' James said to her. 'No doubt you'll have heard this more recently than me.' No matter that he still saw it in nightmares.

'Very well,' said the woman, nodding. 'I'll tell it the way my parents told it. About how you might wake in the night and find him there in his top hat, impossibly tall, his face pale white and without features.' She shook her head. 'He'd swallow you up in the darkness, they'd say. If your family saw you, they'd think you were only dreaming. But you'd have dropped through a gap in the world, into a place where it was only you and him.'

As she spoke, James saw the story unfold before him as

though in the pages of book, the images smudged and blurry from years of fingerprints. He saw the shapes of a bedroom painted in the moonlight's eerie hues, saw the Tall Man lean forward towards where a young girl lay in her bed.

He had no face. He had no features, no eyes, no mouth, nothing; his face bore all the contours of an expression, but it was as empty and blank as a theatrical mask.

At first she was terrified, but her terror quickly dissipated. The Tall Man did nothing but watch her, with that strange, eyeless face – didn't pounce on her and rip out her throat, only sat, waited and watched. The night air seemed to be charged with electricity, and she could feel a strange energy emanating from the creature.

Finally, after what might have been hours, he spoke in a voice that seemed to come from everywhere and nowhere. 'Terribly sorry to have woken you, young mistress,' he said to her, 'but your father tells me you've been somewhat unhappy lately.'

'That's right,' she said, startled by how calm and kind-hearted the fellow sounded. 'My father is unhappy,' she told him, 'I fight with my brother; often I feel as though I should never have been born.'

'Is that so, is that so,' said the Tall Man, leaning closer, his fingers knitted together. 'You feel like you don't belong here,' he said, 'is that so?'

'Yes,' she said. 'That's exactly right.' And she was a fool to say it.

Because once she had, that eyeless face pulled up into a

grotesque parody of a smile. 'What if I were to tell you,' he said, 'that you never belonged here at all?' And then he said, 'Come with me,' moving to the side of the girl's bed, and before she knew it she was up in her nightshirt and taking his hand.

He promised to take her to the Kingdom of Faery. A place where the cold never entered your bones, where the machine hadn't captured your mind, nor the worm entered your heart.

'Those things you feel,' he said to her as she walked through the darkened rooms of her home and out into the moonlight, 'about not belonging, it's a sign. The call of Faery. They're what brought me to you.'

And hearing those words, she felt her heart thrill. At the thought of being known, being seen. But then a thought struck her, the first kernel of doubt about this world she'd been promised. 'Where is it?' she asked. 'The Kingdom?'

'Why, deep underground,' he said. 'Where it's warm.'

So she let him take her over the fields, past darkened farmhouses and through the wood until, scratched by thorn and briar, she reached a cave. Inside it was a hole in the earth, dark and gaping, its walls scratched with chalk marks. The Tall Man's face twisted into a frown when he looked over them, and she thought she discerned a tension beneath his pleasant façade.

'They're a warning,' he told her. 'For years people have feared this place, tried to turn back those who stumbled across it by accident.' He shook his head. 'So many languages,' he said with a sad smile. 'So many incantations. They didn't know what they were afraid of.'

'What are they afraid of?' she asked, hardly daring to hear

the answer.

'They fear me,' he said into her ear. 'They ought to fear the void.'

'The void?' she said, her skin prickling.

He nodded. '*In the beginning the earth was without form, and void; and darkness was upon the face of the deep,*' he said, and when he heard it James knew the words somewhere deep inside him. 'And so it is now. From the void all things were made. But the void's desire is insatiable, unquenchable. It's forever reaching outwards, leaching into the world, seeking to transform it anew.' And then he knelt into a low bow, and at first the girl didn't understand why. 'It is a noble thing, to take the void into oneself,' he said then. 'The greatest sacrifice of all. The gesture of a king.'

And then she looked up into his face and saw his smile widening, and where his features should have been his face seemed almost to splinter, like rotten wood, revealing beneath it something gnarled and dark as arterial blood. 'Thank you for your sacrifice,' he hissed, and then before she knew it the girl was falling, falling down into darkness…

For several seconds the only sound in the carriage was the clattering of hooves and wheels. James was increasingly disconcerted by the man opposite: he'd been listening carefully to the story, a scowl twitching at the corners of his mouth, and what James had taken for a vacant stare now seemed to contain a great deal of intelligence. The man's large hands, one of which had a deep gash of scar tissue cut into it, were gripping the seat beneath him tightly. A phrase came to James's mind, some scrap of a Bible verse surfaced from God only knew where: *you've been weighed and found wanting.*

'I could tell you a story of my own,' the man said after a minute. 'Imagine a young girl. Seventeen, maybe eighteen. The daughter of a groundskeeper at a country house.' He smiled, but his eyes remained thoughtful. 'And you know what the rich are like.'

James felt the prickling of fear in his guts, and forced his face into a numb mask, keeping his eyes fixed on the middle distance.

'This girl falls pregnant,' the man went on, catching James's eye for just a moment. Next to him, the woman was leaning forward, listening intently. 'Out of wedlock, of course. But she carries the child until the appointed time, delivers it alone in her cottage.' He raised his eyebrows. 'For three weeks she cares for the child,' he went on, 'nurtures it like the very best of mothers. Pure instinct.'

The man paused, and in the silence the ragged woman broke in. 'But something happened,' she said, unsurprised. 'To the child.'

'Exactly,' he said, a little colder. 'Three weeks after giving birth to a healthy baby, the girl wakes up and finds it gone.' Again he tried to catch James's eye, but in his mind James was far away from here, home with Gabriel; there was no bloom of fear inside him, no shudder of familiarity. 'Not dead, you understand. Just – gone.' Again he paused, weighing up their reactions. 'If I told you a story like that, what would you say happened?'

The corners of the old woman's mouth were twitching. 'They become like kings and queens,' she whispered with an uneasy smile. 'The nameless saviours of the world.'

The man's expression was stony now, stripped of all mildness. 'You've heard a story like that before, I dare say.'

The woman didn't answer, but went back to picking at the tassels on her shawl, half-watching the village drawing closer, although James sensed she wasn't finished with the man yet. There was an alertness to her, a quick wit he'd not seen at first.

'Someone here saw fit to write to me about just such a girl,' said the man, reaching into the inside pocket of his jacket and withdrawing a letter. 'Didn't give their name, nor all the details, but it was enough for me to piece that story together.' He drummed his fingers against his lapel. 'My colleagues thought it was a hoax – nothing to it, they said – but what kind of a detective would I be if I didn't find out for myself?' He raised an eyebrow. 'So here I am. Herbert Whittell. Inspector with the police.'

And perhaps James should have been afraid that the police were here, but in that moment all he felt was the hand of providence. If Whittell was here, asking questions, that was one more reason for Edward to flee this place.

The old woman rolled her eyes. 'You'll never find him,' she said.

'And who exactly am I looking for?' said Whittell, his eyes hooded. 'This so-called Crimson Man, from the stories?'

'He goes by many names,' the woman said with a crooked

smile. 'None of them fit for your ears.' She rubbed viciously at the folds of skin beneath her neck. James's skin prickled then too, and not only in fear – when he looked down at his arm there was an angry rash spreading across it, as though burned with lye. 'There's rewards without measure for them that serve him willingly in daylight.'

'If somebody in this village took that child,' Whittell hissed, 'it'll be them that answers for it, not the Crimson Man.' He was leaning across the coach now, his face inches away from the woman's. His clenched hand quivered on the edge of her patchwork cloak. 'Keep your superstitions if you must, but they won't blind me to the truth.'

The woman gave a high, girlish laugh. 'You're not the first person to come asking questions about our customs,' she said. 'They all run away in the end.'

'I won't be laughed at,' Whittell said through gritted teeth, staring into her eyes. He withdrew, but the tension stayed in his body. 'Somebody here knows what happened to her,' he snarled. 'And I intend to find her.'

'Ought to have started with that lot up the hill then, hadn't you?' said the old lady with a sneer. 'Save yourself trekking back up there in the morning.'

James was glad of his shabby travelling cloak and battered day-suit then. He looked like any other traveller, not the one-time heir to Harringley Manor.

'Not many down here would want that job,' she said, warming to her theme. 'Got high ideals, that family. Think they're better than the rest of us.'

'Oh, I'll find my way up there soon enough,' said Whittell with a slow nod, tapping his lapel. 'But first I'd like to get the lay of the land. Understand how people think around here.' His eyes flicked to James, and James had the sense then that the inspector had been watching him the whole time. 'I take it you've heard similar mutterings? About what happened?'

Somehow James managed to get the words out without stammering. 'I'm not sure this is the place to speak of it, Inspector.'

Whittell's smile was without humour. 'Maybe you ought to let me be the judge of that.'

He wasn't even sure where he'd start. He'd seen so much that felt wrong already: those overgrown trees, blotting out the sky; his father's forgetfulness. The disconnect between Edward and his father's perception, and Sophia in the middle of them both, the child in her arms, trying to carve out a place of safety somewhere in those vast, cluttered rooms.

'I've – I've heard enough to give me pause,' he said, honest in spite of himself. Gabriel had spent years telling him he had nothing to be ashamed of. Maybe that was true back home.

'Would you care to elucidate further?' said Whittell, his gaze intense.

James swallowed hard, finding himself again without a place to hide. 'I – I can't, Inspector,' he said feebly. 'Or at least I won't. Not here.'

'Is that so?' said Whittell, not breaking his gaze, but somehow, miraculously, James managed to stay silent. Somewhere in Whittell's lip a muscle twitched, and when he spoke he sounded terse. 'Well, do seek me out in the village, sir,' he said. 'I'll happily stand you a drink when you're more willing to talk.'

Whittell's confidence was almost touching. He'd not seen what had happened to the others who'd set foot inside the house – all those governesses maimed or maddened or driven to suicide within its walls. This place had its way of breaking people like him.

The stagecoach's inhabitants sat in an uncompanionable silence as the hazy smudge of the village grew steadily larger and more distinct. As they drew closer James became aware of a low, throbbing hum, a steady bass beat that seemed to reverberate through the coach and into his body. It was not unpleasant: it was as familiar as a heartbeat, almost hypnotic, and James became aware once more of the deep weariness in his bones. In spite of himself, he was beginning to feel drowsy, had to force himself back to alertness more than once.

All that changed when the coach rolled along the village's main street, and the ragged woman elbowed him in the ribs. 'We're here,' she said, nodding out the window. 'Before long you'll forget you were ever away.'

'This isn't my home anymore,' muttered James, but she didn't seem to hear.

Beyond the window, marching along the main street, a group of villagers were hollering at the sky in a call-and-response pattern whose words James couldn't make out. At the front of the parade was a tall woman with blonde hair and impossibly dark eyes, dressed in a flowing white gown that seemed at once to conceal and expose her body.

She danced with bewildering abandon, and the others followed in her wake – not matching her gestures, but the spirit of the dance, its wild, dark heart. Behind her the village green was filled with figures in motley clothing: harlequins and travellers, a vagabond in clumsy face paint drawing rough caricatures of the people in motion.

James had never seen it like this, the swirl of movement and rhythm and wild laughter. Somehow it was both alien and familiar, speaking a language he understood; as if the very melodies here had been playing for years in some dark recess of his skull, and he'd only now come to realise it.

The coach pulled to a halt in a rutted patch of shadow just next to the inn. 'Stopping here for the next few hours,' the coachman yelled. 'Don't even think about sleeping on the coach. I've spent one too many nights cleaning piss off the benches.'

James clambered down, trying to avoid a hard landing, and joined Whittell, who was staring at the festivities, searching for a route through the crowd. At the sight of the inspector, one of the women peeled off from the parade and slunk close, running her hand down his arm. She was not unattractive; her hair was a mass of flaming curls, her smile wide and somehow unmarked by holes, but Whittell recoiled from her with a look of revulsion.

Startled, the woman stumbled back, her eyes wide, then something hungry and wild entered them; she looked like a young dog, rebuffed and becoming ever more playful, hurling itself at its trainer. Whittell answered her grin with a low growl, then slipped away from her down the side of the parade, pressing himself against the walls to evade the crowd. The woman watched him go for a second or two, shaking her head in amusement, then turned to James and spoke with a lucidity he found startling.

'I hope he's no friend of yours,' she said.

'Just another outsider who thinks he knows this place from its census records,' muttered James off-handedly, although he too watched Whittell closely as he crossed the square.

She smiled, an oddly forced expression that he suspected was an attempt to flirt. 'You know what it's about? Tonight?'

James nodded. 'You're celebrating still being here,' he said. 'Didn't realise that was all that much to celebrate.'

'Things are dark in these parts,' said the woman, her eyes bright. 'So much blood shed in this place. So many lost.' She shook her head. 'But the darkness hasn't swallowed us up yet. We're not beaten.'

He furrowed his brow. 'You mean the void.' He lowered his voice, leaned in, not sure who might be able to hear him if they had a mind to. 'Are things worse now than they were?'

The woman snorted. 'They've been going bad for near enough a quarter-century,' she said, 'ever since that old fool on the hill promised us his "better way to live".' She rolled her eyes. 'This place asks a lot of its people. But at least it used to give something back in return.'

'So all of this — it isn't a way of giving thanks,' said James, gesturing at the festivities that whirled around him. 'It's a mark of defiance.'

Her face broke into a grim smile. 'Exactly,' she said. 'Tonight's the night we say, "Fuck the Harringleys, and the Tall Man too!"' And with that the woman kissed James on the cheek, and plunged back into the crowd without warning. He stared after her for a moment.

Ahead of him he saw the sign of the Hare Inn, its icon leaning and misshapen. He groped his way towards it like a drowning man, assailed on all sides by voices, hands, without purpose, without discernment. The square of golden light opened into a long, oak-panelled hallway, at the end of which sat a low-ceilinged bar. Behind it stood the skeletal owner, familiar in a tweed waistcoat, who raised his eyes as James's shadow crossed his doorway. His look was of the mildest curiosity, but there was more cunning in those eyes than he let on.

'You look lost, sir,' he said with a smile, raising an eyebrow. That level of familiarity was expected: James could hardly pass as a gentleman anymore. He supposed the barman didn't recognise him. All the better.

If there'd been another option for lodgings he'd have taken it. This place was far too close to home. But it was four miles across the moors to the next settlement, and walking there by day meant taking a path lined with the bones of unlucky sheep. Crossing the moors by night was an easy way to meet the same fate.

'Looking for a bed for the night,' he said. 'Can you help?'

The bartender stuck out an underlip and looked James up and down. It was a brisk, thorough appraisal, taking in everything from the cut of his jacket to his height, bearing and manner. 'You travelling through?' the man said. 'Here for the festival?'

'Catching up with some relatives. I'm from this part of the world.'

Just a hint of a frown on the man's face then. 'You'd never know it,' he said.

'To my shame,' said James, the words hollow and unconvincing as they left his mouth. 'I've been away from here a long time.'

Still the barman watched James out of the corner of his eye, a sly smile flickering at the edge of his lips. As though the man possessed some secret knowledge, knew it all already, enjoyed watching James squirm. 'How long?'

'Near enough a decade.' *Seven years*, James thought, but that would give him away.

Another of those appraising nods. 'But you came back,' the barman said.

'Do all your guests get this kind of interrogation?' said James, trying to keep his tone light. 'Anyone would think I'm not welcome.' From outside there came a great roar of laughter, but James forced himself to stay focussed on the barman.

'Oh no,' said the barman, his surprise genuine. 'You're most welcome, of course. Only we have some unusual customs here.' He gave a tiny shrug. 'Might take a little explaining.' He pursed his lips, gave a thin smile. 'But you'll be well acquainted with all that, I suppose.' He knelt and retrieved a glass from beneath the bar. 'Stand you a drink?' he said, setting it down. 'Toast the coming of spring?'

'Very kind,' said James, setting down his bag, although the

tension remained across his shoulders. 'Brandy, if you have it.'

'Certainly,' said the barman, removing a sticky bottle from the highest shelf and scraping away at the layers of caramelised liquid around the rim with his paring knife. 'Been a while since anyone ordered this,' he said conversationally. 'I'll get there soon enough, mind.'

'Not to worry,' James said. 'Most things taste better when they've had chance to mature.'

'Oh, I don't know about that,' said the man, still scraping away in the grooves. After an eternity of pulling and sawing, the stopper came out and the barman poured a decent measure of sticky ochre liquid then slid it across to James. 'Enjoy,' he said, and James tried to muster a convincing smile. He was exhausted, uncomfortably aware of his aching back, and surely it showed. 'After that we'll see about finding you a room and something to eat.'

The glass was shabby and stained with finger marks, and the brandy left an oddly bitter taste on his lips, although its warming effect was undeniable. James sipped gingerly at it, waiting for the inevitable questions, but the barman seemed quite willing to remain silent, watching James with a quiet intensity.

'Will you be joining the festivities later, then?' said the barman as James took a final sip of his drink and pushed it from him. The bar was still almost totally empty, its only other inhabitant a small man in a long black coat who sat slumped over a table next to the low fire. 'They're quite the spectacle.'

'Not sure I share their enthusiasm,' James said, raising his eyes. He'd all but forgotten the chaos outside; now he was aware of it again: the throbbing bass of drums, the screech of fiddles in a fragmented, torturous jig. There were shouts, drunken laughter – not the sounds of a party dying down. 'Time hasn't been kind to this place.'

'It's not so bad,' said the barman with a tiny shrug. He rubbed his chin. 'Way I hear it, things are getting darker everywhere. Least our children aren't living in slums.'

'No. They met a much worse fate,' muttered James, almost without realising, and at the look on the barman's face he knew it was a mistake.

He frowned at James, stared at him for a moment or two, apparently trying to make him out. 'They did a great thing, those children,' he said. 'And their parents too.' He sniffed. 'You're from round here,' he said. 'I'd have expected you to understand the debt we owe them.' There was real anger in his voice, and James could feel the threat of violence radiating from him. He glared down at James's glass and then swept it away from him, tipping the dregs into a heavy pewter tankard. He looked James in the eye, challenging him to speak up.

'Forgive me if I said something wrong,' said James with a deference he didn't feel, fearful of being cast out. 'I've been away a long time.'

The barman's frown showed no sign of softening. 'I'd best see how the food's getting on,' he said coldly. 'Come on,' he said, moving out from behind the bar. 'I'll show you up to your room first.'

6

THE ROOM was located directly above the bar, a low, cramped space with three small windows along one wall, looking out over the village square. A lumpy mattress lay on top of a rough wooden frame, a small pile of scratchy-looking blankets at one end. Opposite the bed hung a picture, clearly painted by the same artist who'd crafted the hare for the inn's sign: the style was instantly recognisable, intricately detailed and yet oddly childish, realist and somehow distorted.

The painting was a scene of rustic gloom: it depicted a traveller, a woollen cloak thrown over his shoulders, walking a long road from the mountains. At his arm stood the silhouette of a man, tall and skeletally thin, filled from top to toe with golden light. On first glance, the picture seemed to be of a man supported on his way by a bright angel. But if you looked again, you'd see the traveller was grimacing, stumbling – weighed down by the presence of his companion, warped somehow by proximity to him.

Outside the window was a thin, cobbled alleyway in which the coach was parked. It was lit by a shaft of light from the main street, and in it were two figures pressed up in an embrace against the wall. James couldn't see their faces, but it was hard to shake the sense that one of them was looking straight at him.

He settled himself on the bed and closed his eyes, exhausted. As expected, the mattress was lumpy beneath him, the sheets scratchy on his skin. The rash he'd felt on the coach had spread across his neck and the back of his arms, the skin of them as red and mottled as if he'd been stung by nettles. The top layer of skin was flaky, peeling away like wallpaper, and beneath it his wrist was red and swollen. Even looking at it was painful; he had the sensation that something was moving beneath his skin, that the pulse in his arm was not blood flowing through his veins but some insect burrowing out, poised to emerge at any moment.

He closed his eyes, tried to remember the city, his apartment, even Gabriel's face – but nothing would come. His mind felt like it was still on the coach, unable to be quieted, shifting from one thing to another. Sophia's pale, anxious face; the child's fists, closing and unclosing in its crib; the dark snarl of branches overhanging the driveway.

And then, right on cue, he heard a sound that was all too familiar from years spent living next to Newcastle docks: there was something in the walls. He could hear the scratching, scrabbling sound of its claws, as though trying to dig its way out. He kept his eyes closed, tried to track it – that worked at home – but the sound seemed to be all around him.

James rose from the bed and listened to the sounds shift and pulse across the room until they seemed to settle beneath the picture. He crossed to the wall in slow, measured steps. He couldn't make out the sound – it was too large to be a rat, surely, too heavy and clumsy – and it sounded as though whatever was in there was holding onto something, pulling his wall away in chunks. When he reached the spot where the noise seemed loudest, he was startled to see it throb with what looked like a heartbeat.

It was impossible. He recoiled, and stared again at the spot for thirty seconds or so, waiting for that same flicker of life – but there was nothing. He pressed his hands to his temples, feeling the beginnings of a dim pain at the back of his skull, then looked at the wall once more, trying to convince himself there was nothing to see. Rats, nothing more.

Now the wall seemed almost to glisten. He moved towards it, the scratching still in his ears, more intense than ever, and reached out, pressing his fingers to the plaster. At the first touch it was spongy, like raw meat, but when he pressed a little harder the plaster dissolved like wet paper on his fingers, the very fabric of the room turning to an ashy paste.

He shuddered, recoiling from the walls, wanting to be as far away from them as possible. His stomach roiling, he closed his eyes in a desperate attempt to still the nausea, but there was no peace here: the room kept pressing in on him until he flung open the door and threw himself into the corridor.

He'd felt fear like this before. The memories came in flurries, one after the other, seeping in like rain after a storm. He was in the house, a boy of sixteen, running towards an oblong of darkness where the panels had been pulled back in the walls. And as he ran he felt the presence behind him, felt the rush of wind as someone dived on him and drove him to the ground. His forearm collided with the hard floor, the breath knocked out of him.

Oh God, please not this – not again—

He heard his father's wrenching howl of despair, so visceral and furious it sounded inhuman, and then the old man was over him. Pounding James with his fists, landing blow after blow, crying all the while.

'I'm doing this for your own good,' he said, over and over, between blows. 'One day you'll understand. I'm doing this to save you.'

And so it went on, as it always had, the pain as awful now as it was then, winding and bruising and snapping—

And then he was out on the estate, a boy of twelve in a rainstorm. In those days he'd taken to avoiding the house, suffocated by its atmosphere. Ever since that day in the woods, he thought his father regretted the wide boundaries he'd set for James – telling his eldest son he could go wherever he chose, provided he stayed on the boundaries of the estate, effectively meant James and his father met only at mealtimes. But James was certain his father was still watching somehow: the servants had been instructed to follow him at a distance, perhaps, and check no calamity had befallen him.

He recalled being unsure how often his father patrolled the boundaries of the estate, whether he knew how poorly defined the boundary lines were. The fences were decaying and tumbledown, where James could find them at all, and often overgrown by bushes or sinking into the mud– the earth was reclaiming its territory, as though to make a mockery of his father's attempts to set limits upon it.

It was those boundary lines that James found most interesting – perhaps it was just the frisson of danger he got from being where he shouldn't be, or perhaps he'd wrung out the novelty from every other corner of the estate by the age of twelve. That was where he'd been on the day of the rainstorm, out on the edge of the hill, at the bottom of which the village was dimly visible. The fence was still standing there, albeit rickety and uneven, and he sat with the woods at his back. It wasn't as though there was much to see from there, but even watching the carts making their way to and from market was oddly hypnotic.

It was late afternoon when James saw the rain clouds rolling in across the village, vast and imposing; saw the flashes of lightning from afar, felt the cold wind sweep across him – and then with a hiss the great bowl of the valley was filled with torrential rain, so heavy and dark that it seemed as though the whole world had been shaded over in charcoal. The rain hadn't reached him yet, but it was only moments away, so he shuffled backwards into the shelter of the trees.

When he was safely under cover, he looked back at the landscape and saw it – the silhouette of a man, top-hatted and formal, making his way up the hill. His stride was upright and purposeful, as though the weather hadn't even registered, and he seemed impossibly out of scale, as though he'd been somehow elongated. And what's more: there was no way James could have missed him approaching, nowhere he could possibly have been hiding while James looked down the hill. It was as though he had emerged from the earth itself.

There was something about his movements that were wrong, a stiffness to them, a faint delay to the swing of his arms that gave him a strange, herky-jerky quality.

'Stop,' James said, mustering his courage. He took a couple of steps forward out into the sheets of rain, forcing himself to summon his father's voice from somewhere deep within. 'You can't come past this point.' At a distance the figure seemed like a man without a face, without features. 'Do you hear me?' James called again, louder now. 'This is private property.'

But the figure didn't stop: it approached the fence and paused for a moment, as though considering James's words – and then, looking straight at James with that strange, eyeless face, it stepped over the fence and continued walking towards him with long strides.

It was then James felt a blank terror grip him. He backed away from the figure until he felt the trees behind him, and then he turned and ran, ran without looking back, his arms torn to ribbons by the branches in his path, panic gripping him whenever he stumbled and went flying on to his knees.

When he reached the low bed of a stream he paused. He wasn't sure how long he'd been running, but his lungs felt like they were filled with lightning and he could taste blood in his mouth. When he turned to study the woods he saw only a twisted mass of tree trunks, spindly and distorted, stretching back as far as he could see – there was no sign of the figure who'd pursued him.

Keeping his eyes on the woods, he bent to the water and cupped his hands, drinking as best he could.

Whatever that thing was, it wasn't human. Some creature of the land, formed from the soil. This was what his father was afraid of, this was why the old man had warned him not to stray too far. In his guts James felt a sick thrill that might even have been excitement – there was more to this world after all.

He glanced back up at the woods again, and then he saw it: a flicker of movement, one of those trunks seeming to uproot and move towards him with great purpose. He blinked back the impossible vision, trying to take it in, and moments later his terror caught up with him. He was frozen with a mad panic, his stomach roiling, his every muscle tensed.

He was going to die here, he knew it. There was no protection within the boundaries of the estate, nothing special about this land – this *thing*, whatever it was, would keep coming, implacable.

'What do you want?' he heard himself call. 'I've done you no harm.'

There was no answer: only the wind rustling in the branches, the low hiss of rain in the distance.

'You don't want me,' he heard himself call. 'I'm nothing.'

When he glanced at the woods now there was no sign of movement – but the strangest thing, that sensation of being watched, as though whatever was out there was dead still, head cocked, listening.

When he heard the voice it seemed to come from all around him, from the very woods itself, although it left no trace of an echo.

WE BOTH KNOW THAT IS UNTRUE, he heard it say.

That was when he began to run again.

He stumbled back through the doors of the house an incoherent mess; even Ransford seemed taken aback at his red face and torn clothes. He was covered all over in nicks and scratches, although he didn't remember catching his clothes on anything.

'Come on, sir,' said Ransford quietly. 'Let's clean you up before your father sees you.'

Except Ransford was too late: James's father had already emerged from his study at the sound of a commotion, and was now surveying James from the balcony. James craned his neck to look up, his eyes blinded by the sunlight streaming through the window.

'Father,' he said. 'I'm sorry – the woods – I saw something—'

His father's jaw was tight as he descended the stairs. 'What did you see?' he said. 'Those woods are dangerous.'

James felt tears prickle unexpectedly in his eyes, a weakness in his limbs that threatened to uproot him entirely. 'I kept to the estate – like you said – but it wasn't enough—'

'James,' said his father, kneeling next to him and addressing him with a surprising tenderness. 'This place is set in its ways. Its villagers cherish their traditions.' He looked James in the eye, and held his son's gaze until the threat of tears had subsided. 'They'd rather I kept things as they've always been,' he said, with a sigh. 'I suspect that's what today was, an attempt to threaten you. But it won't stand. I won't be bullied.' He raised his eyebrows, tried a smile. 'Now tell me. What did you see?'

James thought back to what he'd seen and heard – that strange, echoing voice that seemed to come from everywhere and nowhere, like nothing he'd ever experienced. 'There was a man – or something like a man,' he said, finding words inadequate to the task. 'And a voice that came from the woods, and from nowhere.' He sniffed. 'It's hard to explain.'

His father was silent then, his smile gone, his eyes hooded. 'And you're sure you were on the estate when this happened?'

'Yes. I swear. Near the boundaries, but on the estate all the same.'

'That can't be right.' He shook his head, visibly concerned. 'It can't be.' He stood up, glancing over James's head in the direction of the woods, a frown etched on his face. 'You shouldn't have been that far out, James, not after what happened when you were a boy.' He couldn't even look at his son. 'You know it's not safe out there.'

'But I did everything right—' James hated the whine in his own voice.

'That's enough,' said his father, fixing James once more with a hard stare. His concern had turned into exasperation. 'It's like you can't resist searching out trouble,' he said. 'After all I've done to protect you and your brother, I'd have expected a bit more sense from you.' He turned to Ransford with a sigh. 'Get him some fresh clothes, Ransford,' he said, already striding off. 'I can't let this carry on any longer.'

And then that terrible night in the village came back to him too –
standing over Emily with her stomach sliced to ribbons, her
guts spilling out past her fingers. He saw her try to rise to her
feet, to walk with her hand pressed tightly to her abdomen…

And his father, stepping out from a doorway, catching Emily
as she began to fall, and hissing into his son's ear: 'What have
you done?'

And then James was running into the woods, the trees
closing in on all sides, the night darker than he thought possible;
his head pounding, praying his foot would not stumble.

The memories lasted only moments, but they left him bruised;
there was a sharp pain in his chest and a pounding at his
temple.

Below him, in the bar, he could hear people were laughing –
deep, untroubled belly laughter. The low murmur of chatter
sounded convivial, conspiratorial. Up here he could hear
only the scratching, somehow even louder and more insistent
now. Several long, hard strokes, followed by a flurry of shorter
scratches. Something in his room was trying to claw its way
out, he was certain of it. It sounded agitated – or at least he
hoped it was panic, the terror of being trapped in the dark,
rather than impatience.

Enough. He couldn't stay in his room all evening. Let them
ask who he was, and he'd tell them. Tell them why he left too,

even. Give them something to talk about over their beer, some new stories about Harringley Manor.

He flung open the door, grabbed his cane and jacket from the chair where he'd left them, then made a quick exit. If he had to stay here for the night, so be it — he could at least make sure he was unconscious first.

7

D INNER WAS a thick, dark stew, some meat he couldn't determine cooked for hours in stout. It was rich with barley and sweet lumps of root vegetable; rustic fare, without any polish, and when it was set before him James felt an instinctive anxiety, certain that his table manners would give him away. All around him red-faced and sweaty labourers sipped their drinks and acted like they weren't trying to figure him out.

The sleeve of his jacket chafed every time he lowered his fork to the bowl, the itching almost unbearable. He wanted to dig his fingers into the swollen skin, could just imagine the sweet relief of tearing away at the flesh until the blood flowed freely. It took a concerted effort to force himself to think about something else, and he dreaded the thought of lying in bed later with nothing to distract him.

A short way down from where James sat was Inspector Whittell, looking less rattled than he had amidst the festivities. In the pub's dim light James thought he was in his mid-thirties, a little shabby and scuffed around the edges, with a kind of haziness to him: his cuffs were starting to wear thin, his jacket fading to grey. He was handsome in a gruff sort of way, but tired too; as he lifted a mug to his lips his every movement was weary. He noticed James watching, jerked his chin up in an unexpected gesture of welcome.

'Oh, hello again,' he said. 'Come and join me if you like.' There was a Yorkshire lilt in Whittell's voice, but only a faint one.

At James's hesitation, Whittell smiled, his demeanour softening. He looked James properly in the eye. 'It's alright,' he said, raising his eyebrow. 'I don't bite.'

'Does your offer of a drink still stand?' James heard himself say, as the image of his room with its pulsing, flaking wall came into his mind, along with the sound of agitated scratching. Drinking with Whittell felt like a less risky option than another minute in there.

Whittell patted the table next to him. 'Sit down with me,' he said. 'Finish your stew.' He nodded over to the bar, and made a confident gesture to summon more beer.

James shuffled down to where Whittell sat.

'Good man,' Whittell said. 'You look like you've had a long day.'

'Like you wouldn't believe.' He was surprised how easy it was to slip back into the vernacular of the city, and how comfortable. This was where he belonged, in the company of normal folk.

'Have you come far?' said Whittell, with a long sip from his beer, and cocked his head at the puzzled expression on James's face. 'Your accent. You don't sound like a local.'

'No,' said James on instinct, then frowned. 'I'm not. Not anymore.' His tongue felt heavy and uncooperative in his mouth; he sounded clumsy and stupid, and he hated it. The arrival of a heavy tankard filled with stout was a welcome distraction.

Whittell's eyes were bright with amusement. 'You don't sound sure,' he said

'I mean…' James sighed. 'I grew up around here. But that was a long time ago.'

'And what exactly brings you back?' said Whittell.

'I have family here,' said James, and Whittell frowned.

'Here?' he said, incredulous. 'In the village?'

'Is that so strange?' said James, although some part of him could already tell he was on dangerous territory, off the beaten path and into the woods. He lifted the tankard to his lips and drank a quarter of its contents in a single go.

Whittell stuck out his lip, still thinking. 'You'll have to excuse me saying so, but to me it feels very strange.' There was still a spark of amusement in Whittell's eyes, as though all of this was a parlour game. 'You seem awfully refined compared to our drinking companions,' he said, glancing round with a touch of theatricality.

'People do manage to escape this place, you know, Inspector.' James heard the petulance in his voice and knew it was a mistake. Perhaps all of this was a mistake, but it was done now. Another large mouthful of stout, and with it the promise of oblivion.

'It seems like remarkably few people manage it,' said Whittell, his eyebrows raised, 'at least if reports are to be believed.' He sat back in his chair and surveyed James, his arms folded, his lips pursed. After a couple of seconds, he nodded, as though confident in his deduction. 'You're him, aren't you?' said Whittell. 'The Harringley boy. The one who ran.'

James sighed. 'Was it that obvious?'

'Terribly so,' said Whittell, a smile prickling at his lips. 'But then you have to remember that I've been doing this detective thing for some time.' He paused, perhaps considering whether he'd overplayed his hand by exposing James. 'Listen,' he said eventually, 'how would you feel if I asked you some questions about your family?'

To his surprise James felt no panic, only a grim resolve – after all, if Edward wouldn't take the threat seriously, at least Whittell might. 'How do I know that you're not going to smear my family's reputation in the dailies?' he said, studying Whittell's reaction.

'Oh please,' said Whittell, somehow managing to remain jovial in spite of his apparent exasperation. 'I'm not some kind of yarn-chopper. I'm interested in finding out what happened to that girl, and nothing more.' He took another sip of beer, and when he resumed there was a hint of steel in his tone. 'But ask yourself this, sir. If your family had something to do with what happened to that girl – to Janey – then wouldn't you think they deserve to have their misdeeds shouted from the rooftops? Wouldn't it be better if they were?'

Again James drank. His tankard was almost empty now, and Whittell had already motioned to the bar to summon another. All the better: perhaps if he was drunk, Edward wouldn't accuse him of deliberate sabotage. 'Is this trying to convince me to tell you our secrets, Inspector?' he said, hearing the slightest of slurs in his voice.

'So you admit you have secrets?' Whittell said, his smile widening.

James paused then, taken aback by the confidence of this strange, forceful man. 'How about we start with you, Inspector?' he said, emboldened by alcohol. 'If I were going to tell anyone about what it's like living up in Harringley Manor, why should it be you?'

Whittell rubbed his chin, thought for a moment or two. 'Because I know families like yours,' he said. 'They think the world belongs to them.' A flicker of distaste crossed his face. 'I'm telling you this because I think you agree. I think that's why you ran. Tell me I'm wrong.'

He wasn't, although James didn't want to tell him that right away. 'I'd like to know just what makes you so confident of that fact,' he said, with a heartiness he didn't feel.

Again Whittell thought before he spoke. 'Well, I imagine they're the ones to blame for your leg,' he said, nodding towards James's stick. 'So I'd say you know exactly what they're capable of.' He paused, and James saw his lip curl, despite his best efforts. 'I could tell you stories that would turn you white, sir, believe you me. You'd not believe some of the crimes our aristocracy have committed.' Whittell rubbed at a deep scar on his wrist. 'I got this from a landowner in Kirkby who liked knocking his servants about a little too much,' he said. 'He didn't take too kindly to me when I pointed out they weren't paid to be punching bags.'

They were interrupted by the appearance of two more

tankards of beer. 'Are you sure you haven't already decided they're guilty, Inspector?' James said slowly, taking a long sip from his mug. 'This wouldn't be some kind of vendetta, I hope.'

Whittell looked stung, but he maintained his composure. 'I'm not trying to destroy them, sir,' he said levelly, 'I assure you of that. But in my experience, families like yours prefer to keep matters like this to themselves. To try and keep them out of the light. And that's where the rot grows.' He ran his tongue over his teeth. 'We all feel that rot, sir. Every one of us.'

In the silence that followed James studied Whittell's face. There was a glowing anger in the inspector that scared James. He needed an ally to shake Edward out of his complacency, but letting Whittell through the doors of Harringley Manor could easily light a fire that burned beyond James's control.

Be shrewd as serpents and gentle as doves, the priest told him once. Now was the time.

'What exactly do you want from me, Inspector?' James said, leaning across the table.

Whittell tapped his index finger against his tankard. 'I want you to help me find Janey,' he said. 'To go where I can't.'

'You want me to spy on them.'

'No,' said Whittell, a little more tersely. 'Just to watch them, and tell me what you see. Nothing new. And then when you have, you let me buy you a drink, and we talk.' He was silent a second, running his finger round the rim of his glass. 'I think you used to watch them, sir, and wonder. And something tells me you need someone to talk to now.'

James ran his hands through his hair, trying to maintain

his resolve. Sooner or later he'd have to bring up the Tall Man: if he lost Whittell, it would be then. 'They'd kill me if they knew I was talking to you,' he said with a sigh.

A tiny smile flickered across Whittell's lips. 'Would they now?' he said, a little wryly.

James didn't match his smile. He was exhausted, as though the tiredness of the past two days had slammed into him. 'They're not very keen on outsiders, Inspector.'

Whittell nodded, his expression becoming more sober, more business-like. He was silent for a moment, then asked his question as casually as if they'd been talking about Janey all night.

'The girl who vanished,' he said. 'Did you know her?'

'Not well,' said James, drinking again. 'Not for a long time.' The last time he'd seen her she'd been eleven or twelve, stocky and awkward from helping her father around the estate. He couldn't imagine her nursing a child.

'But you did know her,' said Whittell.

'Sure. She grew up on the estate. Was a few years younger than me.'

'Shall I tell you what I think happened to her?' said Whittell, raising an eyebrow, and James felt an unexpected flicker of irritation with this man so enamoured by his own cleverness.

'Go ahead.'

'I think the child was your father's,' said Whittell. 'Why else would he choose to keep her on when she fell pregnant?'

James narrowed his eyes. 'That's pure speculation, Inspector,' he said coolly. 'You don't know my father at all.'

'You're right,' said Whittell with a nod. 'But from the stories

I've heard tonight, he sounds like a man who believes God put him on earth to single-handedly rescue every widow and orphan out there. Almshouses and rent waivers and worker's pensions—'

'There you go again, Inspector,' slurred James. 'I wouldn't believe everything you hear by the bar.' He found to his surprise that he was gripping the edge of the table, the wood pressing hard into his flesh. His cup was empty again, and Whittell had already motioned for another.

'You'll have to excuse my theorising here, sir,' said Whittell with a genial smile. 'It's not intended to be distasteful. Merely thorough.' He tapped the edge of his mug, impatient to continue. 'So your father gets her with child,' he went on, 'and she gives birth.' He took a long draw from the fresh tankard. 'And then – then she starts talking about money. How on earth she could provide for the child, how she might educate him. Starts to talk about telling people who the child belongs to, maybe.' Whittell rubbed his chin. 'And your father – that's when he gets worried.' He let the last statement hang in the air.

James was drunk, but he wasn't a fool. 'You think my father killed her,' he said icily. His head was spinning now, and in his hazy state Whittell's logic seemed horribly plausible.

'I didn't say that,' said Whittell with the air of a man who chose his every word carefully. 'Maybe it was an accident. Janey took some liberties, your father got angry, and she got scared. Ran away, hurt herself.' He sniffed. 'I don't want to jump to conclusions. For all I know she left the child on the church doorstep and took a coach to York. But you do understand I have to consider every eventuality.'

Except the Tall Man. James remembered how Whittell reacted on the coach: the inspector would never give the Tall Man anything more than a cursory investigation. Not unless he had no other option. 'You don't know this place, Inspector,' he heard himself say, his words slurring in his mouth. 'You can't hope to understand it.'

Whittell frowned. 'You've too little faith in me, sir.'

'I saw it in your eyes. You've no interest in the stories.'

'And you think that's important?' he said, sounding almost amused.

James leaned across the table, keeping his voice low. 'I don't think you'll ever understand what happened to Janey's child if you don't listen to the stories they tell in this place,' he said. 'Honestly, I don't think you'll ever get close.'

Whittell's frown deepened, a trace of anger creeping into his voice. 'Who said I wasn't listening?'

'But you don't believe any of it.'

Whittell thought for a moment. 'No,' he said, resolute. 'No, I don't.' He raised his eyebrows. 'You're telling me you do?'

James tapped the table with two fingers. 'Exactly,' he said. 'Because if you want to know what happened to Janey's little boy, I'd swear the Tall Man's involved.'

'The Tall Man?' said Whittell, leaning in a little closer. 'I thought he was The Crimson Man?' There was a touch of exasperation in his voice now. 'So they're one and the same, these two? The Crimson Man and your... Tall Man.'

James nodded, more vigorously than was perhaps wise. 'That's the name by which I knew him.' He swallowed hard.

Despite the beer, his throat was strangely dry and scratchy, as though something were trying to stop him speaking. 'This isn't a good place, Inspector. There's a darkness under it. Even you can feel it.' Again he cleared his throat, took another sip from his tankard. 'I think maybe it's been here longer than any of us. Forever threatening to drag this place into the earth.' He sighed. 'The Tall Man offered them a way to make all that stop.'

Whittell's eyes narrowed, and he gave an imperceptible shake of the head.

'You're talking about—'

'You know what I'm talking about,' said James firmly. He was conscious of their fellow drinkers, and nothing would draw unwanted attention like the phrase *human sacrifice*. 'They give him their children – and he holds back the void.'

'The void?' said Whittell, looking mystified.

'Don't you know your Bible, Inspector?' said James fiercely. '*In the beginning the earth was without form, and void; and darkness was upon the face of the deep?*' He took a long drag from his beer and sighed. 'The void is the raw material of life. Ancient, and limitlessly powerful.' He could see Whittell's confusion. 'It's what everything in this world was made from. But all that power didn't just vanish when the world was done. It's still there, beneath everything. And that's the problem. It wants to keep shaping what it made.'

Whittell closed his eyes, making almost no effort to hide his dismay. He spoke with a sigh, as one might talk to a madman: 'And you're telling me this – Tall Man – that he's somehow involved?'

'He's – an emissary, I suppose. You might call him a broker.'

Whittell was silent, stony-faced, lost in thought.

'Why are you telling me this?' he said.

'Because I think whatever happened with Janey is connected to the Tall Man. And if he came for Janey's child, then soon he'll come for my brother's.' James felt a sinking feeling, as though a chasm had opened up inside his chest. 'I can't let that happen.'

Whittell shook his head, his lip now curling once more with apparent distaste. 'This isn't the first time I've heard men claim to be demon-possessed, sir. It strikes me as an awfully convenient way to deny any responsibility for your crimes.' He narrowed his eyes, holding James's gaze. 'I've yet to see any evidence that convinces me.'

'What if I could get you proof that the Tall Man exists? That all this is his doing?'

'I'd say you're drunk, sir,' said Whittell, one tooth digging into his lip. 'It's not possible.'

'I'll march you up there right now,' said James, getting unsteadily to his feet, 'except I don't think you'd believe it even if you saw it. I don't think you'd want to.' The steps up to his room seemed like a long way away, and his legs were uncooperative.

'Are you sure you don't need some help, Mr Harringley?' said Whittell, still seated. His eyes were narrowed and his stare intense, and he was watching James carefully.

'That's exactly what I need,' James muttered, and then began walking, keeping his eyes on the destination, steadying himself on whatever he could find.

8

THE NEXT morning there came a knock at his door. James woke slowly, his head pounding, his body refusing to rise from the bed where he lay. In daylight the room was no better than he remembered: the wallpaper was speckled with damp and the walls still seemed to throb according to the beat of an unseen heart.

'Just a second,' he called out. His voice was parched and rasping, and there was no water to be found anywhere. He hauled himself across the bed like a dying fish, until he was close enough to the edge to persuade his feet to touch the floor. As soon as he was upright he became immediately aware that he was still drunk, the ground unsteady beneath his feet as he pulled on his jacket and hobbled over to the door. 'Who is it?'

'Beg your pardon, sir,' came a voice through the door. 'Your brother's downstairs.'

At the words James felt a sudden, inexplicable stab of fear. An image of his father flashed into his mind, his hands bloody, disappearing into the woods with Edward's child – a thought he couldn't account for. He opened the door a crack, saw an awkward-looking man in tails, one he didn't recognise from the house.

The fellow looked a little abashed, and James wondered how long he'd been knocking. He hated to think what he must look like: his face grey, his hair dishevelled. It had been a long time since he'd last drunk himself into oblivion.

'It's nothing to worry about, sir, I can assure you of that,' said the servant affably. 'I believe your brother wants to buy you breakfast.'

In the bar downstairs James found Edward, looking no less tired than the previous night. He was scowling down at two plates of steak and fried eggs ringed with greasy fingerprints; the yolks were speckled with black fragments, but the smell made James's mouth water. There was no sign of Whittell this morning. He was grateful for that.

'Did you sleep?' said his brother before James had even chance to sit.

He could hardly tell Edward about the previous night's drunkenness, even if his brother's question had been sincere.

'I've slept better,' James said, taking a seat and picking up his cutlery. 'Are you not eating?' he said, nodding at his brother's untouched plate.

'I've lost my appetite,' muttered Edward, picking at the yolk until it burst, spreading across the scorched surface of his steak. James picked a couple of bits from the top of his eggs, wiping them on the table, and then began to saw through his steak. He'd eaten plenty of bad meals in his time, and this was far from the worst. Edward watched him with a flicker of disdain – James couldn't tell if it was his manners or the food – and then sighed.

'Listen,' he said. 'I need you to come back up to the house. It's important.'

James frowned through a mouthful of steak. 'I thought something must have happened. You only sent me away yesterday.' When he tried to swallow, the meat stuck in his dry throat, but on peering into his mug he found it filled with more ale. 'Go on then,' he said, taking a tentative sip. 'Tell me everything.'

Edward's eyes were closed, his face a picture of dismay. 'He was wandering, late at night,' he said wearily, 'but not gentle wandering. He was agitated. Scrabbling at the door, tearing at his fingers until they bled, trying to fend me off when I tried to help him.' He swallowed. 'Then he made a break for it, through the kitchens and into one of the old priest holes, but he tripped and fell as he was climbing in.' He sat back in his chair, his arms in his lap and his head bowed, as though he were the one to blame. 'He's pretty badly bruised.'

'Did he say anything?' James's stomach was still growling at the smell of his eggs, but it was hardly the time to take another mouthful.

'Nonsense. Gibberish, really. *There was something in the darkness*, he said, *the darkness was alive.*' He frowned. 'Oh, and *the cracks are widening.* Or something like that. I think he was trying to get out to the woods.'

'He's hardly going to listen to me,' said James. 'We both know he doesn't want me there.' He scooped up another forkful of egg, then raised an eyebrow. 'What exactly do you think I can do?'

Edward looked uncomfortable. 'I want you to take him out of here. Take him back to Newcastle with you.' He glanced at his hands. 'If he's led the Tall Man back to our family – if his presence in our house is putting my son at risk – then he can't stay.'

James set down his fork and stared at his brother. So Edward was taking this seriously, after all. He supposed he should be glad of that. But to take his father back to the city – the place where he'd started again, the sanctuary he'd carved out with Gabriel – it would be ruinous. He'd always be at his father's mercy, no matter where he lodged the old man. He'd always be within reach. 'I can't do that,' he said, finishing his mouthful.

'You owe it to him,' said Edward with a curt nod. 'To the family.'

'I don't owe you anything.'

Edward's tone was withering. 'Why did you even come back?'

His thoughts were flurries. 'I need to think, Edward,' he said. 'I need time.'

With a sigh, Edward sat back in his chair. 'If you need time, you need time.' He thought for a moment, as though trying to find another line of attack, and then, failing, he got to his feet. 'You've seen him now,' he said, 'the state that he's in. If you really want to protect this family, you'd better do it soon. There might not be much left to protect in a week or so.'

Before James knew it, he was getting up too. 'I'm coming,' he said, hurrying round to Edward, uneasy at this abrupt change in his brother's mood. There was a heaviness in his guts now, and it wasn't all from breakfast.

They stepped out of the Hare into the mid-morning sun. Compared to Newcastle's bustling streets, the village's smattering of scattered figures made it seem eerily deserted, although he could see the green was every bit as churned up as Ouseburn's on market day. Edward stayed close to the Hare's outer wall, as though hoping to avoid being seen, but to no avail. Before either James or Edward could reach the carriage, a familiar cry came from down the road. Whittell.

'Hello there!' said the inspector, raising his hand, and James saw his brother glance up at the approaching figure and grimace. Out of politeness Whittell addressed James, but Whittell couldn't hide his interest in James's companion. 'I was hoping I'd catch you, sir.'

'Inspector, please allow me to introduce my brother, Edward Harringley.'

Whittell held out his hand with an affable smile. 'A pleasure to meet you,' he said. 'Herbert Whittell, detective inspector with North Yorkshire police.' Edward shook his hand with a brief, cold formality, but Whittell didn't flinch. 'I've been hoping to make your acquaintance, sir,' he said. 'About your missing servant.'

'Hmm?' said Edward, apparently preoccupied. 'Oh, you mean Janey.' He gave a tiny nod. 'Yes – we're concerned for her welfare, naturally, but I'm sure she'll surface soon enough.'

He looked over towards the stables. 'You'll have to excuse me, Inspector,' he said with an air of exasperation, meeting Whittell's eye again, 'but my father's ill and we're expected at the house.'

For the first time Whittell seemed a little taken aback. 'We're talking about a woman in your father's employ,' he said, cocking his head. 'Surely that counts for something.'

Edward inhaled deeply, as though swallowing his irritation. 'I'm afraid she's not my priority right now,' he said.

'You have a duty to her, sir,' said Whittell with a frown, 'and to the law.'

'And I have a duty to my father, Inspector,' said Edward, his anger now impossible to disguise, 'that's higher than them both.' James wondered if his brother might simply walk off and leave Whittell standing in the shadow of the Hare — which would be both foolish and rude, but Edward truly seemed to want to be anywhere but here.

Whittell chuckled, as though amazed. 'I believe the courts would say otherwise.'

'Then the courts can take it up with me,' said Edward briskly. 'If some judge wants to come all the way from York to see me then I'll serve him tea. But if you'll excuse me, I don't want to spend another minute away from my father.' He was already turning, heading for the stables; Whittell glanced over at James for a moment, apparently hoping for an ally, but James had no power over his brother either.

'That's very honourable of you, sir,' Whittell called after him. 'More honourable than most gentlemen.' Edward stopped then, alert to Whittell's tone, apparently unsure of how to react. 'Your father's lucky to have such a dutiful son.' James thought he detected a trace of irony in Whittell's words, some kind of trap.

'You're too kind, Inspector,' said Edward, not hiding his sarcasm.

'You won't mind if I come up to the house and ask some questions in the next few days?' said Whittell casually, raising his eyebrows.

'Not at all.'

'Of course, I might have found the girl by then,' he said with an off-handed shrug. 'Some ragged fellow at the bar claims he saw her skulking around at last night's festivities.'

Edward's eyes flashed. 'Then why are you wasting your time with us?' he scowled.

Whittell studied him. 'It's not a waste, sir,' he said slowly, 'I assure you of that.'

'Shouldn't you be out there finding her right now?' said Edward, in no mood for Whittell's games.

'I'm not interested in simply finding her, sir,' said Whittell, more assured now. 'I'm hoping to understand.'

Edward shook his head. 'I'm not sure I understand you at all, Inspector,' he said. 'Good day.' He continued on to the stables, not looking back.

Whittell's expression was thoughtful. 'Not much of a conversationalist, is he?'

'He's got a lot on his mind,' said James, equally struck by Edward's rudeness – their father would have been appalled. 'You'll find him on better form up at the house.'

'Yes,' said Whittell wearily, 'I certainly hope so. Make sure he doesn't bar the door, eh?'

'James!' Edward called from the stables.

'Good day to you, Inspector,' said James, faintly apologetic.

'Good day, sir,' said Whittell, but he appeared to be deep in thought, hardly present at all.

The stable was low and dark, ripe with the smell of mouldy hay, and when James entered he found a stable boy examining their horse's hooves, his face set in a look of concern. Edward was standing over him, his arms folded and his face tense.

'We were supposed to be long gone by now,' Edward muttered. James wasn't sure who Edward was addressing: he exuded a kind of generalised irritation.

'Not sure that's going to happen, sir,' said the boy, with the kind of wariness that came from being casually beaten. 'Your horse's picked up some kind of infection.'

A low growl escaped Edward's clenched jaw. 'How the devil did that happen?' he said. 'We've only been here an hour.'

'Search me, sir,' said the stable boy, shuffling back a couple of inches, apparently to put himself out of Edward's reach. 'Splinter from the road, maybe, or trapped stones – poor thing's foot looks rotten.'

Edward knelt, his face a picture of disgust. 'Let me see.'

'I'm not sure you want to do that, sir,' said the stable boy, holding out a hand, but Edward just brushed it aside.

'Get out of the way.' With surprising tenderness he lifted the horse's hoof so he could see its underside, then winced. 'Dear God, that smells awful,' he said, his voice choked and his eyes watering. James caught a glimpse of raw, red flesh and the shocking white of oozing pus.

'Is there anything you can do to patch it up?' James cut in.

'There's creams, sir, ointment. Your coachman is fetching some as we speak.'

'And they'll fix this?' said Edward curtly, rising to his feet. He was pressing a handkerchief across his nose and mouth to mask the smell and looked a little faint.

The stable boy stuck out his lip, obviously unhappy about being the bearer of bad news. 'Not fix it, sir, no,' he said slowly. 'But patch it for long enough to get you home perhaps.'

For a moment it looked like Edward might take his anger out on the boy, but he was spared by the entrance of the coachman, absurdly out of place in his livery. In his cupped hands he carried a small stone mortar, filled with a stark green paste. 'Sorry, sir,' he said, bowing to Edward. 'I know you don't like to linger.'

'No, I most certainly do not,' said Edward. 'What have you got there?'

'It's a poultice, sir,' said the coachman with a grimace. 'Local recipe.'

'I suppose it's the best we're going to get,' said Edward with a heavy sigh.

'You'd be surprised, sir,' said the stable boy, brightening at the sight of it. 'Our local remedies are powerful.' He scooped some up on his fingers and lifted the horse's hoof.

Edward sniffed hard, his expression one of distaste – although

James could smell soil and fragrant herbs, a recipe he remembered from long ago. 'I'm well aware of your local remedies,' said Edward tersely. 'Now get that on there and let's get going.'

The family's hansom cab was hardly big enough for two, and Edward made no secret of his displeasure at being squashed into such close proximity with his older brother. He spent the journey up to the house staring gloomily out of the window as the road climbed and the moors vanished behind thick woodland. James shouldn't have been surprised – they were hardly close – but his brother's awkwardness filled him with a longing for home, and the man who knew him better than his own blood.

He recalled the day that Gabriel had strolled into his offices in the centre of Newcastle. James had been at Samuel Clyburn's nearly four years, one of a half-dozen clerks, faceless in his black work suit. The job didn't ask that much of him, not really: some light book-keeping, letter-writing, note-taking. They were more interested in a certain kind of bearing, a refinement that you could recognise from the second a fellow walked in the door. Sometimes James felt as though he'd joined a secret society, every one of his colleagues cut from the same cloth, all burying their trauma behind a certain reserve. They weren't close, didn't fraternise much. Perhaps that was part of the appeal.

Gabriel had appeared in the doorway in an immaculate grey waistcoat and shirtsleeves, a sledgehammer at his side – and from the moment he stepped in, he instantly looked more solid than anyone in the room. He glanced around at the rows of scribbling young men as though trying to determine who was in charge, and decided in a moment where the power lay. He crossed the room to Mr Clyburn's office in long strides, without hesitation, and James was immediately struck by Gabriel's self-possession. *It must be nice to know exactly who you are,* James recalled thinking.

After no more than five minutes, throughout which James kept his eye on the office door as furtively as he could manage, Gabriel emerged, folding a banknote neatly into his pocket. He looked around, caught James's eye, and gave a single, curt nod. James went back to his papers, embarrassed at being singled out.

He'd intended to eat his lunch in leafy Jesmond Dene, but he abandoned that plan when he stepped outside to see Gabriel leaning against the wall, tapping his sledgehammer against his boot. 'You were watching me,' were Gabriel's first words, his voice low enough that James had to move in close to hear him, and some part of James wondered if he was about to be ambushed. 'Why is that?' Gabriel said.

'I don't know what you're talking about,' said James with a laugh that was only partly convincing, making to walk on, but Gabriel laid a hand on his arm. For a moment James just stared at it. Gabriel's forearm was criss-crossed with thick scratches, his hand rough and strong where it lay against the white of James's shirt. He couldn't recall the last time anyone had touched him – maybe not since he'd left the house. Gabriel's flesh was warm through the fabric.

'You do,' said Gabriel, leaning in, his hand still on James's arm. His lips were pursed, his eyes thoughtful. 'What is it you think you see?'

'I – I just wondered what you were doing in our offices,' James muttered, discomforted less by Gabriel's proximity than by what his colleagues might think if they saw James had been singled out. 'It's not every day a man arrives holding a sledgehammer.'

'Your boss,' Gabriel said, 'he hired me to expand his library.' Gabriel raised an eyebrow. 'Didn't strike me as much of a reader, but what do I know?'

In spite of himself, James laughed. Samuel Clyburn was a desiccated shell of a man, the folds of his suit filthy with dust, his skin pale and flaking. 'You're perceptive.'

Gabriel removed his hand from James's arm. Took a step back, looked James up and down, his eyes wary. 'You've done his accounts,' he said. 'Is he doing this for the money? Building up a collection of books he can sell on?'

James cocked his head, puzzled. 'What's it to you?'

A slight, one-armed shrug. 'Got to know the people you're working for,' Gabriel said, as though this were obvious. 'Give them what they want.'

James felt a tiny kernel of disappointment, and caught himself. What an idiot he'd been, to think Gabriel had recognised something in him. The last time he'd done that, he'd barely escaped with his life. 'And you think I'm going to help you get in Clyburn's good books?'

'I can make it worth your while,' Gabriel said. 'I can pay, I mean.'

'I don't need your money,' said James, surprised by the strength of his own reaction. 'And I don't think you know men like Samuel Clyburn at all.' Again he made to walk off – in his jacket pocket he had four slices of thickly buttered bread and some leftover roast beef – but Gabriel held a hand up.

'See, I knew I had the right man,' he said. 'You don't belong in there.'

The old fear. 'I'm sorry?' said James, bewildered.

'Yeah. You're not like the rest of them,' he said, nodding slowly, his eyes fixed on James's. 'Your colleagues are half-asleep in there, but you're not. This isn't you.'

Now James mustered all the assurance he could find, all those years he'd spent being trained in deportment, and looked Gabriel straight in the eye. 'Who are you?' he said.

'Gabriel Waldron,' he offered a calloused hand. 'Day labourer.'

James hesitated for a moment before taking it. 'James Harringley,' he said, waiting to see if Gabriel reacted to the name, but there was nothing. Mostly people didn't. Names were cheap here, and there were plenty of ruined aristocrats to go round.

'Pleasure to meet you, Mr Harringley,' said Gabriel, holding James's hand a second or two longer than expected. 'Now,' he said, a smile pricking at the corner of his lips as he lifted the long hammer from where it lay against the wall. 'How do you fancy helping me knock down Samuel Clyburn's wall?'

From outside, Clyburn's house looked like any other red-brick Jesmond terrace. That was the problem with places like this — you just never knew what went on behind their doors. Everything had a veneer of respectability since they'd cleared out the slums; it made it too easy for the darkness to hide.

The library was tucked away in the centre of the house's second floor, lit by a small window. There was a faint mustiness in the air that suggested it wasn't well used; the whole edifice had an impractical air. The shelves were too high to reach, the room too dark. *You could read in here,* thought James, *but it wouldn't be much fun.*

Perhaps Gabriel disagreed: when he entered the room, he gave an admiring shake of the head. 'Still gets me, how big this place is,' he said. 'You'd never expect it of him, would you?'

James rolled his eyes. 'For all you know, he starts the day with an epigram from Virgil.'

Gabriel shook his head. 'From our short acquaintance, I'd say that's thoroughly unlikely.'

'You don't think a man like that can surprise you?'

'Not a man like Clyburn,' said Gabriel. 'See, I reckon he likes stuff. Things. All those files of his. I bet he's not touched them in a decade.' He looked around him. 'No, this is his collection. He could just as easily collect beetles.' He raised his eyebrows, as though daring James to argue. 'Go ahead, tell me I'm wrong.'

'You're a good judge of character.'

Gabriel's face broke into a smile. 'Of course I am,' he said. 'I spotted you.'

'And what exactly am I?'

'You're a mystery,' said Gabriel. 'What exactly are you doing here, mouldering away in an office like that? You've not given up on life yet.'

'I'm here to knock down Mr Clyburn's wall,' said James. 'Like I was promised.'

Gabriel held onto the hammer for a moment, studying James, and then handed it across to him. 'Go ahead,' he said, patting a patch of the wall. 'You want me to show you how?'

'It's not that hard to break things,' said James. And he was right.

It didn't take much to shatter the orderliness of Clyburn's library – three blows from a sledgehammer – and James would have been lying if he said it wasn't satisfying. Beyond lay ragged timber and sheeted furniture, a work in progress. Still more books, propped against the wall waiting to be repositioned; he recognised the names of the classics in hardback leather. *The Odyssey*, *The Iliad*.

Gabriel stepped up behind him and peered into the hole. 'Impressive,' he said. 'I wasn't even sure you'd be able to lift that thing.'

'You're very rude, you know,' said James, wiping the dust from his face. 'Stand back, would you?' Gabriel did as he was told and James swung again, sending hard wood cracking and splintering beneath his blows. It took only a few minutes for the hole to appear, and when it did he stared into the void beyond, and waited for his eyes to adjust to the darkness there.

When James next paused for breath, he set down the hammer against the wall, feeling an unfamiliar sense of peace. He was good at his work, but he could never lose himself in it – not like this.

Gabriel didn't speak right away; instead he gazed around at the room, taking in the statues sat in alcoves cut into the wall, the soft gaslights set in black mouldings at intervals. It was opulent even covered in debris. 'Can you believe this place?' he said, half to himself. 'He didn't even bother clearing it out.'

'And there was me thinking you were a good judge of character,' said James. 'Men like Clyburn can always get someone to tidy up after them.' Gabriel stuck out his lip, thoughtful. Despite himself, James felt the pull of intimacy, that desire for a real conversation he tried his best to bury. 'You'd really want to live somewhere like this?' he said after a moment. Dangerous conversational ground, but at least James was the one steering them over it.

'Course I would.' Gabriel's eyes widened. 'You mean you wouldn't?'

'I've been in enough places like this,' said James, just vague enough to deflect further questions. 'They're not all that special.'

'It's a different world, isn't it?' There was something like awe in Gabriel's face.

'Not the good kind of different,' James said. 'It's not much of a life.'

Gabriel was shaking his head as if to block out James's words. He shuffled over to the alcove nearest him and ran his hand over the hip of a marble goddess. 'My God, though,' he said, staring up at her figure. 'Imagine having money to waste on that.'

With the toe of his shoe James shifted the rubble into some kind of pile by the hole, nodded up at the statue. 'Work a little harder,' he said, 'and you might be able to afford one of them someday.'

Gabriel chuckled. 'You'd not say that if you saw where I'm living.' He picked up the hammer, tossing it from one hand to the other. 'I'm happy enough as a day labourer.'

'There are worse jobs.'

'Sure there are. Anyway, I've been doing something like this since I was a boy. It's a damn sight better than being up a chimney.'

The remaining sections of brick were at floor level. James aimed a swift kick at one, knocking it down. 'Do you not have colleagues?' he said, keen to keep Gabriel talking about himself. 'Some sort of – labourer's guild?'

'I work alone, mostly,' said Gabriel. 'Took over from my dad last year.'

'What happened to him?'

'He got ill,' said Gabriel quietly, and then sighed. 'And then he died.'

'I'm sorry.'

Gabriel rubbed his cheek and shrugged. 'Happens. It's a dangerous business.'

'It sounds more satisfying than doing Clyburn's books.' He didn't say: *it sounds like a good death. Pure. Untainted.* And yet

Gabriel's eyes were searching his face, as though they knew all of it already.

'I guess so,' said Gabriel eventually. He stepped through the hole and looked back from the dusty antechamber through to the splendour of the library. 'Well, you've got potential here, Mr Harringley,' he said. 'If you ever fancy a change of career.'

'I'm not sure my leg can stand it,' said James. 'I'm hurting already.' He'd not thought of his injury while swinging the hammer, but now the adrenaline had worn off it reasserted itself with fresh vigour. 'Not to mention that my father would be appalled to see me talking to you.'

Gabriel raised an eyebrow. 'And how exactly would he know?'

'Sorry,' said James, embarrassed. 'That's an old habit.'

'Well,' said Gabriel. 'Assuming you can bear the shame, I'll be here for the next week or so, knocking down your employer's house. Feel free to keep me company in your lunch break.'

And so James had gone back the next day, and the next, to eat his leftovers among the ruins of Samuel Clyburn's library. Of course he did: it felt like coming home.

When James and Edward arrived at the house, Ransford had already fetched their father down to lunch, dressed in clothes that were rumpled and ill-fitting. He looked like a recalcitrant child, slumped in a massive chair, glowering over his plate of meat. It was venison, redcurrants gleaming on one side like garnets. The gravy on top was thick and congealing, already losing its sheen.

The old man glanced up as James and Edward took their

seats, his expression sour. 'He invited you back, then,' he said to James. 'Still thinks you might win me round.'

'Edward said you needed me,' James said, still unsure how to treat his father – whether he needed gentle handling. 'Something happened last night.'

'Your brother thinks I'm getting old,' said his father curtly. 'Forgetting things.'

'You are, though, aren't you?' Edward said.

'Forgetting what kind of things?' James asked.

'He claims I never told him Janey ran away,' Edward said, in a tone of gentle exasperation. 'That yesterday was the first he'd even heard that she was gone.' He shook his head. 'As if I'd keep something like that from him.' He turned to his father, addressed him directly. 'What would I stand to gain from doing it?'

'You were embarrassed by her,' their father said. 'Embarrassed I let her stay.'

Edward looked taken aback, as if he'd not expected his father to speak so candidly. For a moment or two he seemed as though he were scrabbling for words, but ultimately he couldn't hide his disdain, his face twisting into a scowl in spite of himself.

'Alright,' he said with a sigh. 'If I must, then, you're right. I was. Embarrassed.' One hand fingered his steak knife while he tried to keep his eyes on his father. 'You're not the one who'll inherit this place,' he said, his discomfort obvious. 'Who has to live with the rumours.'

His father's jaw was clenched, his expression furious. 'It was the decent thing to do!' he shouted, horribly and unexpectedly loud.

Edward's next sigh was even deeper. 'Just think what they'll say about you in the village—'

'You think they don't talk about me already?' their father bellowed. He looked angry enough that he might leap from his seat and throttle Edward at any moment.

'Enough,' James warned, his voice raised, glaring at them. 'Can you not even speak civilly to each other?'

There was a heavy silence.

'You're awfully magnanimous all of a sudden,' said Edward eventually.

James bit hard on his lip, the pain a vivid and welcome distraction from his brother's goading. 'Unlike you, I remember my manners,' he said in a tight voice.

His father inhaled wearily and lowered the tip of his knife to the surface of his steak, poking it gently through the crust, then speared it with his fork and cut off a tiny corner. He chewed mechanically, trying not to look at either of his sons, eyes fixed on a point just beyond James's shoulder.

They sat without speaking for two minutes, maybe three, the only sounds those of cutlery and chewing. When he was sure they were calm, James spoke to his father again.

'What would you have done if you'd known?' he said.

'Hmm?' said his father. He looked almost dazed, hardly there at all.

'If you'd known about Janey – about her leaving.'

His father took a long sip of his wine and then wiped his mouth with a napkin. 'Who are we talking about again?' he said blankly. 'I'm losing track.'

'She didn't want to stay,' Edward cut in. 'If you'd only been able to see that.'

The old man glared at him for several seconds. 'You're talking about the groundskeeper's girl, aren't you?' he said coldly. 'When did you last speak a kind word to her?'

Edward stared back, his anger every bit as obvious as his father's. James wasn't sure he'd ever seen the resemblance between the two of them so clearly.

'I was plenty kind to her,' Edward said, 'but I always knew my place. That's where you and I differ.'

His father's hand tightened around his steak knife. 'You think I don't know what you're insinuating,' he said, 'but I do—'

'It's not proper!' yelled Edward, slamming his hand on the table.

There was a low, animal growl – James was startled to realise it came from his father. 'Do you really want to talk about what's not proper?' he said, his voice low and dangerous. 'Letting her dump that child on a doorstep somewhere instead of—'

'Oh, you don't know that's what happened,' said Edward with an airy wave of his hand. 'Nobody's found her or the child. Maybe she took to the road, found somewhere she could be free.'

'You should have told me—' the old man said, glowering.

'I did tell you!' Edward said, exploding again. 'We spoke all about it!'

'Then why don't I remember a word of that conversation?'

The silence hung in the air, weighty and horrible.

'Exactly,' said Edward slowly. 'Why indeed.'

His father took a low, shuddering breath, obviously rattled. 'I don't like this,' he said, pressing a hand to his temple. 'I don't like this at all.'

'You see what he's like?' said Edward, turning to James.

James could hardly bear to look at his father. 'So he's getting old,' he said, trying to hide his father's shame. 'That doesn't mean he's mad.'

'He was the one who told me she'd gone, James.' There was something like vindication in his brother's voice, and it was ugly.

'And?'

'All I have to go on is his word,' said Edward. 'Who knows what he did to her.'

At that his father's eyes snapped open again and he sprang up from his seat. 'How dare you,' he growled. 'I knew Janey from a girl. I'd never have harmed a hair on her head—' He grabbed clumsily at the knife by his plate, first knocking it away then succeeding in grasping it.

'What are you doing?' said Edward, looking disgusted. 'Put that thing down.'

But the old man was already making his way around the table, holding its edge with one hand to keep himself upright, the knife clutched in the other. 'I won't be treated this way,' he said. 'After all I've done for this family.' He was half a dozen steps from Edward now, but Edward looked only angry, not afraid.

'You're not going to assault me,' he said, shaking his head. 'I'm your son and heir.'

There was a moment, then, where their father seemed to hesitate. Seemed to catch himself, consider the ramifications of what he was about to do. And then, with a look of utter resolve, he launched himself at his youngest son, closing the distance between them in an instant, driving Edward to the floor. The knife was raised, poised to strike Edward's neck, when on pure instinct James hurled his arms around his father, pinning his elbows to his sides.

'Don't do this,' James hissed into his father's ear as beneath him the old man bucked and rocked with surprising strength. 'You know him.'

'I ought to put him in the ground,' he shouted, spittle flying from his lips.

'You don't mean that,' James said, shocked in spite of himself – not so much by his father's rage but by his lack of inhibition. Edward had shuffled backwards against the wall, and was watching the scene play out with a look of blank revulsion.

'He doesn't want you here either,' said his father, nodding to Edward.

'Let me talk to him, Father,' James said. 'You're better bred than this, both of you.' He wasn't so sure about that, but he had to appeal to their better nature somehow.

'Let go of me,' said his father, dropping his steak knife on the floor with a heavy thud. The tension had gone out of him and he was breathing heavily; when James released him he slumped forward onto his arms, panting. A moment later, his father sought out Edward, and fixed him with a glare. 'This isn't over, boy,' he said, 'you hear me?'

'Good to know what you really think of me,' said Edward laconically. His father gave a hard, shuddering sigh, looked around at them both as though weighing up his chances, and then decided against it. Instead he pushed himself to his feet and stormed off into the hall, and they could hear him stomping up the stairs to his bedroom.

James allowed himself a moment's breath to calm himself, turning to his brother only when he was confident he could do so without losing his temper. 'You're riling him up on purpose,' said James. 'It's not fair.'

Edward stepped forward from where he was leaning against the wall. 'Maybe that's the best way to get him to see sense.'

He couldn't believe how childish his brother was being, how petulant. 'Have you even bothered to go down to the village and ask around before throwing out this kind of accusation?' he said, knowing the answer. 'Find out if anyone actually saw Janey or her child?' Edward's demeanour said it all: he wouldn't meet James's eye. 'No,' James said. 'I thought not.'

'They won't talk to me,' said Edward with a sulky little shrug.

'Hard to blame them,' James shot back. He caught a flash of anger in his brother's eyes then: so he'd got through to him after all.

'If you're so interested in proving him innocent,' Edward said, 'then maybe you ought to be the one asking the questions down there. Make it worth your while coming back.'

James looked at his brother, stunned. 'I just saved you from getting a steak knife through your neck!'

'But you're not going to be around forever, are you?' said Edward in a voice dripping with contempt. 'So it's going to take a damn sight more than that to save this family.' His brother half-turned, then, like he might march off upstairs just as his father had. But before Edward's feet could carry him away, he seemed to catch himself.

Shaking his head, his eyes on the ground, he said in a much quieter voice, 'I'm sorry. That wasn't what I intended from today at all. He's – he's good at riling me up too.'

'Thank you,' James said. 'You didn't have to say that.'

'And I am grateful. Truly.'

'It's fine.' James sighed, still unsure how to deal with this unfamiliar, emotional side to his brother, and keen to get to safer ground as quickly as he could. 'Listen, is there anything else I can do to help? While I'm up here?'

Edward frowned thoughtfully. 'Well, I've been hoping to get a look at Father's correspondence for a while,' he said. 'See if there's anything in there about what he's seen. But the old fool's lost his key, and Ransford won't let me in without Father's agreement.'

'There's a way in, you know. A priest hole that leads right in there.'

'You're joking,' said Edward, his eyes widening. 'I never did find that one.'

James could hardly hide his own surprise; all those years he'd thought he was the only one who'd figured out how to move around the house unseen. 'You knew about them?'

'Of course I knew,' said Edward off-handedly. The contempt wasn't entirely gone from his voice, but there was a flush of real excitement in his face now. 'If you could get into the inner sanctum – that would be extraordinary.'

'Come on, then,' James said. 'I'll show you the way.'

But for some reason Edward hesitated. 'I don't much like it in the walls,' he said. 'I'm always afraid of getting lost, or – trapped in a dead end somewhere.'

'There's nothing to be afraid of,' said James. 'You know your way around this house better than anyone. You'll be able to work out where you are.'

'Even so,' said Edward, chewing on his lip. 'You know those passages better than me. You go through, and open the door for me. He must have a spare key lurking somewhere in his study. In his desk, maybe.' He passed a hand across his face and for the briefest instance James thought he saw pain flicker across it.

And then, without warning, Edward was turning on his heel, striding away across the great hall and up the stairs to the West Wing – leaving James standing alone in that great, wood-panelled room.

James was startled to discover he felt sorry for his father. Maybe the old man had been tupping Janey, but it was more than sex: he cared enough about her to let his mask of decorum slip before his sons. Surely she'd not have left him without sending him a note to explain.

His head felt fuzzy, and nothing made any sense. At the inn, Edward had seemed like a changed man, willing to do whatever it took to save this family – but all his resolve had disappeared when he and the old man got in the same room as one another. There was history here that James wasn't seeing, he was sure of it, and if there were any answers they'd be in his father's study. If he could find something in his father's correspondence, it might be enough to both salve the old man's distress and get Edward off his back.

Already he could see the thought forming in Edward's mind – that his father was capable of murder, might even have been driven to it by Janey's ingratitude. If she'd refused to stay locked in these walls—

He gave an involuntary shudder then – bad memories – and tightened his hand on the grip of his cane. *Nobody's forcing you to live with that pain except you,* Gabriel had said.

All of a sudden he wanted more than anything to be out of this place, out in the sunlight. But some part of him still needed to know. One way or another.

9

OUTSIDE IN the main corridor, James let his hands drift along the walls, feeling for the familiar latches disguised in the panelling. They were all but invisible to the naked eye, but he could find them in his sleep. A single turn of a key exposed the house behind the house.

Even in Newcastle, James still felt the pull of that darkness: to disappear, to be nothing and see everything. He'd felt that same sensation, upon waking, every day for the past decade. He'd got good at resisting it. You couldn't live that way, but that didn't mean the temptation went away.

It felt like only a moment before James was slipping into his father's sanctuary and pulling the door shut behind him. He was shocked to find every surface covered in paper. Books teetered from atop cabinets, a spray of documents emerging from beneath their covers. The floor was a carpet of faces and smudged text, the low fire behind the desk filled with crumpled-up balls of kindling, and from the walls stared down sketches of a family tree he distantly recognised. Their faces were filled with shadows of his own, the hollows and grooves etched out again and again in an unbroken pattern throughout the years. There was an intensity to each of them, a common glare; it was almost unbearable, the weight of tangible history.

James set down his cane and stepped carefully into the room, trying to avoid catching his arm on one of the many piles set on all sides. On top of several were teacups without saucers, their surfaces thick with a scum of milk, their contents the greying colour of rotten things. There was no way to avoid stepping on the sheets on the floor: there were several layers of them, the bottom dissolving into a kind of mulch, the top already marked with footprints. He supposed that if he looked at the corridor leading to the study he might see the faint trail of newsprint, a ghostly set of footprints tracking back and forth.

On the desk was a stack of papers, on top of which sat a small painting of James's grandfather. In the image he was in his late fifties, trim and established, with the confidence that came from knowing exactly who he was. His shirt smart and neatly ironed, his beard cut short, the artist had captured him mid-laugh. It was an image James had never seen before, and he didn't remember it being painted; it was so casual, so lacking in propriety, and he was startled his grandfather had allowed it. Maybe it was intended as a statement: *this is a happy family.*

Beneath it was an autobiographical sketch of surprising skill, his father's face sombre and angular, and even further down sat renderings of James and Edward. On these James lingered only a moment, more compelled by the sheets of paper covered in his father's thin, spidery handwriting, apparently a short essay about his ancestry. From the opening sentence James had a sense of transgressing, stepping upon holy ground, and yet from the moment he began reading he was unable to stop, devouring not only this document but the others, in awe of the treasure he'd almost given up hope of finding.

The first line of the document read:

What destruction we wreak upon the ones we seek to protect.

It was an account of his family legacy – how his grandfather's wanton, profligate life had filled the house with men whose names James's father never even learned, and how as a boy James's father spent his life pressed up against walls trying to make himself invisible. How his great-grandfather so gave himself to drink that the housekeeper abandoned him, and the servant's quarters turned to rot, and when the old man came out of his stupor and hired a replacement six months later there were mushrooms the size of dinner plates growing from the walls and the house had begun to slide into the earth.

On, and on, and on it went, catastrophe after catastrophe somehow averted: gambling scandals, adultery, murder. The house should have been burned to the ground, should be an empty shell – and yet somehow it was still standing, the fortune miraculously intact, the reputation untarnished. Accusers had ripped out their own eyes, had cut out their own tongues, or had vanished into thin air; they had recanted their confessions against the family, rewritten their sworn statements, insisted they'd been possessed.

It was him, James was sure of it. God only knew what he'd

shown them – if he'd forced them to relive their children's final moments, or if he'd given them a glimpse of the void itself – but it scarcely mattered. He'd done it all for the Harringleys. The old woman had said as much on the coach: *There's rewards without measure for them that serve him willingly in daylight.*

James had only ever seen him as a curse, a blight on his family – but it hadn't always been that way. The papers didn't lie. It was the Tall Man who'd secured the Harringley legacy, again and again. He'd made them what they were today.

What had his father been searching for in this sea of paper? James couldn't make any sense of it. It was all too snarled and baffling, and he was too close.

He could hear Edward pacing back and forth outside the door. He glanced around the room, searching for a glint of metal. Nothing. When he opened the desk he found it, too, filled with paper, but there, buried beneath the sheets of paper in the top drawer, lay a long iron key. He wasn't sure his father knew it even existed.

When the door swung open, Edward's expression was one of awe. James could see why: it was like seeing the chaos of their father's mind writ large. All those years the old man had been pretending, putting on that grave and austere façade, while beneath the surface this insatiable curiosity was blooming.

'My God,' Edward said. 'Look at it.'

For the first time James felt wary, as though he'd given away too much, revealed a secret that was not his to share. 'Are you sure you want to see all this, Edward?' he said. 'Maybe it's better to be ignorant.'

Edward's joy faltered. 'You've seen the old man, James,' he said. 'He can't manage this place anymore. Hasn't been able to do so for a long time. I'm going to stop it sinking.'

'You're going to take control of the estate?'

'Well, yes,' said Edward, as though this were obvious. 'Once I have the ammunition to do so.' He sniffed. 'That's always been the plan.'

'But that will destroy him.'

'No,' said Edward, but he sounded very much as though he was trying to convince himself too. 'No, it won't. He thinks it will – and it will undoubtedly be painful at first – but I'm not planning to rub it in. Just to take the burden from him.' Edward glanced up at his brother, and James's hesitation must have shown on his face. 'It's the right decision,' he said. 'I swear it is.' He moved over to James, and laid a hand on his shoulder. 'Thank you for this,' he said. 'You've no idea how grateful I am.'

'I'd like to stay and help you sift it,' said James, his unease growing, 'if I may.'

Edward was already leafing through the piles of paper, only half-listening. 'Hmm?' he said, glancing over his shoulder. 'Oh, don't worry, that won't be necessary.'

James thought of his room at the inn – the all-consuming rot and decay, the scratching inside the walls – and suddenly the idea of sorting his father's papers until he passed out felt welcome. 'Please, Edward,' he said. 'For my own sake.'

This time Edward held his gaze. 'I'd prefer you don't, James, if that's quite alright,' he said. 'There's family business here that I need time to digest properly.' Again there was a challenge in his tone, as though defying James to argue. 'I'll let you know what I find. On that you have my word.' Edward had learned his iron resolve at their father's knee: there'd be little point in fighting against him here.

For the first time in years, James almost regretted cutting himself off from this family.

A couple of weeks after their first meeting, Gabriel gave James the most beautiful thing he'd ever seen. It was twilight and they'd been heading back toward Gabriel's rooms; that was the pattern they'd fallen into after that first week, and by then James couldn't imagine going back to his former isolation.

Gabriel lived in the shabbier side of the city, in a ground-floor apartment a far cry from the perfumed City Centre halls where he'd been working lately. There were holes in the skirting boards, a low mattress on the floor, a battered bureau pushed into a corner with a set of charcoal sketches pinned above it.

When they'd come in, Gabriel had nodded towards his armchair. 'You take that,' he said, opening the bureau with a small key and removing an unlabelled bottle of dark liquor. 'You keep hobbling around on that leg of yours like it's a badge of honour, but it's got to hurt.'

James was taken aback. He often felt that way when he realised he'd been seen. 'Suppose I just learned to live with it,' he said, trying to sound casual. 'Hardly notice it anymore.'

Gabriel looked unconvinced. 'Your face says otherwise.' He found two tin cups and poured a healthy measure into them. 'How'd it happen, anyway?'

For a moment James wanted to fall back on habit: to change the subject, steer away from the past. But in Gabriel's eyes he saw a real curiosity, one without an agenda. Perhaps it was time James found another friend: it had been so many years since he'd lost Emily. 'It was my father,' he said quietly.

Gabriel stuck out his lip, nodded. 'Did you deserve it?' he said, after a short pause.

James stared at him, not sure how to answer. 'That's a hard question.'

'I'm sorry,' said Gabriel, crossing the room and handing James the mug with its handle outstretched. When their hands touched Gabriel didn't pull away for a second or two: the warmth of his rough skin was shocking. 'Whatever the reason.'

'Thanks,' said James, a little choked. He took a sip from the mug: whisky, and bad whisky at that, brewed in somebody's cellar. 'I tried to run away.'

Gabriel set himself down on the bed, frowned. 'And he broke your leg?'

'Yeah.'

'That's a terrible thing.' Gabriel took a long slug of whisky. He didn't sound alarmed, just affronted. 'I don't know how you forgive a man for something like that.'

James gave a short, disbelieving laugh. He'd borne this secret alone for more days than he cared to count, and he'd never imagined this reaction. 'Yeah.'

'You must hate him,' Gabriel said with a shrug. 'I'd hate him.' He shook his head, stared down into his mug. 'But he's a long way from you now, I suppose,' he said after a second. 'Back in Yorkshire.'

'It wasn't just him who was the problem,' James said. 'That whole place was rotten.'

'Don't let him off the hook that easily,' said Gabriel, a warning in his voice.

James was silent for what felt like a long time. These days everything that had happened at the house felt like it happened to a different man. It was better that way. 'He tried his best,' he said lamely. 'He wanted to protect me. Except he – he didn't know how.'

Gabriel gave a harsh laugh. 'I'll say.'

'He gave his whole life to that village. Didn't leave much for me and Edward.'

'That's very admirable. But it doesn't excuse what he did.'

'I'm not the only Yorkshireman who walks with a limp because of who their father was.'

'No, I suppose not. But I'm glad he can't do it to you anymore.'

Perhaps that was the moment James knew he loved Gabriel. There was no pretence in him, no politics; he knew what was good in this world, and he embraced it. He was the first man James had met who seemed to know how to live.

James tried to keep his tone casual, although he felt himself on uneven ground. 'It's better off forgotten,' he said. 'What my father did.'

'I'm not trying to argue with you,' Gabriel said gently, rising from his chair, 'although I've something that might make the process of forgetting a little less painful.' He was already heading towards the door, apparently without the faintest concern that he'd left James alone. 'Won't be long,' he called over his shoulder.

At first James stared after him, unable to comprehend this kind of casual trust, but when it became clear after a minute or two that Gabriel wasn't coming back, James pushed himself painfully to his feet and made his way across to Gabriel's open bureau. Across it was spread a mass of pamphlets, and a sea of paper that looked like Gabriel's journals.

Above the desk, he could just make out Gabriel's charcoal sketches in the lamp light – the sun breaking over the city, a study of a hand, and – and James's own face. It was startling in its accuracy, as though he'd been caught in a candid moment. The eyes were haunted.

The room dimmed, and James turned to see Gabriel silhouetted in the doorway, a stick of dark wood slung over his shoulder; even in the gloom James could see that it was gnarled and distorted. It had been polished to a high sheen, and the gas light flickered over its surface as Gabriel entered the room.

On seeing James sat at the bureau, staring at the sketch, Gabriel raised an eyebrow. 'I hope you don't mind,' he said. 'We've spent a lot of time together lately.'

'Of course not,' said James, his mouth dry. 'I'm honoured.' He thought that was true, although at least some of what he felt was terror.

Gabriel's face softened into a smile. 'I want you to take this,' he said, holding the stick out across his outstretched palms.

'Nobody's forcing you to live with that pain except you.' James stared at it, unable to take it in. It looked expensive.

'It's beautiful,' James said. 'I can't let you—'

'Don't you dare,' said Gabriel. 'It's a gift. And one you sorely need.'

James could see in Gabriel's eyes there'd be no argument here. He rose to his feet and took the cane, ran his hands over its surface, marvelling at how an object so contorted could look so refined. He set it on the floor and rested his full weight upon it, and felt an instant swell of relief through his back, his calves, his feet.

'I don't know what to say,' James said, his voice a little choked.

'Don't say anything,' said Gabriel, setting himself back down on the mattress. 'I don't want to hear another word about it.'

And then he poured them both another cup of whisky, and another – and when night came they found each other in the darkness, and James had never left since.

As he walked the road back into the village, James's mind was a swirl of disordered thoughts. He felt like he'd stumbled into a trap constructed by his forefathers. Now he was being eaten alive, his skin a mass of searing flesh, prickling and burning beneath his shirt.

He wanted to be shut away, far from awkward questions, out of sight of the house. But even on his bed there would be no rest. Somewhere out there, beyond the hills, was Gabriel: the very source of his comfort. How many nights Gabriel had held him close, whispered into James's ear that the past was gone. He needed that stability, now more than ever.

The first thing he did on returning to his room was to sit at the tiny writing desk and begin a note to Gabriel. His words were hasty and scribbled, improper, without even a veneer of respectability. But what did it matter now? Let the postboy read them. Perhaps he knew all about James and Gabriel already.

Gabriel,

I should never have come here. You knew better than I ever did how long a shadow this house still cast over my life, & I was a fool not to listen.

If only you could see this place, then perhaps I could make you understand how my life came to be the way it is today. It's a void, swallowing up everything that's good and right in the world. Sometimes it feels like I dreamed up our house in the city, the light falling on your face from the holes in our window frames.

Whenever I start thinking that way, I remind myself of the postboy knocking at the door, & that letter that brought me back here. That look of sorrow in your eyes, like a man defeated. I'll never forgive myself for making you feel that way.

I thought I was strong, Gabriel. Thought this place had no power over me anymore. But it was only ever you that made me strong. I'm a parasite, a leech.

One day you'll read about this place in the papers. They'll dig up the bones underneath & talk like they've discovered some great scandal. Maybe soon.

I doubt anyone will ever understand how far the roots of this place go, how much of this country has been tainted just by its existence. It should have been torn to the ground years ago. Not only for me, but for us all.

I remain forever yours,
James

10

THE LETTER completed, the room reasserted itself with fresh violence. The scratching in the walls, the scratching in his arms. The mutterings from the alley, the smell of rot. When he closed his eyes he felt as though somebody was watching him, some half-glimpsed figure in the corner of the room who flickered out of view when James looked in their direction.

Another night of oblivion, he supposed. He fetched his jacket from the chair, his stick from where it lay against the nightstand, and made his way slowly downstairs.

When he found Whittell at the bar, the inspector was thumbing through his notebook, his ale untouched at his side. Whittell picked up the thread of their previous conversation at once, as though James had never been away.

'I stopped by the church earlier,' Whittell said as James set himself down on the next stool and ordered a stout from the barman. 'Place looks totally derelict.'

'That so?'

'Mm-hmm,' said Whittell, sipping his beer. 'Grass so high you can hardly read the gravestones. Knocked on the door, but nobody answered.' The man looked harassed and tired, as if he was being held together by pure stubbornness.

'You tell them who you were?'

'Course. Guess I made quite the fool of myself too, as when I turned around I had an audience.' He rolled his eyes. 'Bunch of grinning fools, the lot of them, acting like they'd caught me with horseshit spattered up the back of my waistcoat.'

'Nobody who'd take in a child then?'

Whittell grimaced. 'I wouldn't leave a child there,' he said. 'Pay a visit yourself if you don't believe me.'

'I've never been,' James said. 'My father wasn't much of a churchgoer.'

'He wasn't?' said Whittell, pausing mid-sip, that familiar gleam of curiosity back in his eyes again. 'Surely he asked a churchman to teach you your catechism, your Scripture?'

'Once,' said James, staring down into his stout. 'But he came to us, we didn't go to him. Actually he taught Edward and me for several years, longer than some of our governesses.' He drank cautiously then, still feeling the after-effects of the previous night's excess. 'I think my father quite liked him,' he said after a moment. 'Preferred his company to the villagers, anyway.'

Whittell gave the tiniest of nods, as though some private hypothesis had been proven right. 'For a man who gave his life to serving them, he doesn't seem to much like them.'

James shrugged. 'They've taken a lot from him,' he said. 'From all of us. If it weren't for them, he could have gone anywhere in the country. Started anew.'

'Hmm.' Whittell took another long slug from his tankard and wiped the back of his hand across his mouth; an unexpected, unguarded motion that he had the good grace to look a little embarrassed by. 'How is your father?'

James hesitated before answering. 'Edward asked me to get him out of here. Take him back to Newcastle with me.'

Whittell couldn't hide his surprise. 'And you're considering it?' he said, setting down his tankard mid-sip. 'In light of what he's done?'

'You've no proof he's done anything,' said James firmly.

'I've got a reasonable suspicion, though,' said Whittell, matching his stare.

'Then write to the police in Newcastle and tell them to watch him. Keep digging.'

'You can't deny it's suspicious, sir,' said Whittell with a sigh. 'Spiriting him away from here like that.'

'It might be the only way to save him,' said James. The inspector wasn't wrong, but he had only part of the story – he couldn't understand the danger of the Tall Man, or wouldn't.

Whittell sat back in his chair, drumming his fingers on the table. 'You really believe this?' he said finally, his expression troubled. 'This superstition?'

'You don't have to dig hard to find evidence of him here, Inspector,' said James, fixing his attention back on his tankard of beer. 'Ask anyone and they'll tell you the stories. A decade ago George McKinley drove a pickaxe through his wife's skull and tried to kill three men who came to restrain him. He said she'd been consorting with shadows, that she'd crept naked into their beds.' He shook his head, thinking back to the many stories Emily had told him about this place. 'Just before I left, Agnes Kilmarnock got lost for three days inside her own house, and when she came out she was half-starved and raked with scars like she'd met some kind of beast.' His tankard was empty again, and he'd scarcely been conscious of drinking. 'How many people have lost children here? How many houses have been swallowed up by the earth? How many people have torn apart their husbands, wives, neighbours?'

'You'd find that anywhere in the country,' said Whittell, although he looked uneasy.

'Maybe you're right,' said James, motioning for another beer. 'But this is a small place. A few hundred people at most.'

'And you think the Tall Man explains all this,' said Whittell, his eyebrows knitted into a deep furrow. 'Gives you an answer.'

'What more proof do you need of the void?'

'I need to see it, Mr Harringley,' said Whittell after a moment's pause. 'Need to see it for myself.' He fixed James with a hard stare. 'But I don't suppose you can show me, now can you?'

You don't know what you're asking, James thought, but he didn't say a word.

11

Two of the governesses their father hired went mad. The first hosted a parasite the doctors later found eating away at her brain, while the second had the kind of madness that makes you cut off your own skin. 'Flaying' James discovered it was called, when he searched his encyclopaedia later that night.

Another governess disappeared. Left one night, walking back home through the woods, and was never seen again. There was a search party, a group of labourers from the village who walked the trails for three days and found no trace of her at all.

Some fared better than others. One, a pale girl who was so thin her limbs looked like branches from a silver birch, lasted nearly eighteen months, although when she left for the city of York she did let slip that she'd not slept longer than an hour in that whole time. Another was carried off, vomiting blood, after just a few months.

And amongst it all were two little boys for whom life carried on. When there was no governess, Edward accompanied his father into the village on the old man's trips to collect rent; James sat in one of the library's wingback chairs and worked his way through whatever adventure novel he could lay his hands on. There were bad dreams for a week or two, of course, and on more than one occasion both Edward and James woke from sleep with chests tight, clutching at their throats, but what good was there in dwelling on that? It would hardly make the dreams stop.

When Martha cut the skin from her own arm, Edward was eight. He was the one who found her in the school room, the knife in her hand, drawing a line from palm to elbow. He didn't run right away. He stayed watching while she peeled the skin back, staring down at the mess of gore as though mesmerised.

He sought James out later that night in the library.

'Do you think she did it because of us?' Edward asked him, interrupting his reading.

'No,' said James, setting down his Jules Verne novel. 'It wasn't us.'

'Father says it's because our governesses come from the village. He says they're inbred.'

'He shouldn't have said that.' James sighed. He could hardly brush Edward off – his brother needed someone to comfort him – but even at twelve James knew he was hardly the right person to do it. 'He's upset too, Edward. I think he's just not very good at showing it.'

Edward stuck out his lip, making him look petulant. 'I'm sick of learning history anyway,' he said. 'I don't need it.'

'It's important,' said James. 'Teaches you about the world outside of here.' He nodded over at the window, where the moors were distantly visible over the trees.

'But we're never going to leave here.' There was no sadness in Edward's voice – to him it was a statement of fact.

James spoke carefully. 'You could if you want.' Edward could be a contrarian child, inclined to oppose something just because you'd had the temerity to say it.

'Why would I want to do that?' said Edward, his bewilderment apparently genuine.

James studied him for a moment, startled by how little he knew this boy with whom he'd shared a home most of his life. 'Surely you don't mean that.'

'You should see the way they look at Father down in the village. Like he's the king.'

'They don't think that,' said James with a frown.

'Maybe not a king. But he's the richest and most powerful man here. He made this place.' Edward was speeding up, warming to his theme. 'He says that without our family, there wouldn't even be a village down there. We opened the mine, we built the cottages, we started the farms.'

'He might be powerful,' said James. 'I don't know if they like him.'

'Does it matter?' said Edward, shrugging.

'I suppose it doesn't.' The sight of his brother so enthused made him feel uneasy. He'd expected Edward to be melancholy, thoughtful – not manic. 'You shouldn't believe everything he tells you,' he said quietly.

'Why not? He's right.' Edward glanced around at the library, filled with more books than one man could read in a lifetime. 'Look at everything we have.'

'All of this was given to us. It was given to him, too. He never earned any of it.'

Edward rolled his eyes, a little sulky. 'If you say so.'

'I'm right, and you know it,' said James, glad to be back on stable ground. 'Don't you want to stand on your own two feet?'

'Father says we've a duty to the village. We're to be good stewards.'

James hesitated, unsure how much to disclose to Edward, and how much of what he said would get back to their father. But Edward needed someone to talk to, or at least somebody real, who wasn't paid to talk to him.

'Not me,' he said. 'I don't owe this place anything.'

Edward lounged back against the shelves, silently thinking. 'It needs us,' he said decisively after a minute or so. 'Look at what happened to Martha. And the others.'

'You think we could have helped them?' said James, stunned.

'Maybe.'

'Maybe it was this place that did it. This house. Maybe they couldn't stand it.'

Their father couldn't have entered the room at a worse moment. James leapt up from his chair, the book falling from his lap onto the floor, while Edward pushed himself forward from the shelves to present himself upright. Their father's eyes lingered on James only a moment, just long enough to let him know that the old man had heard what he said, and then settled on Edward. 'I understand you witnessed Martha's – deterioration – first-hand,' he said stiffly. 'I'm sorry that you had to see that. I expected better of her.'

'Will she be alright?' said Edward, his voice a little higher than it had been before.

Their father grimaced. 'I'm not sure she was especially well to begin with.'

Edward looked over at his brother. 'James says this house is cursed.'

'I didn't say that!' James pleaded, but his father's look was withering.

'It's not this house,' he said coldly, still addressing Edward. 'It's this place. The whole village. It gets inside people.' He gave a heavy sigh, as though exhausted by the thought of it. 'It doesn't have to be this way, boys. We can help them. Show them a better way.' He glanced over at James then. 'But that means staying here, no matter how difficult it is. Not running away at the first sign of trouble.'

He let the unspoken criticism hang in the air. James was the first to break the silence.

'That's it?' he said, appalled in spite of himself. There'd been so much blood spilled in this house. 'You're just going to let our governesses keep dying in front of us?'

His father spoke carefully but firmly. 'There are limits to what we can do, James,' he said. 'I suppose you'd have me watch these women at all times, lest they turn the knife on themselves, but I'm not their keeper.' He closed his eyes, as though he too was visualising Martha's flayed arm. 'I give them a home, a wage, and a moral example. That's more than most.'

'It's not working,' said James bitterly.

'Well,' said their father with a nod of acknowledgement, 'I happen to think you're right. So from next week you'll no longer have a governess.'

And so it was that his father enlisted a priest, a slight young man from down in the village with prematurely grey hair and a faint tremor in his left hand. He found the man waiting for him in the gloom of the library, a set of books spread out on the reading table in front of him.

'Hello, James,' he said with a tentative smile. 'Have a seat.' He seemed watchful, on edge, well aware of his status as an interloper. 'I don't know how much your father has told you about these sessions?' he said after a moment. He spoke slowly, his voice snagging on the edge of his words with a faint but distinct hiss.

'Not a great deal, sir,' said James quietly. 'I assume he wants you to teach me about, well, the Christian faith.'

The priest shook his head, gave a little grimace. 'Actually,' he said, 'your father wants me to do no such thing. He expressly forbade it.' He gave a tiny, embarrassed chuckle.

'Then why bring you here at all?' James knew that, as a twelve-year old, he couldn't get away with being so blunt anymore, but he couldn't find a polite way to ask the question that had been eating at him since earlier that morning.

'I asked him that very same thing,' the priest said, raising his eyebrows ruefully. 'I believe he has concerns about what you might hear from a teacher who'd grown up in the village.' He paused, seemed as though he was searching for the right words. 'They're superstitious folk.'

'I'm surprised you agreed to come.'

'I'll tell you what I told your father,' said the priest. There was a smile pricking at the corner of his lips now. 'This faith of mine – everything is tied up with it. History, politics, literature – anything worth knowing – there's no unpicking faith from them.' His smile widened. 'He didn't much like that, James. But nor could he argue with it.'

'Not many people can leave my father lost for words,' said James, impressed.

'I'll choose to take that as a compliment,' said the priest. 'Now. Let's start with some basic mathematics, shall we?'

James liked the priest. He didn't fit in here either. With his ancient stories and his unearthly politics, his way of considering the smallest question as if it might save a man's soul, he was like some exotic plant plucked from far away and planted in a greenhouse to wonder at.

But the priest saw things other people missed. He didn't often show his hand, but he was watching everything.

There were days when he seemed weary, weighed down by it all, as though being among these walls was draining him.

That was when the priest was most distracted, when it was possible to get him talking about ancient kings and their vicious tortures, or about etymologies. He'd lapse into great, rambling monologues, lost in a reverie, sometimes forgetting James was even there. James thought those might have been when he learned the most from the priest, as though every tangent was a coded sermon about how things truly were.

'Your father's not a happy man, is he?' he blurted one day, breaking off from a history lesson in which he'd been tentative and preoccupied. 'Outwardly he does everything right,' he said, frowning. 'But I've seen the life he's built for you and your brother here. Sometimes it gives me pause.'

James couldn't meet his eye, couldn't even speak; it felt as though if he did he might break. He'd known there was something wrong here his whole life, even if no one else had ever acknowledged it. He'd almost given up hope that anyone ever would.

'Are you happy here, James?' the priest said after a moment or two, with such sadness in his voice James was shocked, but before he could answer the priest had answered his own question. 'Oh, I don't suppose it matters much,' he went on. 'I'm hardly that happy myself most days. And the Lord can work miracles in even the most unpromising situations.' He glanced back at James. 'All the same, I worry,' he said, inhaling deeply. 'It's quite a burden you have here. The expectations your father puts on you and your brother. To serve this place, I mean.'

'It's the only life I've ever known,' James said, his voice a little uncertain.

The priest nodded. 'Let me talk to your father,' he said, as though he'd only half been listening. 'I've a few friends down in the village. Perhaps they can help widen your horizons.'

'He'll never let me out,' James said glumly. 'He's said as much himself.'

'Leave it with me,' said the priest with a tiny smile, rising from his chair to pat James on the shoulder. Then he straightened his spine and visibly brightened. 'I'll see what I can do.'

But when help came, it was from another, more unexpected place – not from the priest, but from inside the walls. James recalled sitting in his room, reading, when he heard the faintest of clicks, followed by the sound of wood running along a groove. He had only a moment to register what was causing it before she pulled back the panel in his room and materialised from the rectangle of darkness.

It wasn't until much later that he realised she must have known he was there all along, but if anything, that made him admire her boldness more.

She was a couple of years older than him, fifteen or sixteen he thought, with light brown hair pulled back into a ponytail. All those details that would soon become so familiar, he noticed right away: those intense, thoughtful eyes, her lips a moment away from breaking into mockery. She wore that maid's outfit like she was playing a dressing-up game, without the stiff formality of the other servants. As though it didn't own her.

'You shouldn't be here,' he said. 'My father doesn't like it when we mix with the servants. He'd kill you if he knew.'

She cocked her head and surveyed him. 'Probably,' she said, sticking out her lower lip in consideration. 'But something tells me that you could use a friend, servant or otherwise.'

Her response left him momentarily baffled: he wasn't used to being spoken back to. 'It's not up to me,' he said. 'I don't make the rules in this house. Not for servants, at least.'

'No,' she said, frowning. 'I can see that.'

He stood, arms folded, waiting for her to make her apologies, to turn and go. 'You're still here,' he said eventually.

'You're observant.'

He smiled despite himself. 'Nobody talks to me like that.'

She shrugged. 'So tell me to go.'

'I already have,' he said, nonplussed.

'No,' she said. 'You haven't.' Her eyes widened, a glint of defiance in them, as though daring him to answer. 'I'll go, if that's what you want. Just say the word.'

And yet he found he didn't want that at all: he wanted her to stay, more than anything, although he couldn't say it in those words. Instead he ignored her question, tried a different tack.

'How did you get in here?' He thought he saw her bristle then, just momentarily.

'That?' she said, nodding over her shoulder. 'We call it the house-behind-the-house. It's a set of tunnels that runs through the walls. They used to be called priest holes. You know, to give the Catholics an escape route if they needed one.' She cocked her head, amused. 'You've never wondered how the servants manage to clear away your dirty dishes?'

James's silence said it all: he'd never even asked himself the question.

She gave him a crooked smile. 'No, I thought not. Still, it's not like anyone's been in here for a while,' she said, with a nod towards the piles of books and dirty teacups scattered across the room.

She raised her eyebrows, and he couldn't tell if she was amused or shocked. 'I'd better get to work,' she said. 'If you'll excuse me.' And without waiting for permission she crossed the room, stacking up his teacups and tidying his books while he watched. She shouldn't have been here, of course – servants never cleaned in the presence of the family – and yet seeing her reaching for his things, without the slightest fear or pretence, he was filled mostly with gratitude.

'Do you have a name?' he asked, slumping into an armchair, trying to look casual. He was acutely self-conscious, desperate not to drive her away.

She glanced back and met his eye. 'Emily,' she said. Then, as an afterthought, 'Sir.'

The word gave him a shock of revulsion. 'Don't do that.'

'What?' she said, turning properly now. Again he was struck by the force of her gaze, the dizzying sensation of eye contact.

'Don't call me sir.' He sniffed. 'Please. Call me James.'

'Alright, then – James.' His name sounded cold and unfamiliar in her mouth. It occurred to him how few people in this house used it. 'Do you want to see what this house is truly like?'

He stared at her, bewildered. 'What are you talking about?'

'The house-behind-the-house, *James*. I can show you the way in.'

'You're a servant,' he said. 'Why would you do something like that for me?'

'You stand to inherit it soon enough,' she said. 'Best that you know exactly what this house stands for.'

He should have told his father about this; he knew that right away. But his father would never believe James wasn't involved, that he hadn't asked for this – and Emily felt like the first real ally he'd found in this house. 'I'm ready to see it,' he said. 'Show me.'

She looked him up and down and then nodded, apparently satisfied. 'You'll need one of these,' she said, reaching into the pocket of her apron and withdrawing a long metal oblong, a little thicker than a pencil. She handed it to him; it was heavy, cast-iron.

He passed it from hand to hand, unimpressed. If he'd found it in the grounds he'd have left it there. 'All the servants have these?'

'If they want them,' said Emily with a shrug. 'Lot of people don't like to go into the walls. They get frightened.' She sniffed. 'It's dark in there. They say they've heard things moving.'

'You mean rats.'

'Maybe.' Emily worried at her lip. 'You ever hear rats scratching in the walls?'

James thought for a second. 'Never.'

'Me neither,' said Emily. 'But whatever they think's in there, I'm not scared.'

He could see that. That was why he liked her.

'I don't let myself get scared,' she said, a little proud. 'They don't know how much they're missing out on, the cowards.' She caught his eye, a smile flickering on her lips again. 'Come on,' she said. 'I'll show you how to get in.'

When she opened the wall, it was like she'd ripped the fabric of the world itself. She'd taken his hand from where it rested by his side and placed it on the wood panelling – the shock of her touch made him shiver – then moved his fingers to a seam, a join in the panels that had no place there, out of which flowed a light breeze. His fingers sought out a keyhole unbidden.

The panel slid back into an inky darkness; he could make out the turning ahead, but beyond that nothing. The walls were roughly plastered, half-finished, and there were no sconces to hold a candle or oil-lamp as far as he could see.

She was right behind him, at his ear. 'Are you afraid?' she whispered.

'No,' he said, and he meant it. 'Not of this.'

From then on, if he wasn't in lessons with the priest, he was with Emily. She showed him the way into the kitchens, where he learned both how to steal food from the larder, and which dishes were best avoided; showed him how to peer into his father's study, where he saw the old man poring over his paperwork, head in his hands; and together they watched servants discreetly fumbling in alcoves, their hands reaching inside the other's clothes, their soft moans of pleasure not as hidden as they thought.

To him, Emily was a character from a storybook, the orphan wild and free; she was the Artful Dodger, able to blag her way out of trouble, or she was Pip and Copperfield, working herself up to respectability. She was Mowgli, the noble savage raised by wolves; she was Jane Eyre, better than this world that tried to constrain her.

She told him he read too many books. The life of an orphan, she said, was a hard one. Nobody looked out for you. Everything was a fight.

And so, as his gift to her, he taught her to read – or at least beyond the basics they'd taught her for work. She already knew her letters, or most of them anyway, but he showed her how to lose herself in a story. Some of the skills he hadn't realised he even possessed. How to modify her voice so she wasn't heard. How to alter her posture to lend herself greater authority. How to disappear.

It was easy enough for he and Emily to sneak off into the library. Edward never went there, and their father preferred his study. So when the priest strolled in one afternoon while James and Emily were lounging in the two vast wingback chairs that sat in the centre of the great rectangular room, he got something of a rude awakening.

It was no accident. He knew they'd be there. He'd sought them out.

At the sight of him, Emily leapt up from her chair as though scalded, only settling back into her usual defiant pose when he turned first to James. 'Your father's no fool, you know,' he said, with a hint of amusement. 'He's aware of what you're doing.'

'And he sent you to tell me this?' said James, who'd stood when the priest entered. He felt a little stung that his father had sent an emissary.

'He's concerned,' said the priest. 'Concerned that you'll make some grave error and lead the family into disgrace.' He glanced over at Emily, who dipped her eyes. 'I'm not sure he thinks Miss Emily is the most appropriate companion for someone of your position.'

Emily sounded alarmed. 'Why wouldn't he send me away? If he knew all along?'

The priest stuck out his lip and thought about this. 'He's a dutiful man,' he said eventually. 'A good man, even. He knows your condition in society, and how difficult it would be for you to live without parents. Don't presume he's ignorant of your situation. And I implore you, don't push him too far.' He raised his eyebrows. 'I assume you have work to be doing?'

Emily took the hint, slinking off through the walls with only a single, alarmed glance back at James as she left. The priest looked down at the book James had left open on his chair.

'What are you reading?' he said conversationally.

'*Gulliver's Travels.*'

'Are you enjoying it?'

'I've hardly got much to compare it to. I've lived in this village my entire life.'

'Yes,' said the priest with a nod. 'I can see why that would feel somewhat constraining.'

'Does he want me to stop seeing her?'

'He's not a tyrant, James. I believe he just wants you to be wise. And to be *subtle*.' His brow furrowed slightly. 'Do you recall the words of Jesus, when he entreated his followers to be wise as serpents and gentle as doves?' He studied James's face, hoping to see the bloom of revelation there. 'Every one of us has our secrets,' he went on. 'None of us disclose ourselves fully.' The priest gave a little sigh then, and James wondered what his secrets were. 'But for men like you, and your father, it's important to portray a certain image to the world. An image of virtue and integrity. If you can maintain that…' He tailed off with a faint shrug.

'I can't believe he'd send you to do this for him,' said James, appalled.

The priest gave a wan smile. 'I'm a dutiful man too,' he said. 'I know my place.' He gave a tiny pause. 'I suppose I could go back and tell him you'd rather have it out with him directly,' he said, the words catching slightly in his throat. 'But maybe it's better this way. Cleaner.'

James thought for a second or two, irritation bristling within him. 'Tell him you've done what he asked of you,' he said.

The priest's eyes remained fixed on him. 'And you?' he said.

'I've heard what you're saying,' he said. 'Don't you worry.'

For the longest time it seemed that the priest was impervious to whatever darkness had destroyed the governesses. Somehow he seemed able to resist it, to stop it affecting him. Whatever weariness he felt at his duties in the house, tutoring two adolescents, one of whom – Edward – made no secret of his scorn at the priest's faith, it seemed not to grind him down.

He was good-humoured, affable, gracious; even James's father seemed leavened by his presence there. Sometimes James saw the two of them taking a turn around the house after his lessons, deep in conversation, his father listening almost deferentially while the priest expounded some theory. He was full of theories, the priest, and not only theories about Scripture. He had views on compulsory schooling, architecture, the study of Classics, spoke at length about the soil in which one grew, the nourishment that one took from one's surroundings.

For a little while James thought the priest might be his salvation, his gateway to a world outside the house. He even seemed like he might convince James's father to look beyond the village, and did it as though it was the most ordinary thing in the world.

Was the priest naïve? Didn't he know about this place, about the Tall Man? James asked him that once, at the end of a lesson, and the priest just smiled and said, 'I know enough about this place not to be scared of it, don't you worry. *The light shines in the darkness, but the darkness has not understood it,* dear boy.' He raised his eyebrows like he'd made some great joke, and seemed disappointed that James didn't recognise it. 'John's gospel,

James,' he said, with a distinctly teacherly air. 'It's one of the most famous bits of Scripture.'

All the same, his confidence was infectious – although when James told Emily about it on one of their night-time kitchen raids, she didn't seem to share it. 'You haven't heard the way they're talking,' she said. 'Your father's got some idea in his head. Thinks the priest can perform an exorcism, rid this place of its demons.'

James thought of the Tall Man, clothed in shadows, his voice seeming to come from the trees and the wind. There was something ageless in him, something eternal, which it felt like folly to even consider facing off against – and yet the priest had lasted this long, hadn't he?

'Maybe he can,' he said aloud, trying to convince himself as much as Emily.

'You're wrong,' she said. 'And he is too.' She shook her head, said grimly, 'There's been a village here for nearly four hundred years, and nobody's figured out how to beat the Tall Man. They learned to live with him. Because that's the only way.'

'What if he's right, Emily – what if his god really is strong enough to fix this?'

'You don't believe that.'

'Something's kept him sane this long.'

'He's stayed sane this long because he's got something to believe in – something that isn't the Tall Man. That doesn't mean it's true.' She pressed her fingers into her eyes. 'Your father took on the Tall Man, and look at what happened to this place.'

'What happened to it?'

'Of course,' she said, 'up here you don't see it, do you?' She sighed. 'The void – it won't be contained. It keeps reaching out. There's woods that weren't there before, trees so twisted and deformed that you'd barely even recognise them as nature at all. Thickets filled with thorns as long as a man's arm. Calves cut out of their mothers with strange growths on their shoulders, as though their shoulder blade had tried to repeat itself once, twice, three times more.' She swallowed hard. 'It's your father's doing, that,' she said. 'You do know that?'

He glared at her. 'It's the Tall Man's doing,' he said. 'He's the one to blame.'

'No,' she said. 'Your father was the one who opposed the Tall Man, told the villagers that things could be different. Told them the Tall Man had no claim on their children.' Her eyes were bitter. 'What he did destroyed this village. And it'll destroy him too, one day.' She could hardly look at James. 'Maybe it's already destroying him. Because there's no way the Tall Man has given up on someone as powerful as your father. I'd swear to that.'

'You make it sound like it would be better if he'd let me die.'

She was silent for a very long time. 'This is much bigger than you,' she said eventually. 'Imagine having the Tall Man visit you every night, and whisper in your ear. Telling you exactly what will happen if you carry on down this path, and how to stop it.' She sniffed. 'How long do you think you'd resist?'

∞

James supposed that whatever plan his father had been hatching with the priest – and it was not one the priest would discuss, although James tried his best to get answers – was a form of resistance. But it didn't work. When the house was awoken one night by the sound of a man screaming, clawing at the inside of the walls – when the servants opened up an old priest hole and saw the priest tumble out, his clothes ragged and his eyes wild, James wasn't watching him.

Instead he was watching his father, and the look in his father's eyes. There was disappointment there, a deep disappointment, and terror, and an impotent rage – at himself, and at the Tall Man, and at the god he'd briefly let himself believe in.

The priest was muttering, over and over, under his breath, *'What profit is there in my blood, when I go down to the pit? Shall the dust praise thee? Shall it declare thy truth?'* For ten minutes he sat against the kitchen wall, rocking back and forth, his head almost touching the knees of his dust-stained trousers. Over and over, muttering words from the Psalms, until James's father knelt down by him and laid a hand on his shoulder. The priest had looked up, two tear-tracks visible through the grime on his face, his eyes desperate.

'We'll no longer be requiring your service,' James's father said coldly. 'I'll see that Ransford arranges somebody to take you back down into the village.' And then he turned on his heel and was gone before the priest could even cry out to him.

After that James retreated to the safety of the house-behind-the-house. He never felt safer than when he was there in the darkness with Emily, her arm pressed up against his as protection from the cold. He'd thought she felt that too, until the day she turned to him and said, 'We're not the same, you and I.' She'd paused, waiting for him to answer, but he couldn't find the words. 'I mean, you might live in a prison,' she said, 'but at least you're locked in here with your family.'

They were not equals, he and Emily, no matter how much he felt the warmth of her hand next to his, no matter how much they had in common. Her world was altogether different to his, and even this kind of closeness carried with it the taint of scandal.

'Did you ever consider running?' James said quietly. 'After they died?'

'No,' she said after a pause. 'I was only a girl.' She sniffed. 'Thank God your father took me in. I don't know what I'd have done otherwise.'

The darkness made him bold: in the walls, it felt possible to ask the impossible questions. 'You never told me how they died,' he said after a few moments, dreading her response.

She paused for several seconds before she answered. 'It's horrible,' she said, swallowing hard, and then she took a deep breath, continued in a stronger voice. 'I'm not sure how much I trust my memory anymore,' she said, with a cynicism he didn't find convincing. 'When I think of what I saw – it's impossible, I swear.'

'Try me.' His voice was more confident than he felt too: not even shaking.

'You'll never believe it.'

'You do.'

'Only just.' She waited then, as though to see if he'd press any further, but he already knew she'd made her decision. Not so long ago he'd taught himself how to use reticence as a pose, a way of deflecting unwanted attention, and this wasn't that. She wanted to talk, same as him. She'd not have been here otherwise.

'They were out in the fields,' she said, 'pulling in the harvest. Wheat, that year. I was helping, as much as a girl of five can help anyway.' She paused, sighed. 'My father had the scythe, my mother bundled the crop, I tied the knots. We'd been doing it for days, we were nearing the end of it, and that was when we saw him come.'

'Who?'

'A man,' she said. 'It's hard in the fields; your eyes get tired against the sun, you only see shapes. He was tall, taller than you'd think a man could be, and so spindly his limbs looked like tree branches. Looked like he'd break apart if he fell, but then I guess not every tree is brittle, only the dead ones. Some of them are springy, tough. He was one of them.'

She was scared, he could tell, hiding still from what happened. There was a tangible reluctance in her words, although she was forcing each sentence out anyway.

'He came over the fields and my father stood, leaning on his scythe, watching. He didn't look afraid, just curious. And then, before the man reached us, he bent down and scooped up a handful of dirt, held it cupped in his hands.' Again she swallowed hard. 'Do you really want me to tell it to the end?'

He stayed silent. He wasn't altogether sure anymore, knew only that he was closer to the heart of this house than he'd ever been, that some threshold had been crossed from which there was no returning. So she'd seen him too, seen that same figure James saw on the day of the rainstorm.

'He approached my father,' Emily said with a faint tremor, 'and my father got up from his scythe to greet the fellow, a smile on his face even then, and then the man lifted his hands and blew the dirt into my father's face. My mother gasped, but not like she was afraid, like she thought it was funny, and it kind of was, really.' She was silent for what felt like too long. 'Except when my father looked up, I saw the blood streaming from his eyes, and it was like – his face – like it was – coming apart at the seams.' She exhaled heavily. 'My mother saw it at the same time I did, and that was when she screamed at me to run.'

Her voice was barely a whisper now. 'So I did. I ran for the woods, and the last thing I saw was my mother supporting my father's weight, trying to help him limp towards the woods, and the Tall Man striding up behind her and putting his hands over her eyes.' She sniffed. 'Then I just ran, ran and ran until I saw something that looked familiar, and it was the groundskeeper's hut, and he was outside tending his herb garden, and I'm not sure how I managed to get the words out but somehow he understood anyway. But it was too late.'

He felt her draw away from him slightly, a fresh wave of cool air against his arm. 'If I'd known that was the last time I'd see them,' she said, then tailed off. 'Maybe I'd have stayed. Fought. For all the good it would have done.'

'I'm sorry,' he said. 'Truly.' He was silent, thinking of the Tall Man, and the strange things he'd seen in the woods. The embers of a burning curiosity beginning to catch flame.

'My parents broke the rules,' she said, not bothering to hide her bitterness, 'and they suffered the consequences. They knew they were doing it, and they did it anyway.'

'What rules?' Once more he became aware of the occult world beneath him, of which he lived out so much of his life in ignorance. He'd never felt so much like a child. 'What are you talking about, Emily?'

'This is your father's fault, James,' she said. 'He told them there was a better way. That they didn't have to give me up, and that they could resist. I suppose he was wrong.'

12

THERE WAS no wall around the church or its graveyard. A few headstones sticking up like lone teeth from diseased gums, half-swallowed by long grass. It was a strange place, the church, an obscure monument on the edge of the village. James shivered, aware of the low and looming clouds overhead and the afternoon's unexpected cool, and headed for the door.

It was weather-beaten and beginning to moulder, the whitewash flaking away to reveal the wood underneath. When he knocked there was no answer, but the latch turned easily when he tried it. Inside was only darkness. He didn't allow himself to linger on the threshold. To do so invited a question he preferred not to think about for too long.

What are you afraid of?

His eyes took a moment to adjust to the gloom. The high windows let in shafts of light, accompanied by smaller beams from scattered holes in the roof and walls. There was the sound of water, dripping occasionally as though from a great height, echoing in the quiet of the sanctuary. Two rows of heavy wooden pews stretched back from a lectern at the front of the church, behind which squatted a low altar.

The lectern was vast and shabby, carved from dark wood. It was in the shape of an eagle, wings outstretched and head bowed, although the years had not been kind to it: there were great chunks missing from the beak, and chips flaking from the wings, giving it a ragged, scabrous appearance. Atop it sat a huge Bible, its pages open for the congregation. James approached cautiously, the tap of his cane louder than he'd like on the flagstones. He was fearful of disturbing the silence: this was a holy place, no doubt of that, a place set apart.

But then came the sound of a door thrown open, deafeningly loud in a space like this, and from the vestry emerged a tall, bald man in a black robe; his cheeks were gaunt, the hollows of his eyes grimed with dirt, his expression furious. 'What do you want with me?' he bellowed. 'I've done nothing to harm you.'

He made his way across to James, every step accompanied by a grimace, and as he drew closer James saw the skin of the man's forehead was covered in overlapping blotches of yellow, maroon, crimson. He looked like a walking bruise.

'Answer me,' the man said. 'Tell me why you're here, or get out. This is a sanctuary, man, and God won't be mocked.' His voice caught on the word *sanctuary*, the faintest hiss that he couldn't hide, and then James saw him clearly.

'It's you,' he said. 'Don't you remember me?'

The priest squinted up at James, his eyes painful and encrusted, and then realisation passed across his face. 'You're the Harringley boy,' he said in a tone of wonder, reaching up towards James's face but restraining himself before he touched skin. 'They said you were – gone – I assumed…' He put a hand to his forehead, and James saw it was quavering. 'Forgive me,' the priest said with a sigh. 'I've come to expect the worst.'

'I was hoping you might be able to help me,' said James, and the priest looked up, his expression eager but vacant. 'The girl who disappeared – Janey – she took a child with her.'

'Hmm?' said the priest, but he wasn't looking at James now, was glancing back towards the vestry, and James suspected he hadn't heard a word. He couldn't tell if the priest was eager to be back within the vestry's walls, or terrified someone else would slip in while he was absent.

'Is everything alright?' James said, trying to keep his tone gentle; it wouldn't be hard to spook this battered, damaged man and send him scuttling away. 'We don't have to stay in, uh… the sanctuary.' He could barely speak the word. It felt ludicrous somehow. 'We can speak in the vestry if you'd prefer.' There was the flicker of candlelight within; James almost wondered if it would be preferable.

'No, no,' said the priest absently. 'No, it's not that…' A strange, sad smile spread across his lips. 'It's——' He sighed. 'Could we share communion?' he said, and when James hesitated the old man laid a firm hand on his arm. The skin was flaking like James's own, a multitude of angry reds that made him look like he was burning up. 'Please,' he said, his breath stale. 'It's been so long.'

'Of course,' said James, wincing at the priest's touch, and

the old man gave a watery, tight smile. He hobbled off across the flagstones towards the vestry.

Everything in him wanted to run. If this was the place Janey had chosen for the child then things were desperate. He could only imagine what future awaited the boy – a church orphanage, dormitories and lumpy mattresses, a lifetime of kneeling to pray on cold floors before bed. Maybe he'd make it to adolescence, but at fourteen he'd be out on the streets again, sweeping up horseshit or working in a match factory.

Thank God he'd run when he had the chance.

There were rustling noises coming from the vestry, the old man wheezing while he pawed through his things. 'Is everything alright in there?' called James, his voice coming back in half a dozen hollow echoes. 'Do you need some help?'

'Hmm?' said the priest, peering round the door. He had something in his hand, but in the gloom James couldn't see what. 'What was that?'

'I asked if you needed some help.'

'Oh no,' said the priest. 'No, no, not at all.' He emerged from the vestry with a tarnished silver cup and a hunk of bread, stumping back towards the pew where James now sat. When he reached it, he sank down next to James, a heavy sigh escaping his chest apparently against his will, his head bowed as though he was dizzy. Finally, he began to murmur the familiar words.

'On the night he was betrayed, the Lord Jesus Christ took bread and broke it, and gave it to his disciples, saying: this is my body, broken for you, that you might have eternal life.' He tore off a piece of the bread and placed it in his mouth, chewing mechanically, then handed it to James. 'This is my blood of the new covenant,' he said, holding up the chalice, his voice still muffled. 'Shed for you, for the forgiveness of sins.' He swallowed hard, gave two wet coughs into his hand, and then swallowed again. When he spoke, his voice was hoarse. 'Do this whenever you meet, in remembrance of me.'

There was something off about the words: they weren't in the order James remembered, different in subtle ways. Surely the priest couldn't have forgotten them.

He looked down at the bread in his hands. It was grey and rock-hard; when he tried to tear off a strip it crumbled into shards. He took the fragments and thrust a handful into his mouth, the jagged pieces jabbing him in his cheeks and tongue. They tasted of dust and stale flour, wood shavings and mouse droppings, and the bloom of decay made him want to vomit. Hastily, he took the cup from where it sat on the pew in front of him and took a substantial sip of the dark, oily wine.

It was on his tongue only a moment before he spat it out again, but he wasn't sure he'd ever forget the taste. It was rancid, almost vinegar, but with a deep, earthy quality that made him feel like he'd washed his mouth out with soil.

'Forgive me,' he said, spluttering. 'I'm sorry.'

The priest brushed crumbs from his robe. He offered a weak, conciliatory smile. 'No,' he said. 'No, no. It's my fault. I should have offered you something worthy in honour of what he did—' He swallowed hard, seemed almost on the verge of tears. 'It's been so long,' he said in a choked voice. 'I'd almost given up hope.'

He seemed so sad, sitting there, that James almost didn't want to ask – he already suspected the answer he'd get – but he had to know.

'Father,' said James. 'Nobody left a child here, did they?'

'What?' said the priest, glancing up from where his hands lay in his lap, something like terror lurking behind those red-rimmed eyes.

'That girl who ran away from the Manor – Janey – I thought maybe she left her child with you, to pass on to an orphanage…' He could feel his words tailing off, could hear the improbability of it all.

'Dear God,' said the priest quietly, staring down again, shaking his head. When he spoke now there was an unmistakable bitterness in his voice. 'Nobody in this village would be fool enough to leave a child unattended, not even in the door of a church.'

'You've no idea where she'd have gone?' said James.

The priest was silent a moment or two, his eyes dark. 'If she'd any sense,' he said, 'she'd have gone far, far away from here. You too.' He rose from the pew, took a long, steadying breath. 'I've work to do,' he said. 'I'd like you to leave.'

In spite of himself, James was shocked at how abruptly the priest's manner had changed, his sudden bitterness. 'I can't stay just a little longer?' he said, rising from where he sat too, sure their history had to count for something.

The priest stared at him, his expression impenetrable. 'I thought I could save your family,' he said after several seconds. 'Thought I could be a blessing to you.' He closed his eyes. 'I was wrong.' He stumped over to the door and held it open. From his pocket he removed a heavy iron key and slung it around his wrist, then watched as James approached.

James felt a weariness deeper than his bones. 'They ruined me too, you know,' he said as he stood in the light of the doorway. 'That's what I'm trying to put right.'

The priest began to laugh then, a nasty, bitter laugh that morphed into a wheeze. 'Put it right?' he said incredulously, when he'd got his breath back. 'You can't put it right, sir. You don't even know what you're trying to fix.'

And then he shut the door, and locked it tight.

13

WHEN HE returned to his room that night he couldn't sleep, despite having drunk three tankards of dark beer. He couldn't shake the image of his father living in Newcastle, wandering the street in rags – imagined him there in the corner of their apartment, watching Gabriel and James embrace at the end of their long day, his eyes uncomprehending and terrible.

The room was cold tonight, his breath condensing on the windows, and when he wiped it away his fingers were marked with grime. There was a patch of rot blooming at the skirting board near one of the writing desk's legs, seeping into the floorboards. He'd not noticed it the previous night, and so to his checklist of half-realised fears he added something new – the prospect of the floor collapsing below him in the night. Perhaps not being able to sleep was a blessing. At least if he kept watch, he'd know what was coming.

And then, from somewhere behind him, came the sound of distant footsteps. At first he thought they were coming from within his room – the same old dream, the same terror – but when he turned it was clear they were coming from the alleyway.

From the window he saw a figure approaching, wrapped in a long woollen cloak, its face obscured. It was staggering from one side of the street to the other, knocking on whatever door it came to, its shadow stretching in the gaslight. Something about it seemed familiar, as though it came from the darkest reaches of his memory.

And then she lifted her head to the sky and shouted at the top of her voice, and the sight of her felt like a miracle. 'Aren't any of you going to help me?' she howled, the thin windows hardly blocking out her words. 'Remember he said we had a choice? Said we could choose a better way?' She gave a hoarse, ugly cackle. 'Where was my fucking choice then? Where's my better way?'

Before James knew it, he was down the stairs, yelling for someone to open the inn's front door. For several minutes no one came – until the barman finally emerged in his nightshirt, barely even a shadow among the gloomy inn. 'What are you shouting about, sir?' he said quietly, and James thought he detected a trace of fear in the man's voice.

'Good God, man,' said James, 'don't you hear that? There's someone out there, calling for help!'

The barman frowned, cocked his head towards the door in a show of listening, but he was a poor actor, the gesture unconvincing. 'I don't hear a thing, sir,' he said after a moment.

James stared at him across the darkness. There was something liberating about standing so close to the man and yet scarcely being able to see his face – James had always felt like that, as though in the dark you could speak with an honesty denied you in the light. 'You're scared,' he said. 'Scared of the Tall Man – of the void.'

'Don't—' said the barman fiercely. 'Don't speak of him. Don't draw his eye.'

From beyond the door there came another unmistakable cry – Janey was singing. It was a terrible off-key sound, a half-remembered folk song wrung from a throat hoarse with screaming. 'I'm not asking you to go,' he said. 'Just let me out. I can't leave her out there alone.'

He heard the barman suck on his teeth. 'Very well,' he said, pulling back the deadbolt and then unhooking an iron key from somewhere to unlock the door. 'But you're on your own out there, sir.'

The night air was freezing as James barrelled out onto the main street, hurtling after Janey. He saw her a little way down, silhouetted in the moonlight, and called out her name – but his voice sounded tiny amidst the darkness of the village green, and she didn't turn. He hurried over to her, pulling his jacket tight to protect himself from the bitter cold, and called out again. This time she turned to him, the hollows on her face stark.

'Janey,' he said. 'Do you remember me? James Harringley?'

'Aye, I remember you,' said Janey with a sullen look.

'Janey, tell me what happened. Tell me, and I can help.'

She widened her eyes, fixing him with a cold, pitiless stare. 'You know what happened,' she said. 'He took my boy. Gave him to the Tall Man to hold back the shadows.'

He felt icy fingers grip his heart. 'You saw this?'

'Don't you go doubting me now, sir,' she said viciously, pulling back from him as though she might stride away in disgust. 'You know it's true.'

'Of course.' He put a hand to his forehead, all too aware he had nothing to offer her. 'And I'm – I'm so sorry. But if you come with me, you can help me stop this from ever happening again. Stop the Tall Man once and for all.'

Again Janey laughed that hoarse, bitter cackle. 'Your father promised that very same thing,' she said. 'Look at how well it worked out for the rest of us.' She shook her head, turning away now. 'People like me don't matter to your family. Haven't you realised that yet?'

'Janey, please,' said James, reaching out to grab her arm; her dress was shockingly thin, far too little protection from the cold. 'I can get you out of here. Get you away from all of this.'

'Take your hands off me,' she said, bristling. 'I don't want anything to do with you, or your family. They've done enough damage to me already.'

But in his mind's eye he saw Edward's son in the crib – saw their father bending over him, lifting the tiny, sleeping body up in the night to hand to the lord of shadows. The fight had gone out of the old man, he could see that now, and all his father's attempts at resistance had left this place in ruins. Someone had to take up the mantle.

'No. No, I won't. I've seen what happens if you leave this place to do its worst to people.' He moved round in front of her, determined not to let her get away. 'You asked for help,' he said, 'begged for it, even. And nobody from the village came.' He put a hand up to try and stop her fleeing, daring her to listen. 'Well, I'm here. Come with me.'

In the moonlight, she held James's gaze for several seconds, then knocked his hand away. 'I don't want your help. You're just like your brother.' She was already marching off down the main street, heading for the darkness beyond the village. It took James a moment to register what she'd said.

'What does Edward have to do with this?' he called after her.

Janey didn't bother to turn, just let her words hang in the air. 'People don't get pregnant by themselves,' she said witheringly, 'at least not outside of fairy stories.'

'The child is his?'

'Didn't take a genius to work that out, did it?' said Janey, still striding away. 'Now get away from me. I can't stay here another minute.'

Already she was growing smaller and dimmer – in a matter of seconds she'd be gone, swallowed up by the darkness, while he stood dumbly in the street staring after her. 'Janey, wait.'

But she was already out beyond the village's last few houses, the front of the blacksmith's looking as insubstantial as boards on a stage. She was little more than a silhouette on the moonlit road, and James found himself hurrying just to keep her in view. The road out of the village was long and straight, only curving upwards when it reached the distant hills, barely visible in the moonlight.

He couldn't let her go, not now. He had to know. How many

years had Edward been fucking her? How many secrets had he kept from his wife?

Edward was more like his father than he cared to admit. They both were, James supposed.

'Janey!' he called again, but she didn't turn, didn't give any sign of having heard him – only continued walking, steady and resolute, her destination unknown and to all intents and purposes irrelevant. James had done the same once before – run from this place without a plan, determined only to be elsewhere, to carve out a life on his own terms.

His head was spinning and there was a roiling in his guts. The road seemed to shimmer and distort in front of his eyes, its boundaries unstable, the darkness reaching out towards him. Out there, in the dark, he'd swear there were shapes starting to unpeel themselves, clambering over each other in their haste, stretching out impossibly elongated limbs.

He hardly dared turn his head to check how far they'd come: he feared that when he looked back again, Janey would be gone, the path empty. They were a long way from the lights of the village now, he could sense that much, nothing but the moon lighting their path. But he'd travelled this road before, by carriage, and he couldn't recall it being so long; he didn't seem to be making any progress.

'Janey, please!' he called again. 'Tell me what happened with Edward.'

The same implacable silhouette, the same refusal to turn, as though she were a marionette, or a figure on a magic lantern screen, created to do one thing only. Exasperated, James picked up his pace, began to run, but still she remained beyond his reach, forever a few steps away. His lungs were beginning to burn, his head swam, and he felt like a man lost at sea, far from any kind of anchor.

There was something wrong here, he knew that. They'd slipped through some crack in the world, emerged in a place that belonged to the void. He could see it, out there in those teeming shadows at which he hardly dared glance. If he stepped off the path he'd be swallowed up, he was certain of it; he could almost feel the choking sensation as the darkness entered his lungs, the crack of his bones as they elongated and snapped themselves into a new shape, the rending of his flesh and muscle.

He'd seen the power of the void first-hand, once. That darkness from which the world itself was made, its limitless power; forever straining at its bounds, seeking to recreate the earth in its own pattern. But he'd spent enough of his life forming himself anew from the dirt. He'd not let it swallow him again.

'Janey, stop,' he called. 'Please. Listen to me.' Against all odds, she stopped; he could see her trembling, shudders coursing up and down her body. 'This place – it isn't safe.' He paused. She still hadn't moved, and he supposed that was a good sign. 'There must be a path back. But I'd rather we find it together. I've made it out of this place once before.'

And now – thank God – she was turning to face him, the shadows carving her features into deep hollows, and so it was a moment before James registered that her eyes were fixed not on him, but on a point beyond his shoulder, her expression one of sheer horror.

He turned to see a figure in a top hat and tailcoat, his silhouette impossibly tall and spindly in the moonlight. He'd seen that silhouette in his dreams every day since he'd left this place. It was him. The Tall Man. Striding along the path, with one hand outstretched as though in an entreaty – his form at once human and grotesquely distorted, made of shadows and yet distinct from them – already seeming to tower over them.

'No,' he heard her say. 'No, get him away from me. What more does he want from me?' She took a step backwards, not letting her eyes leave the Tall Man as he drew closer and closer. 'You told him this would be enough, that if my boy gave his life it would hold back the dark…'

Again the shadows were moving all around them, pulsating – and now James saw something break off from the woods, another blot of darkness that twisted itself into a huge, misshapen creature.

YOU HAVE PLAYED YOUR PART, JANE, said the Tall Man in that voice that seemed to come from everywhere and nowhere, which James had until now never been entirely sure wasn't being spoken directly into his skull. I HAVE NOT COME FOR YOU.

'You want me?' said James.

YOU KNOW WHAT LIES BENEATH THIS PLACE, said the Tall Man, and although James could not see his eyes in their deep hollows, he knew the Tall Man was holding his gaze. YOU KNOW THE PULL OF THE VOID, ITS STRANGE POWER. He paused, his tone leisurely and unhurried. It was the tone of a man used to being listened to. YOUR FATHER DEFIED ME. IT IS NOT TOO LATE TO MAKE AMENDS.

James wanted to laugh: surely all those years living in squalor disqualified him from being a pure, untainted sacrifice. 'I'm no use to you,' he said. 'I'm too old, too broken.'

YOU UNDERSTAND WHAT MUST BE DONE.

'I've told you – you've missed your chance.'

NOT YOU. YOUR BROTHER'S CHILD.

His breath caught in his throat: he'd never imagined the Tall Man would ask this of him. 'No,' he said, swallowing hard. 'No, dear God, no.' He shuddered. 'This is what you want?' He imagined his brother's features distorted by rage, his sister-in-law weeping over an empty crib. 'I won't do this, do you hear me? I couldn't do that.'

YOU UNDERSTAND WHAT MUST BE DONE.

'Why me? What is it you think I can do?'

LOOK AT THIS PLACE. THE VOID IS MAKING IT ANEW. The Tall Man took a long, rattling breath. WHO AMONG YOU WILL DO WHAT MUST BE DONE?

'My father understood who you were. You're a trickster, a charlatan.'

The Tall Man's words came with an unexpected violence, a terrible roar as though of waves breaking on the shore. YOUR FATHER UNDERSTOOD NOTHING, he said with venom, but the anger seemed to last just a moment. IT IS HIS ACTIONS THAT LED THIS PLACE ASTRAY, his voice normal once again. IT IS HIS ACTIONS THAT UNLEASHED THE VOID, THAT BROKE THE BOUNDS…

And then came a scream. James turned to see the darkness – somehow – reaching out to Janey. He saw arms as thick and glossy as tree branches, misshapen hands dragging her away towards the woods, and ran to her, grabbing at her arm.

'Please,' she cried, and now he knew she was addressing him. He could hear the panic in her voice, the catch in her throat that told him her body was being wrenched out of shape. 'Don't let him take me too.' He pulled with all of his strength, trying to drag Janey out of the dark, but his feet couldn't find purchase and some vast, polished limb shot out towards him, sending him flying backwards into the dirt.

Scrabbling to his feet he called out to the Tall Man with a terrible, futile cry: 'This is your doing! Call them off!'

THEY ARE NOT IN MY POWER. THE VOID HAS A MIND OF ITS OWN. I HAVE NO AUTHORITY OVER ITS CHILDREN.

'Janey!' Once more James hurled himself into the undergrowth, trying to fight off the darkness, but the creatures were vast, sinewy, merciless – he would never stop them. They were stronger than him, and as he peered into the gloom he saw shapes from whom all humanity had vanished, like some grotesque distortion of a human figure.

And it was happening to Janey too – her body beginning to distort, as though she were being pulled into a whirlpool, wrenched in impossible directions. Her face was contorted in agony, her grip failing, and James made one last lunge for her – a last, desperate attempt to wrap his arms around her – only to find himself struck across the chest with an extraordinary blow, one that sent him flying through the air, and in his last moment before he hit the ground he saw Janey's neck break, her very skin beginning to split...

❧

When he came to, it took him a moment to orientate himself. He could see the road leading into the village, a few scattered shafts of sunlight breaking through thick grey clouds − and, when he pushed himself upright, the figure of Herbert Whittell, standing over a long, cloth-covered bundle. Whittell wore a thick overcoat and a waistcoat, and as James came to his senses he realised why − last night's chill hadn't entirely dissipated, and James was bitterly cold.

At the sight of James stirring, Whittell walked slowly over to him. His expression was grave, all his former warmth and cordiality gone. He didn't offer James his hand, but instead let him push himself painfully to his feet.

'I hope you've got some sort of explanation for what happened last night,' he said, looking James up and down dispassionately. 'Although I'm not holding out much hope.'

James's head was pounding. 'Janey's dead?'

'She is,' said Whittell with a frown, 'and nobody in this godforsaken village seems to have heard a bloody thing.' He sounded exasperated. 'I'd have you thrown in jail if there was any sign of a struggle, believe you me, but if you killed her then you did so without incurring a single mark. All the same, I'm going to hazard a guess that you were the last person who saw her alive, so for your own sake I hope you recall what happened.'

James thought back − to the darkness that had teemed with unseen life, the creatures that had hurled him back when he'd tried to save Janey. He'd rather have forgotten. 'You're not going to like the answer, Inspector,' he said. 'It's this place. There's something rotten here.'

'No, sir,' said Whittell loudly, cutting the air with a fierce gesture. 'No, I won't accept that.' He looked incensed; deeply, and personally, affronted. 'She wasn't killed by the earth: she was killed by some creature. Somebody. And you saw something. What was it?'

'You won't believe me if I tell you,' said James heavily.

'I think I already know, Mr Harringley. You're going to tell me it was the void.' He didn't bother hiding his distaste. 'Not that I have a goddamned clue what it might want with her, when from what you last told me it wants children.'

James's whole body was racked with shivers; he felt feverish, on the edge of vomiting. 'She was just a casualty, Inspector,' he said wearily. 'She happened to be in the wrong place.' He sighed. 'This is what I told you. Something needs to hold back the void.' Whittell's look was dark. 'Or else it — it tries to reach outward. Into our world. And people get hurt.'

'And you're suggesting that this *void* is what killed Janey?' said Whittell sharply. 'Perhaps I was wrong, sir. Perhaps you ought still to be locked away, for your own safety as much as for the public's.'

'If you stayed here long enough,' James said, 'you'd find any one of these villagers would tell you a similar story. Maybe it's not madness if everyone believes it.'

Whittell's frown deepened. 'I'll believe it when I see it with my own eyes. No sooner.'

James tried to stop himself looking at the spot where Janey's corpse lay, the spots of blood staining the cloth. 'Listen,' he said, holding back another violent bout of shuddering, 'something reached out of the shadows and wrenched her neck so hard that the bones stuck out of it. Tell me you've seen a death like that before. Who could do something like that?'

'You're right there,' said Whittell reluctantly. He closed his eyes, said as though pained: 'Go on then. I'll humour you. What was it, exactly, this creature that killed her?'

'I don't know,' said James, hearing a note of hysteria in his own voice. 'I don't even know if it was something physical – or if it's this place, some force here that twisted her out of shape. But if you want to know why people here are killing their children, you have to understand their reasons. And I'm telling you this: they're doing it to hold back the void.

'There's a reason I ran away, Inspector. There's a reason I want my family far from here.'

Whittell reached into his overcoat and removed a small leather notebook. 'Tell me what you remember of last night,' he said. 'Every last detail.'

And so James told Whittell the story, or as much of it as he could remember through his pounding headache. Told him about hearing Janey calling in the streets, knocking on every door; told him about her impossible journey into the darkness, and the Tall Man's return; told him everything, in short, except for the mention of his brother. Even now, something held him back. Some misplaced loyalty, some kernel of doubt. Some part of him still wanted to believe.

14

FOR YEARS, after fleeing home, he'd barely thought about Yorkshire. Maybe he wouldn't have thought of it at all had it not been for the newspapers.

There were more and more stories in the national press, terrible things. In Blyth, a woman sleepwalked to her death from the top of a tall building. An Alnwick stagehand fell inside an orchestra pit and didn't resurface for six days, emerging covered in grime and speaking only gibberish. A farmer in Country Durham found his animals mutilated by a beast, their joints shattered, their limbs impossibly elongated, their guts spilling out.

They could have been random – chance occurrences – but the prickle of terror he felt when he read about them told him otherwise. He knew what it meant: it meant the Tall Man was right. The void could not be contained. It was breaking out, leaching into the earth, wrenching whatever it touched into new shapes.

He didn't tell Gabriel, although Gabriel must have been

able to see something was wrong: James wasn't sleeping, was barely eating, was distracted and fearful. He wondered how long it would be before the darkness reached Newcastle, began to eat away at the sanctuary he'd built here.

It all came to a head one night in late February. They'd arranged to meet in the Glassmaker's Arms, a run-down inn near Gabriel's latest workplace. The inn was on the shabbiest side of the village, a low-ceilinged room with exposed beams and windows covered by sacking. When James entered he was struck by the room's suffocating heat: it was lit entirely by candlelight, and a fug of smoke hung in the air.

James arrived first, finding a table and ordering two plates of lamb stew. There was something going on in a dark corner: round a long table sat a dozen young women, dressed as modestly as if they were attending church, and a single man in a grubby waistcoat, a dull-eyed fellow James had seen hawking coffee on the street at dawn. At the head of the table was a tall, broad-shouldered lady in her early forties, dressed entirely in black.

'My name is Angela Weber,' he heard her say, 'but that's hardly relevant. Think of me only as a channel, a beacon for those spirits searching for a way back to this world…'

James was so preoccupied that he didn't notice Gabriel had arrived until he sat down, pale with plaster dust and looking ten years older. His face was drawn, his eyes weary. 'Dear God,' he said. 'Not this nonsense again.'

'You've seen them before?' said James.

'They're a bunch of charlatans,' said Gabriel, accepting

a plate of stew from the innkeeper and falling upon it like a hungry dog. After his third mouthful he grimaced, as though he'd finally realised what he was eating. 'This is bloody awful, by the way,' he said. 'Pure gristle.'

James peered down at it. A small pile of stringy meat sat alongside two greying potatoes and some angular lumps of carrot in a pool of thin, watery gravy. 'Long day?' he said, scooping up a tentative spoonful and trying not to think too hard about what he was eating.

'Mm,' grunted Gabriel without looking up, and James wondered if he was listening more closely to what Mrs Weber was saying than he let on. Lifting the spoon to his lips, James nearly gagged: the stew was vile, the thin gravy somehow tasting faintly of raw sewage.

Gabriel nodded. 'I told you,' he said, still not looking at James. This wasn't like him. 'Try the meat,' he said eventually. 'It's the most bearable bit.'

They picked around their stew in silence for several minutes, James's appetite almost totally gone. In the corner, Mrs Weber was talking about how the netherworld was ephemeral, its contours hard to trace. That wasn't James's experience – to him, it had always felt shockingly tangible.

'Is something wrong, Gabriel?' he said eventually, and he knew there was from the long breath Gabriel took before answering.

'You asked me if today was a long day,' he said, putting down his spoon. 'They're all long days lately, James.' He inhaled deeply, halfway to a sigh. 'Whatever's eating you,' he said firmly, 'you can tell me about it. No, forget that. You need to tell me about it. For both of our sakes.'

James stared across the table at this brilliant, beautiful man – who had given him a new life, helped him out of his pit of loneliness – and in an instant knew he couldn't do it. How could he even find words to describe what he'd seen in the darkness beneath his home-town?

'Gabriel,' he said, 'if I've been distracted – if I've been preoccupied – I'm truly sorry. But I need you to know that all this isn't about you. You're my foundation, my bedrock.' He laid a hand on Gabriel's, and Gabriel didn't shake it off. 'Please don't leave me.'

Gabriel held his gaze. 'It's not like that,' he said. 'I'm not going anywhere.' He released James's hand, and ran both of his own through his hair in anguish. 'I just – I need to know.'

James had known this was coming at some point – he'd just hoped for a little longer. When he told Gabriel, things would change. He knew it. The look of pure, unconditional love on Gabriel's face would falter, even if just for a moment, and James wasn't sure he'd ever be able to trust it again. But the alternative was losing Gabriel for sure, and even a small hope was better than no hope.

He took a deep breath and began. 'I haven't told you the full story of why I ran away from home,' he said. 'It wasn't only about my father.'

'Go on,' said Gabriel, frowning.

'There was a man – except he wasn't a man. Some people would call him… a demon.' Again James sighed, more deeply this time, feeling the weariness in his bones from which he'd been hiding for years. 'He came at night, with the shadows. And he was the shadows.' He stared into Gabriel's eyes with a kind of pleading desperation, longing to be understood. 'He said he was something ageless, something that had been around since the start of time – and I – I believed him.'

Gabriel's brow was furrowed, his expression indecipherable. 'And this – shadow man,' he said, his voice a little strained, 'he drove you away?'

'No,' said James, staring at the table. 'Not really. He was my way out. He promised to help me—' He felt the bile rising in his throat, the familiar terror that came whenever he thought of the Tall Man. 'But I didn't understand what he was offering. I didn't realise what he wanted from me.'

'And what was that?' said Gabriel, leaning forward towards James, his voice hoarse.

'He wanted a sacrifice,' said James, swallowing hard, and at Gabriel's look of alarm he went on. 'I've told you about my village, about what it's like there, but you don't know why. Because—' He raised a trembling hand to his forehead. 'Because for years the Tall Man has been coming to its people, and taking its firstborn children.' He closed his eyes. 'He gives them to the void. To contain it. To hold it in.'

'The void,' said Gabriel, and now there was an edge of anger in his voice.

James felt panic creep into his words. 'You told me you'd stay with me,' he said. 'Well, I'm telling you the truth. Like you asked me to.'

'You are,' said Gabriel, and James could see the effort it was costing him to remain calm. 'So this – void.' He took a deep breath. 'You've seen it? And it wants people's children?'

'There's a line in the Bible,' James said, and at the flash of irritation in Gabriel's eyes he held up a steadying hand. 'Listen, I'm not saying I agree – just that it's the best explanation I have.' Gabriel nodded wordlessly, but his unhappiness was showing. '*In the beginning,*' James said, '*the earth was formless and void, and the Spirit of God brooded over the waters.*'

Gabriel frowned. 'I'm still listening,' he said. 'For now.'

'If you believe the stories, before the world there was… chaos. Void.' He paused, searching for the right words. 'Then, *something* shaped it into being. Created the world we have now.' He searched Gabriel's face, and received only a curt nod in return. 'Well, what if all that chaos didn't just disappear when the world was created? What if it just lay dormant, underneath the world?' He went on, the words pouring out of him after so long buried. 'All that creative power. The power to create a world. If it were to get loose—'

'It would keep creating,' said Gabriel slowly. 'Without anything to contain it.'

'Exactly,' said James. 'So the Tall Man, he – he gave the void something to work upon. A child.' Again he saw the tunnels, the pit, and forced it back. 'Or at least he did until my father stopped it. Told the villagers there was another way.'

'You're kidding,' said Gabriel. 'Your father – the man who beat you half to death.'

'He's not a bad man,' said James firmly. 'At least, not all bad.'

Gabriel thought for what felt like a long time. James let him. He was drained from speaking, and so ravenously hungry that even the stew looked almost appetising. Finally Gabriel spoke again, slowly, quietly, as though testing uncertain ground. 'But if people stopped giving their children to him – to the Tall Man...' He shook his head. 'What happened to the void?'

And James was about to explain – ready to explain everything he'd read in the papers, that darkness leaching out into Yorkshire, stretching out its tendrils beyond the moors towards them – when they were interrupted by an ear-splitting yell. It was the medium, her eyes raised to the sky, her skin pale, her voice huge and furious.

'Ask him how many need suffer for his father's folly! Ask him what gives him the right to decide!' Mrs Weber was pointing a trembling finger towards James, and in her eyes was rage. 'Better for him to have cut the throats of those little ones himself.'

Everyone was looking at them now, instantly alert.

'Enough,' said Gabriel, rising to his feet. 'You know nothing about him.'

Mrs Weber made her way unsteadily towards them, weaving between the tables, her furious eyes the scariest thing about her. 'I know enough to understand what he's done,' she said. 'What it means.'

'And what would you have him do?' snarled Gabriel, loud enough for the whole bar to hear. All around the room, people were starting to mutter to their drinking companions. Before long, they'd have no hope of slipping quietly back into anonymity. 'Answer me.'

'Tell him to go back to the lord of shadows,' hissed Mrs Weber, now only feet from them. 'To plead for his mercy, and then throw himself into the pit. Maybe there is yet hope. Maybe there is still time.'

'We have to go,' said James, grabbing Gabriel's arm, conscious of how many pairs of eyes were on them. 'Now.'

'No,' said Gabriel, shaking him off. 'No, I can't let this stand.' He glared at the medium with unalloyed fury. 'Who put this burden on his family?'

'*They had a duty!*' the medium howled, and there was something inhuman in her voice. 'Those people had a sacred purpose, which his father bid them cast off.'

'Gabriel,' said James, grabbing him by the shoulder and starting to hustle him towards the door. 'We have got to leave this place.'

'It's too much, you hear me?' called Gabriel over his shoulder, as James did his very best to wrestle him out of the bar. 'Nobody ever asked them if they were willing.'

'He sees you!' yelled the medium. 'The lord of shadows knows your name!'

They stumbled out into an unfamiliar part of town, a dark hollow amongst the city's many hills. Down here in Walker the gaslights were poorly maintained, many of them defunct, and so the street was carved into blocks of shadow. From out of the darkness came the head of a horse, and Gabriel jumped backwards to dodge the carriage that followed in its wake.

Only once it was past did he realise his error, and call after the rider, but he was already long gone, the carriage rattling away up the hill. Under his breath Gabriel cursed.

From somewhere out in the darkness came the sound of bells tolling, and James counted the hour – eight, nine, ten – and yet the ringing did not stop, and for a second James wondered if there was a funeral being held, only to realise the folly of that idea. And still the bell tolled, again and again, ringing out its fifteenth strike, its sixteenth, its seventeenth – and James couldn't shake the sense they had slipped through a gap in time.

'Up or down?' he said to Gabriel, keen to put as much distance between themselves and the inn as possible. There was still a clamour behind the closed doors, and he suspected it wouldn't be long before someone was despatched to find them, to question James about those many children who'd vanished into the dark.

'Up,' said Gabriel, turning left. The hill was steep, and James's leg gave an involuntary twitch of pain as though in preparation. 'That's where the job was, anyway. I can get us back to the centre from there.' He was already striding off, and only paused a few steps on when he saw that James was lagging behind. 'Do you need some help?'

'I can do it,' said James, stumping forward as fast as he could on the cane. The only pavement here was a set of wooden boards, pressed into the mud to give pedestrians a kind of stability. James's every step was matched with the resounding *click* of the cane striking the planks beneath, which left him feeling uncomfortably visible. It was hard work, too, and it wasn't long before James felt his leg begin to tremble. 'Gabriel,' he said, calling out to where Gabriel stood waiting a few steps ahead. 'Lend me your shoulder.'

Gabriel didn't say a word, just scooped himself under James's shoulder and helped prop him upright. 'Come on,' he said, his breath a little ragged. 'Let's get out of sight.'

Before James knew it, Gabriel was steering them into the dark mouth of an alleyway, its walls slick with water and who knew what else. It was just in time: from somewhere on the street came a bellowing cry whose words James couldn't make out, a sound distorted and animal. Behind it, the bell was still tolling.

'Further down,' Gabriel muttered. 'Get out of the light.' The ground was boggy and uneven, and James struggled to steady himself. The further they pressed into the alley, the narrower it became, and Gabriel finally reached a point where he had to turn sideways to squeeze himself through; James was wedged too far into it to turn his head again.

'This must be deep enough,' he muttered. 'We're safe here.'

Gabriel shook his head. 'I don't like being trapped,' he said. 'Never have.' He was already trying to squeeze himself through what looked like an impossibly small gap. 'We go through,' he said. 'This ought to bring us out by the river.'

And so James followed, pressing himself up against the walls – the darkness surrounding him on all sides, unmooring him, leaving him afloat in time and in space, with the noise of angry shouting and tolling bells just a muffled whisper far behind – until, miraculously, after what felt like an eternity, he emerged on another narrow, shabby street.

It was deserted, its crooked houses unlit and its few remaining gaslights dim, but Gabriel gave a little bow nonetheless. 'Don't tell me you ever doubted me,' he said, although his smile wasn't quite as broad as usual.

'Do you know where we are?' said James after a moment or two. A few feet ahead of them the street dissolved into inky darkness; there were no landmarks to be seen, no bridge or monument or church by which to orientate themselves.

'I don't,' said Gabriel, rubbing the back of his neck. 'But listen, I'm not sure that's as big a problem as it sounds. Let's just walk awhile. We'll find something that looks familiar.'

James nodded, his leg already paining him, and stumped over to the boards across the street. For several minutes he focussed just on putting one foot in front of the other, keeping his cane from slipping on the muddy wood, following Gabriel, and staying upright. It was tiring work, not helped by the street's unevenness – there were times when he couldn't tell whether he was moving uphill or down.

And then he paused for breath, and they both saw it at the same moment. Gabriel wore an expression of mingled dismay and horror; he put a hand on the wall, staring in through the low doorway to where an inky blackness stretched away. It was the inn they'd left shortly before – if indeed it had been only a quarter of an hour – but impossibly dilapidated, and somehow miraculously relocated. Above the door hung a faded, distorted version of the sign, its colours leached and its images stained as if by water. Where before there had been an old man shaping a bottle from heated glass, now there was a hideously warped figurine that seemed shaped out of black jade. At the end of the blower, the creature's bottle drooped away into formlessness.

'This is impossible,' muttered Gabriel. 'This can't be happening.'

James was glad of the darkness: glad that Gabriel couldn't see his expression, the terror of knowing that the void could reach him even here, that the sanctuary he'd thought he'd found was only an illusion. He felt as though something had gripped his heart and was squeezing it tightly within his chest, had to steady himself against the wall to stop himself fainting—

Something gripped his arm; something spindly and impossibly strong, tough as lacquered wood, and he leapt back in blind terror, landing hard in the mud. Amidst the gloom he could see something darker than shadow, something vast and contorted, and Gabriel was backing away too as it reached for him with a grotesquely elongated limb.

'No!' James heard himself cry, and he knew Gabriel was running now; he could hear his footsteps echoing in the darkness as he fled the terror that James had always known would drive them apart in the end. More of the creatures were approaching now, a half-dozen of them at least, staggering out of the blank mouth of that impossible inn, and he groped around in the dirt for his cane, all the while knowing he could never hope to fight them off – but then came a voice, echoing around the silent street, seeming to come from the very walls themselves:

NOT LIKE THIS.

The creatures fell back, and from behind them stepped

forward a figure in a top hat and tailcoat, the shadows moulding themselves into a face, a body.

YOU KNEW THE COST, said the Tall Man, AND YET STILL YOU RAN.

He had no idea where Gabriel was – perhaps he was dead – and James couldn't make his tongue move, couldn't find the words to answer.

IT DOES NOT HAVE TO BE THIS WAY, said the Tall Man. YOU KNOW WHAT I ASK.

'I'm – I'm not—' stammered James, and he thought he saw the darkness that was the Tall Man's face twist into something like a smile.

WHAT WAS THAT?

'I'm not that man anymore,' said James. 'What use am I to you now?'

ASK YOURSELF THAT, said the Tall Man. ASK YOURSELF WHAT YOU CAN YET DO TO STOP THIS.

And then, with the blink of an eye, he was gone – as if he had never been there at all.

He turned to find Gabriel standing at the edge of the kerb, with his club held loosely at one side and his mouth agape. He was still staring at the inn's black maw. 'What was that?' he said eventually. 'Who were you talking to?'

'It's him. The Tall Man.' James put his head in his hands, on the verge of weeping. He was silent for what felt like an eternity, the darkness stretching time out far beyond its bounds. 'This was coming all along,' he said, feeling a heaviness in his chest, the weight of home. 'I just couldn't see it.'

'You don't owe him anything,' Gabriel said. 'Even if all this is true – if their sacrifices can hold back the void – why should it always be your village that makes that sacrifice?' He knelt to press his forehead against James's. 'Why do you have to bear the weight of this?'

'Because it started with me,' James said. 'Because I'm where it all went wrong.'

'No,' said Gabriel quietly. 'You're not.' He put both hands on James's shoulders. 'You're not, you hear me? You're not the one to blame. And you don't owe them anything.'

Gabriel's resolve scared him: he spoke like a man who still believed this could be fixed. He couldn't see James's downturned face, the weight of his despair.

'You saw what happened here tonight,' James said. 'That's what the void can do. It can make and remake the world, but it can't do it quite right. It's got the power, but no wisdom.' He shuddered. 'It'll devour this city, and everything we care about.'

'And why do you have to be the one who saves it?' said Gabriel, unable to hide his anger.

'Who else then? Who else will do it?'

'I don't know,' said Gabriel, with a heavy sigh. 'But I can't lose you. I can't.' He shook his head. 'You think you're the only one in this city who's lonely, but you're not. I'm sick of having to pretend I'm someone I'm not too, you hear me? I need what we have.'

James couldn't answer him: his throat was tight, constricted from sheer gratitude.

Gabriel pushed himself upright and began to pace around. 'There's something else bothering me,' he said. 'How did he find you? The Tall Man, and those… *things*?' He looked almost pained, as though grappling with this had a physical cost. 'You're a long way from Yorkshire now, and even if the void has reached this far…' he tailed off. He was silent again, thoughtful, and James was too exhausted to interrupt him, his head swimming with what he'd seen, and what it meant. 'Maybe it was her,' Gabriel said eventually. 'The medium. She drew his attention, and you just – happened to be there.'

'You're clutching at straws, Gabriel.' The cynicism in his voice was nothing to what he felt inside.

'No, humour me. What use are you to him now? Why not just find another youngster in your village to throw to the void?'

James threw up his hands in despair; he couldn't fault Gabriel's logic, but then logic was hardly going to save them now. 'I don't see what difference this makes,' he said. 'If he can find me now, he can find me again.'

'Or maybe that's where you're wrong,' said Gabriel with an air of triumph. 'Maybe he only found you because you were unlucky. Because you drew his attention.' There was a slightly manic gleam in his eye. 'You managed to escape him this long. Maybe you can do it again.'

'You're talking about hiding.'

'I'm not,' Gabriel said after a pause, but he must have caught the look of sorrow in James's eyes. 'I swear to you. But you're not the man you used to be anymore. You haven't been for years.'

He laid a hand on James's shoulder; perhaps it was meant to be reassuring, but it felt more like Gabriel was trying to stop him running away. 'I'm telling you not to go back. Don't think about him. Don't go anywhere where you might stumble across him. Can you do that?'

James couldn't meet Gabriel's eye. He felt like something had broken inside of him, some faith he'd once had in a different future. 'I thought I'd finally be free of him.'

'You are,' said Gabriel, but even he didn't sound entirely sure. 'He doesn't own you.'

15

O N T H E way back to the house James felt a presence at his shoulder. The hedgerows were like trenches, hiding whoever it might be from view. He wasn't afraid of being robbed: he could handle himself well enough now. But he wasn't used to being this exposed; this was why he'd learned to melt into the shadows, to make himself nothing.

It was unforgiving country, this. In the city there were places to hide: the corner of a tavern, an alleyway, a crowd. Set your face a certain way, dress like the masses who poured down each day towards the factory, and nobody would ever see you.

Out here he felt like a lone voice, calling in the wilderness; the only person who dared suggest that things could be different. Surely Whittell wouldn't help him now – most likely he thought James a suspect in Janey's death, and he'd be a fool not to – but perhaps James could still reach Edward, show him the danger creeping closer to him.

He felt it again: the sense of being watched from behind the trees. A feeling he knew all too well. So strong was the sensation of being followed that he called out. 'If there's anyone there, then for the love of God show yourself.' In the lanes his voice sounded harsh and unfamiliar, almost like his father's. He tightened his grip on his cane. 'I'm not afraid to defend myself.'

But there was no answer. Only the wind blowing in the trees, a low, insistent snicker that remained behind him with every painful step he took.

Ransford opened the door as James was coming up the driveway. He stood in the doorway of the house, tall and broad, looking in that moment like he could stop all comers. *Or at least he could certainly stop me,* thought James, who was sweaty and flustered despite the overcast day, his head pounding from lack of sleep. He'd been in such a hurry to get here he'd again neglected to eat, and he felt parched and grubby.

Ransford wore a sombre frown. 'Good morning, sir,' he said, as though James were any other visitor. 'I'm afraid Master Edward is sorting your father's papers. It would have been better to have sent word you were coming.'

James felt an obscure pang of anger that might have been homesickness. He wanted to grab this old man by the lapels and shout *this is my house, man.* Somehow he restrained himself.

'He'll want to see me,' said James. His hands were trembling, his breathing shallow. 'This is no small matter, Ransford.'

'By all means, sir,' said Ransford, with a trace of impatience, 'but your brother has urgent matters of his own to attend to.' He paused a moment, as if expecting James to go back the way he came, but eventually he capitulated. 'Go on up,' he said, exhaling gently through his nose. 'I'll set out tea in the drawing room.'

He was startled by the rapid change in his father's study. The decaying teacups had been cleared away, along with many of the piles of paper. He found Edward sitting at his father's desk, his head propped up on his hand, poring over a ledger. He was wearing the same clothes James had seen him in the day before, and his face was pallid. If he had slept at all, it hadn't been much.

Edward spoke without looking up. 'I should have come in here sooner,' he said. 'Should have been more forceful with Ransford. I suppose I didn't dare, not so long as Father was head of the house.' He gave a single, unhappy snort of laughter. 'Turns out he's not been in charge for quite some time.'

'Edward,' said James, hearing the tremor in his voice, 'there's something you need to know. It's Janey—'

Edward was still lost in his train of thought. 'The financials are a nightmare, James. We're in the pit.' He ran his hands through his hair, and when he glanced over at his brother, there was a hopelessness in his eyes that James had never seen before. 'There's no money left, you realise?'

The shock of that knocked James off his stride. 'There's not?'

'No,' sniffed Edward. 'Hasn't been in years, not since the mine dried up. The old man's been living off rents, when he remembers to collect them, but even if they all came in we'd still be in trouble.'

'What will you do?'

Edward was silent for a very long time. 'We'll figure something out,' he said, his voice hollow. 'I suppose we'll have to.'

Edward looked so desolate that James could hardly bear to drop the news about Janey on him – but there were surely only moments before Whittell banged on their door. 'I'm sorry to do this to you, Edward,' he said, 'but there's something else.'

'Oh?' he said, his attention shifting fully to James now, apparently for the first time.

'Janey's dead.'

When Edward lifted his hand to his face, pinching the bridge of his nose, it too was trembling. 'Dear God, that poor girl,' he said, his voice choked. 'Do you know what happened?'

It was not the time to confront Edward about sleeping with her. Let Whittell dredge that up, if he had to. 'It was him, Edward,' James went on. 'The Tall Man.'

He heard the note of alarm in Edward's voice. 'You're sure?'

'I saw him. Spoke to him.'

'You did what?' There was anger, now, amidst his brother's terror.

'He wants your son,' said James, and the relief of speaking it out loud felt almost physical. He swallowed hard. 'He took Janey's child, but it – it wasn't enough.'

Edward was visibly angry now. 'Father was right,' he said, rising from his chair. 'He's taken too much from this village. And its people.' He shook his head vigorously, as though trying to straighten out his disordered thoughts. 'What more does he want from them?'

James stared at him, amazed. 'Are you not listening to me? He wants your son.' He felt his own anger rising, not just at Edward, but at everything that had made him this way, grounded him in ego and pride. 'You've got to get away from here.'

'No,' said Edward with force, striking the table with his fist. 'I won't do that.' He was breathing heavily, furiously. 'We have a duty here, James. Our family. I know that doesn't mean much to you, but somebody has to stand up to him.'

'You can't take him on,' said James, backing away from his brother as though his folly were contagious. 'Whatever's beneath this place – the void – it's stronger than it was when we were young. Whatever killed Janey, I've never seen anything like it—'

'I'm stronger too,' said Edward fiercely. 'Stronger than you realise.'

James felt his jaw clench; there was a sharp pain across his neck from where he was tensed. 'I don't think you understand, Edward,' he said in something like despair. 'I don't think he can be beaten. I think perhaps he's always been there, and always will be.' Against the odds, Edward seemed to be listening. 'You know what he'll say if you go to him—'

'I know exactly what he'll say,' said Edward with a grimace, as though the Tall Man were some unruly neighbour. He took a steadying breath, then laid a hand on James's shoulder. 'But Father resisted him, didn't he? You and I both lived to adulthood. So the Tall Man doesn't win them all – unless there's some murdered sibling somewhere among these pages.'

'You're serious,' said James, feeling giddy, as though he were on the verge of hysteria. 'You're actually going to stay?' He shook his head. 'My God. What about Sophia?'

'Enough, James,' said Edward, releasing him. 'I don't expect you to see it as I do.'

He hated Edward then – or at least some part of him did, anyway – with a hatred that only existed between siblings. He felt at once patronised and slighted and righteous, and perhaps that accounted for what he said next. 'You're a fool,' he said. 'Do you hear me?' He felt appalled by the man standing across from him. 'Last night Janey died at the Tall Man's hand, and now you're spoiling for a fight with him.' He spoke to wound. 'She told me the child was yours.'

That got his attention. 'Keep your voice down,' he hissed.

James glanced over at the door, knowing full well how far voices carried in Harringley Manor. 'That would be one way to get Sophia to leave this place.'

Edward advanced on him, as though to restrain him by force. 'Don't you dare.' His voice was low and carried a real threat of violence.

'Why am I the only one here who understands how dangerous he is?' James yelled.

And then Edward grabbed him, his expression a mixture of terror and anger. 'You're not!' he shouted hoarsely, and then he shoved James hard in the chest, sending him staggering into the wall. 'You're not. I can see what the void has done to this place just as clearly as you can.' Edward was running his hands through his hair again, apparently appalled at himself.

'But you've never made any secret of your contempt for this family, and you've let it blind you.' His brother's face was set in a grimace. 'I can't think with you here,' he said. 'I can't see things clearly with you skulking around the place, and Father in a strop because I got into his papers. I'd like you to go.'

At that very moment, Ransford appeared in the doorway, solid and imposing as a lump of oak. James knew he'd heard the whole thing – the servants always did. There was an implied threat in his presence, and despite the man's age, James had no desire to cross him.

'I'm leaving, Ransford,' he said. 'Tell my father that Janey died last night.'

'Very well, sir,' said Ransford without turning. There was no trace of sorrow in his voice.

He descended the steps hurriedly, crossing the hall without waiting for Ransford to see him out, and he'd have opened the door himself had Sophia not stepped out of the drawing room and greeted him with a low curtsey. She looked pale and weary, as though she'd rather be asleep. 'I hope you don't mind,' she said. 'I heard Ransford let you in. It's good to see you.'

'Don't worry about entertaining me,' he said, still a little shy around her, unsure of how much of this house's culture she'd absorbed in her time here. 'I'm just leaving.'

'Oh, I'm sorry to hear that,' she said warmly, her smile apparently involuntary. 'It's nice to have visitors.' She cast her eyes down. 'It's so quiet up here most of the time,' she said, embarrassed. 'Just us and the servants.'

From upstairs there came the sound of a door opening and

the distant squall of a child crying. 'I'd better go,' he said. 'I hope my nephew's well?'

'Oh, he's a monster,' said Sophia, her face brightening. 'They are at this age. They're wild animals, really, don't know what they need.'

He glanced up towards his brother's room. He couldn't have long before Edward would appear and order him out. He had to take this chance. 'Do you think Edward's enjoying fatherhood?' he said. If he couldn't persuade Edward the child was in danger, perhaps he could still persuade Sophia. That might just be enough.

He'd said the wrong thing, he knew it right away. The lightness seemed to drain from Sophia's face. 'In a manner of speaking,' she said after a moment, then gave a little sigh. 'He's not very good at enjoying himself, your brother. He's intense. Preoccupied.' She gave an unhappy little laugh, her smile wintery now. 'You'll have to excuse me being so frank,' she said. 'I'm a little out of sorts.'

The silence hung between them, pregnant with its secrets. 'Sophia,' James murmured. 'Did something happen? With Edward, or your son?'

Sophia ran her tongue over her teeth, and he could see the calculations behind her eyes: *is this worth the risk?* 'You came here today about a girl,' she said eventually. 'About Janey.'

James could hardly speak, just nodded mutely at first. But Sophia was patient, expectant, and he owed her an answer now. Somehow he found his words. 'That's right,' he said.

Sophia gave a single, brisk nod. 'Is she dead?'

'She is.'

She sniffed, took a steadying breath, then said resolutely, 'And the child?'

'No sign.' Beneath her stare, her defiant attempt to remain upright, he almost felt like the guilty one, like he'd killed Janey.

'Dear God,' said Sophia with a sigh. Her composure was extraordinary, but he could see something beneath the surface had shattered. 'Something like that – so close to here – it gets to you.' She swallowed, trying to modulate her breathing. 'Whenever I mention it to Edward he just tells me not to be ridiculous, but it's not as easy as he makes it sound.' She paused, closed her eyes. 'I don't like imagining what she went through.'

Again the silence hung between them; there was no way back to safe conversational ground now.

'Maybe you could persuade Edward to take you away for a while,' James said, as lightly as he could manage. 'Take an apartment in the city.'

He saw her smile then, faintly, but it didn't linger on her lips – and Edward picked that very moment to appear at the top of the stairs. Sophia took a step back, abashed.

'Trying to lure her away, are you?' Edward said, and though the words had the cadence of a joke their tone was all wrong, felt instead like a kind of threat.

James tried to muster the same level of calm. 'Edward, please.'

Edward descended the stairs in quick strides; it was only moments before he was next to his brother, his face pressed close to James's, his voice a low hiss. 'You were right to leave this place, James,' he said firmly. 'If you come here again, I'll instruct Ransford to bar the doors.'

James took a step back, rattled. 'You're making a mistake,' he said, knowing he'd lost.

'The only mistake I made was letting Sophia invite you back here,' Edward spat. 'Now get out of my house.'

16

H E STUMBLED out of the house in a panic. More certain than ever that Edward's son was in danger, and unable to do a thing about it. Whittell thought him mad – maybe even thought him a murderer – and Edward had banished him from the house.

It was like that first night in Newcastle all over again: he was friendless, hopeless, alone. He thought of Sophia, the panic behind her eyes, and he felt it all afresh – the way the house subsumed you, cut you off, became your whole world. How had he survived sixteen years within its walls?

But you had Emily, he thought, *and the priest.*

And then it hit him. The priest was still here. A broken man, true – shattered by whatever botched attempt he had made to rid the house of the Tall Man – but until then he'd managed to resist the house's pernicious influence, never given in to whatever devoured so many governesses. Perhaps there was sanctuary within those rotting church walls. Or perhaps, in the ruins of the old priest's mind, there still something that might yet help Sophia.

Back, then, to that ruined churchyard, back to that weather-beaten door. It was late afternoon when he arrived, the sun setting beneath the horizon in a hazy glow, the church silent.

Today when he knocked no one answered, but that came as no surprise now – the priest would be tucked away in the vestry, poring over some ancient text by the light of a guttering candle, numb to the sounds of the outside world.

Again James knocked, waited. Nothing. No sound of movement, no footsteps or answering call from within. He reached out for the heavy door handle and turned it, finding to his surprise it moved. He opened the door, stepped into the church's familiar gloom.

'Hello?' he called, and his voice returned only echoes.

The church was not entirely silent. From somewhere there came the faint, distant sound of wood striking wood, a rhythmic clatter that he couldn't place.

'Father?' he called.

And then his eyes adjusted, and he saw that nearly all the church's furniture was gone, as though dragged away for firewood. Only the heavy altar and lectern remained, in which James could now make out thick gouges from where they'd been hit with an axe.

He felt a sudden sensation of vertigo, put a hand to his chest to stop a rising nausea. There was a fury to what had happened here, a malice, and no matter where he set his gaze he could not escape it.

'What happened here?' he murmured, but the only answer was that strange, rhythmic knocking, like dry bones colliding in the dark.

It was coming from the vestry.

He took a candle stub from one of the wall sconces and hobbled across the great space of the sanctuary to the antechamber. He didn't call out again: there'd be no answer.

The vestry was without windows and almost totally black. 'Who's in there?' he called in, but there came no reply. Whatever was in there didn't respond to his footsteps either; the only sound was that knocking, hollow and strangely tuneful.

James held the candle stub out a short way in front of him, and the room came slowly into focus.

There was a man hanging from the ceiling.

James recoiled, the flagstones horribly slippery beneath him, his fingers burning from where he'd touched the candle wick before it fell from his grasp. He couldn't tear his eyes from the sight. The figure was suspended by a rope across his shoulders, and spun back and forth with gravity and the breeze from the room's open door.

The knocking seemed louder now, echoing from the walls of the tiny space, hollow and vacant. It was coming from the man himself. James inched closer, trying to make out what it could be, hardly daring to let himself imagine – and yet the thoughts rushed in regardless: of the man's chest cavity wrenched open, his ribs replaced by branches, his heart by stones.

There was something wrong with the scene. A man wouldn't spin in the breeze like that: he'd be too heavy, would hang like a dead weight. A little bolder now, he pushed himself upright against the wall of the vestry, reached out a hand towards the dead man.

He was made of wood. Long limbs made from jointed tree branches, knocking against each other, and the face a scribbled mass of twigs. He was dressed in a black tailcoat, well-made and surprisingly expensive-looking.

James should have been relieved. But the worst part of all this was its familiarity – the sense that he had been here before, that somehow he knew this thing. He felt tainted by even touching its sleeve, and sure enough his fingers were marked with an oily black residue. For a moment, before he told himself otherwise, he half-wished it had been a dead man after all.

Outside darkness had fallen, but when James staggered out of the church he found himself surrounded by a great arc of figures, people waiting for him to emerge.

'Thank goodness,' he said breathless and a little taken aback. 'The priest – he's gone – and—'

But then he saw their faces. Saw the lack of surprise in their expressions, their sombre and steady gazes, and knew he had no allies here. The silence seemed to stretch out.

'Somebody here knows something about this,' James called, looking from face to face. 'Where is he?'

No answer.

He turned to an onlooker, a little bald man with a foolish grin and wiry tufts of hair poking up by his ears like reeds.

'What have you done with him?' James said, taking a step towards him, newly conscious of his own strength and size. 'He was a good man.'

The little man gave no answer, only bit his knuckle and giggled, a high, piping sound that seemed curiously appropriate. Then, from the back of the crowd, emerged a battered-looking man with a mass of curly black hair.

James recognised Ephraim Miller – once he'd been the village butcher, one of the village's few real success stories, but now he was a ruined thing, his face criss-crossed with burst blood vessels and set in a permanent scowl.

'He was a miserable wretch,' said Miller coarsely. 'Told us the very same thing himself, plenty of times.'

James steeled himself, determined not to appear intimidated by Miller. 'So he deserved to die?'

Miller gave an off-handed shrug. 'Maybe he was taken,' he said. 'Chose to submit himself to a different authority.'

James held his gaze. 'You and I know that's not what happened.'

'I don't know much, sir,' said Miller with a smirk that suggested otherwise. 'Except about that church there.'

'And what's that?'

'It don't belong to God no more, that's for sure.'

17

THERE WAS no sign of Whittell when James returned to the inn. Tonight he was glad of that. He couldn't bear the inspector's disdain, not after the horrors of the church. His whole body itched and he was numb with tiredness; all he wanted was to be in bed, unconscious.

It was too much to hope for a night without dreams. When he closed his eyes he'd see that thing, hanging from the roof of the church, and those scars cut into its walls – but he'd at least be away from this absurd place, however temporarily, where everything was askance and the upright man looked drunk.

When he stepped into the inn, the barman fumbled the pint he was pouring, sending dark beer spraying across his shirt and apron. At least it meant James didn't have to meet the man's eyes, to see the fear and distrust in them. Every patron in that shabby bar knew where James had woken up that morning. It was only a matter of time before they asked.

James acknowledged the barman with a curt nod and made

straight for the steps leading upstairs, but before he'd reached the top he heard the man call after him.

'There was someone asking after you,' the barman said gruffly. 'You only just missed her. Does that have anything to do with what happened?'

James half-turned, not wanting to be here a moment longer. 'Who?'

'Don't know her name,' said the barman with a sniff. 'Recognised her face, though. Stops in every month or so for market day. She left something for you.' From beneath the bar he produced a small rectangular package wrapped in cloth and set it on the bar. 'I take it you weren't expecting this?'

From where he stood James stared at the thing, a riot of terrible images filling his head: it was the bones of Janey's child, stripped bare, or the priest's tongue ripped clean from his head. 'No,' he said hoarsely. 'Not at all.'

He descended the stairs. Lifted the package, shook it. Nothing rattled. Gingerly, he loosened the rope tied around the thing and peeled back its cloth cover. Inside was a stack of paper, twenty or thirty pages at least, written in a spidery and scrawled hand that was strangely familiar. The first sentence read, *My boy is dead. This place killed him.*

He glanced up at the barman, who was watching him intently. 'The person who handed you this,' he said urgently, 'the traveller – which way did they go?'

'Out into the square, sir,' said the barman, raising his eyebrows. 'You may even have passed her on your way in.'

James flung the cloth back over the manuscript, tied it up

roughly and thrust it into the hands of the barman. 'Put this in my room,' he said. 'Don't let anyone see it. And if anything should happen to me—' He grimaced, wondering who would act on it. 'See to it that this gets to the inspector,' he said. 'He'll understand.'

The barman looked flustered, unexpectedly ruddy and animated, as though he'd been at the brandy. 'Right you are, sir,' he said hesitantly, but by then James was already out of the door.

The street was littered with the remnants of market day. Fruit and veg crushed underfoot, their innards bleeding out onto the flagstones. Shattered beams, already breaking into jagged splinters. There was a stench rising from the ground, the smell of something rotting.

When James stepped out of the inn, he caught a flicker of movement in the corner of his eye, a figure peeling off from the shadows. It stood on the edge of a stream, watching him, its face shrouded by a hood.

'I got your package,' he called over, and in the silence his voice echoed. 'You could have given it to me in person.'

The figure was silent. Watching James, implacable and expectant. He felt something like judgement in its gaze, and couldn't explain why.

He took a step towards it, prepared for it to run, ready to give stumbling chase if it did. But it only stood there.

'I don't know what you're expecting from me,' he called,

taking another tentative step towards it. 'Why you sent it to me.'

Now the silence was becoming weightier; he felt it in his chest, like sorrow or grief. It was unbearable. It was like drowning.

'Say something, why don't you?' he called out, hearing the note of despair in his voice. Still the silence lingered, stretching out into eternity, the only sound the echoes of his own words. He took another step towards the figure, then another, and still it didn't move. There was a pressure inside his head, a low, insistent hum. 'I said speak to me, God damn you!' he thundered, and in that moment he felt like the shadow of his own father.

The figure cleared its throat: a harsh, gravelly sound, only half-human.

'You've got a lot to answer for, James Harringley,' it said, in a voice like razors.

He just stared. He knew that voice, he was sure of it, but like him it was changed, its owner's identity buried in some dim recess of his brain.

'I – I don't know what you're talking about,' he said, more quietly now.

The figure shook its head, and when it spoke again it was in the same gravelled voice. 'Not here,' it said. 'Follow me.'

It stepped down into the shadows of a low bridge, and now James felt a dumb terror, the sense that he'd been here before but couldn't recall where this road led. 'I'm not doing that,' he said. 'I won't go in there, you hear me.'

'I'm not the one you need to be afraid of.'

He stood his ground. 'Prove it.'

'And there was me thinking you might remember me,' Emily said, lifting her head. Her face was nicked with scars, her hair streaked with grey and roughly tied back, but the years hadn't dimmed the mixture of sorrow and ferocity he saw in her eyes.

'It can't be,' he said, with a gasp. 'They cut you open – my father told me you were gone.'

At the name she grimaced. 'Your father's got a lot to answer for.'

'But you're alive,' he breathed. 'How can you be alive?'

He could hardly bring himself to look at her. He'd been so certain he'd never see her again; so certain she'd died that night, the servants burying her quietly on the grounds. Even now, speaking with her felt unreal; he wasn't sure how he'd bear it if she were only a figment of his imagination.

'All those years I thought I was to blame,' he said. He wanted to reach out a hand, touch her face, but he thought if he tried it she'd probably break his arm.

Emily shook her head. 'Not here,' she said, turning once more into the darkness. 'You know what this place is like,' she said without looking back. 'I don't know what they'll do if they hear us talking about *him*.'

And then she half-turned, and held out her hand. And this time he took it, and let her lead him into the dark.

18

'THIS ISN'T about you,' she said into the gloom. They were shielded from view beneath the village's low bridge, on either side of a stream that burbled over a scattering of pebbles. In the moonlight James could just make out Emily's silhouette. 'Don't get the wrong idea.'

'Come on, Emily,' he said, hearing the superiority in his voice and hating it. 'I'd never even have known you were alive if you hadn't come looking for me.'

'No,' said Emily sharply. 'It's about Janey.' She took a deep breath. 'Because she deserves someone who'll fight for her. And someone needs to make sure her story's told.'

'You know what happened to her?' said James, louder than he intended, then quietened himself, looking around for Whittell. He'd sworn he'd never forget the dangers of this village – the night he first lost Emily – but time and memory played tricks on a man in the place he was born, could erase every promise he'd made since leaving in the blink of an eye.

'I do.' Emily's face was downcast. 'She loved that child,' she said with a shake of her head. 'I mean, he was never going to have an easy life, but he had something going for him.' Her eyes darkened. 'He deserved better.'

'What happened to him, Emily?'

'He's dead,' she said. 'Don't tell me you're surprised.'

'You can't know that,' James said, his mind scrabbling for a foothold, something to orientate himself. 'How can you know that?'

'She fucking told me, didn't she?' Emily gave a bitter laugh. 'It's all written down in that package I sent you. Took me years before anyone would tell me their story.'

'No,' he said. 'You're here now. So tell me. Please. I need to hear it from you.'

'Very well,' she sighed.

When Emily told the story, James saw it unfold as though he'd been there himself. Janey woke every morning, Emily said, and looked at the gardens from her window. Her list of tasks was endless, but most days it didn't feel like a job. Trim the hedges, prune any loose branches from the shrubs, pull up the weeds, rake the debris. Tend to the flowerbeds – planting, composting, watering – and then the trees. It felt like carving order out of chaos. She found it satisfying.

Four years she'd been managing the gardens single-handed, ever since she'd awoken one day to find her father slumped on the kitchen table. His heart had given out, the doctor said, and it hadn't come as much of a surprise. He'd been tired for as long as Janey could remember. His face criss-crossed with cracked blood vessels, his days marred by headaches so severe that he couldn't even stand the light. She'd been preparing for his death longer than she'd realised.

Bearing a child, though, that took her by surprise. She was not prepared for the sickness that came over her in the mornings, sending her scurrying to vomit under a tree. Not prepared for the bone-deep fatigue that overcame her at the end of the day. Yes, she knew about the physical pains of childbirth, the terror and exhaustion of labour. But what she hadn't known, and what she was only now beginning to understand, was the way her body and mind would be irreversibly changed. She already felt different, inside and out.

She was no fool. She knew what was growing inside of her. Some part of her hoped that all this effort might even drive it out of her, that she might one day feel a shift and a gush of blood and the thing would be gone. But she had no such luck. Three months passed, and then four, and five, and by then she knew the thing was tenacious. It kept growing inside her, and so she kept growing too, and each day her job tending the gardens became ever more difficult.

Her swelling belly stopped her from being able to kneel, her bladder surprised her at inopportune moments with its demand she piss. When the child first kicked inside of her, the tiny flutters a sign of a burgeoning intelligence, she resented it. Only in time did she come to appreciate its companionship – how she was no longer alone, and never again would be.

When her son was born, the Harringleys provided her

with a crib. She scraped together some blankets and pillows, and a few old toys to keep the baby occupied and entertained. It was a meagre offering, she knew that much, but she didn't much care. She'd tended to the gardens for years, taming their disorder, and she'd been good at it. This wasn't so different.

She could provide for this creature, no matter how difficult it was. She'd give it a good life, like her father had given her. A life with order, with stability, with purpose. She'd work every waking hour, if necessary, to make sure her baby never knew hunger or hardship.

She knew her place in the world. She wasn't trying to be anything more. But the father of her child had made her promises. He'd called her little boy a child of destiny, said there was a place set aside for it. She'd thought he meant to take the boy into his home.

And then the boy disappeared in the night and she found herself running through the woods. She'd run out in her nightclothes, hadn't even put on her boots. Her heart was pounding in her ears. There was bile in her throat, sweat circling her neck. She could taste blood, and was sure she'd bitten her cheek.

She wasn't sure how she found it. A tunnel into the earth, a circular orifice ringed by damp, black soil. On the breeze she could taste the stench of old, rotten things, decaying foliage and stagnant water.

And there, before that hole stretching into the earth, stood the child's father. He was holding the little boy in his arms, wrapped up in a tight bundle. Only he wasn't alone. With him was a tall figure in a tailcoat and top hat, clothed in shadows and without a face.

That was when Janey called out to them. You can't take him, she'd said, and the child's father had taken a warning step towards her. You don't understand what this is, he'd said. You don't understand how important your boy is.

He's my child, she cried.

He's not, said the child's father. Not according to your contract. Any court would agree.

A court! she'd said. He's a child. He's not even got a name.

He's my property, said the child's father. Legally. And you are too.

Oh, so that's how it is, she said. Wasn't like that when you were inside me, was it?

And then the Tall Man spoke up. I can make him a king, he said to her. Exalted above all others.

I don't want him to be a king, Janey said.

Then what?

I want him back, she said. Give him to me.

You have not counted the cost, the Tall Man said. You are making a foolish choice.

I said give him to me, she said, and she reached out to pull the child from his father's arms – but he was strong, so strong. He flung her away from him lazily, with a flick of his arm, and in that moment she sensed he would smash the child's head on a rock rather than let her take him back.

Instead she turned to the child's father, grabbing at his coat, pleading with him, telling him through her tears that he could stop this if he chose.

And in return he told her, there is no other way. And he placed his son into the Tall Man's arms. And then he set off towards the house alone, all his tenderness gone, not even offering Janey his coat.

When she turned, the Tall Man had gone too, vanished into the earth with her boy. So she sat on the ground a little longer, without any words, until the cold became too much to bear.

It took her three days to get back again.

At first, when James heard Janey's story, his brain refused to comprehend it. Emily's words washed over him, and only after a minute or so did he finally register what she'd said.

Then came the nausea, the terror. There was a vile taste in his mouth – sour and metallic – and his nerves felt like piano wires.

'You're wrong,' he said. 'Or Janey was wrong.' His mouth opened and closed again; he looked down at his feet, and then back up at Emily. He was appalled, aghast. 'Edward wouldn't – he'd never—'

'He did,' said Emily flatly. 'I'm sorry.'

'My brother went looking for the Tall Man? You're sure of that?'

'Of course I'm sure,' Emily growled.

'How?'

'She told me herself, James. She had no reason to lie.'

'Christ,' said James. 'That's – it's – monstrous.' But he'd known it all along, hadn't he, ever since Janey had told him the child was Edward's? His brother had never loved a groundskeeper's girl. He'd hoped to escape on a technicality.

She had to tell this to Whittell, he told her then. Had to go to him with Janey's manuscript, call in every resource the law had to find her justice. It was the only option, he told her, truly believing it as the words left his lips, until in the moonlight he saw her expression change from curiosity to disgust. He could hear the bitterness in her voice.

'I can't do that,' she said.

'You have to. Please. He's a good man. He can help.'

'No,' she said firmly. 'Don't take it to the inspector.' She closed her eyes, put her head back against the wall, and sighed. 'I'm begging you,' she said, and James could hear what it cost.

'But it's the evidence he needs—'

'It's not, don't you see?' Emily groaned, with something like despair. 'If you give it to him it'll disappear.'

'He's better than that, Emily.' And James still believed that, even after all Whittell had said to him – the inspector was a man searching for the truth, who'd believe it when he saw it.

She was silent a moment, then leaned forward, took his hand from his side and held it in her own. 'This village does something to people, James,' she said, biting his lip. 'They forget.' She shook her head. 'If you leave those pages with Whittell, they'll end up buried here, like every other story that's ever been told about – *him* – and then Janey will have died for nothing.'

'Whittell's not like the others,' said James. 'He's not from here.'

'I'm not sure it matters,' sniffed Emily, dropping his hand.

It hung uselessly by his side, still warm from her touch.

He studied what he could see of her face in the darkness. He still couldn't believe she was real. 'What makes you think I'm any different to Whittell?' he said eventually. 'What makes you think I can stop him?'

'Because you've got a life outside of here,' said Emily fiercely. 'You've got status, connections.' She paused, the bitterness creeping back into her voice again. 'Listen,' she said, 'if I send those pages to a publisher, they'll burn them. But you—'

He thought of his home in the slums, and had to stifle a laugh. 'Those aren't really the kinds of circles I move in.'

He wasn't sure if Emily had heard him at all. 'You're my best hope,' she said. 'I've tried for so many years, but—'

'But what about Sophia, and the child?' he said, thinking of the panic in her eyes, knowing what it felt like to be rotting away within those walls. 'I can't just leave them here.'

Emily didn't try to hide her exasperation. 'You're one man, James,' she groaned. 'I don't care how strong you are, it's not enough. Not to stop him.' She screwed up her eyes, clearly trying to remain calm. 'If you tell that story to enough people,' she said, a little more gently, 'then this place will be flooded with outsiders. And maybe that's exactly what it needs.'

He knew instinctively that she was right. This village wouldn't survive an influx like that, would crumble under their scrutiny – and yet…

'But I mean it – I can't leave them. Edward, or Sophia, or the child. He's coming for them, I'm sure of it.'

'You can't save them on your own,' she said.

Some part of him was appalled by her coldness. It had been there all along, but the years had strengthened it into a hard core. 'This is easy for you,' he said, before he could stop himself. 'You've got nothing at stake.'

Emily's eyes widened, and she hesitated just a moment before answering. 'I've got nothing at stake?' she snarled, obviously furious. 'What do you think the good folk drinking down the Hare would do if they knew I'd given that manuscript to you? My guess is they'd cut me open again without even realising they'd done it.' She shook her head, her hands clenching and unclenching at her sides. 'But I won't run,' she said viciously. 'Any chance I've had, I've fought to show people who he is, and I'm not stopping now.'

James held his hands up in a gesture of surrender. 'You should come back with me,' he said, in an attempt at conciliation. 'To the city.'

'There's nothing for me there,' said Emily, without meeting his eye.

'I can help you find a new life,' he said, warming to his theme. 'A better life.'

Emily's smile was grim. 'I've heard that before,' she said. She took a deep, steadying breath. 'You're kind,' she said, and in spite of her anger he thought she meant it. 'Truly you are. But I won't go until I know this place is free of him.'

'How can you be so certain this will work?'

'I can't,' said Emily, her eyes on her feet. 'But I know him – I've studied him all these years. He likes shadows. So that's what we need to take away from him.'

19

H E REMEMBERED the night he'd first lost Emily. It was a few weeks after the priest had left, and his father still hadn't found a new governess – in fact the old man seemed to have become increasingly irascible and preoccupied, flying off the handle at the servants when they stood too close to his elbow at dinner or failed to saddle his horses quickly enough.

James did what he always did. He escaped to the library, and set himself down in a wingback chair with a novel. But for the first time ever, his strategy had failed him: he found he couldn't lose himself to an imaginary world, his thoughts drawing him back insistently to the priest – his eyes glassy, muttering the words, '*What profit is there in my blood, when I go down to the pit? Shall the dust praise thee? Shall it declare thy truth?*'

For days he tried to shake it off. Took long walks around the estate, slunk into the walls to watch the servants and the kitchens to steal food, but none of it satisfied. It was all so familiar, so rote. In his fifteen years here, he'd seen every paltry wonder this place had to offer, and couldn't live off them for the rest of his life. He needed more.

That night, when Emily slunk out of a hole in the wall, she found James on his feet, waiting for her. 'I have to get out of here,' he told her right away.

She cocked her head, studied him curiously – as if wondering if he were in earnest. She was still dressed for work, her clothes shabby with dust. 'You'd really leave this place to Edward?'

'It's not like I'm going to do it much good,' he muttered.

'Maybe you're the best hope this place has,' Emily said, her brow furrowed. Her usual verve had deserted her: she was sombre, sorrowful. 'Because you can't stand it.'

He'd had this same thought himself. 'It'll never work,' he said. 'You saw what happened to the priest. And anyway, my father's got plenty more years in him.'

Emily took a step backwards, as though hoping to disappear back into the darkness. 'That's it, then,' she said, a catch in her voice. 'You'll leave me here to rot.'

He'd thought of this too. How could he ever leave her?

'You can come with me,' he said quietly.

She blinked hard, twice, and then gave a crooked smile. 'You're serious.'

'Of course I'm serious,' he said, his smile widening to match hers. He felt giddy with the thrill of it. 'We won't have any money. But we can work that out later.'

She took a step forward then, gingerly, and then another, until she was right in front of him. Then, as he watched, she lifted herself up on her tiptoes and kissed him gently, once, on the cheek. He stared at her, bewildered, as she stepped back onto her heels.

'You're a good man, James Harringley.'

'I'm not sure you're right about that,' he said, still a little dazed. 'I can't do anything for the people down there.' He swallowed hard. 'And he'll hate me forever, you know. He'll think I'm shirking my duties.'

Emily studied the ground at James's feet. He'd never seen her like this – now she seemed almost overwhelmed, her sorrow a memory. 'How well do you know the people down there, James?' she said after a second or two. 'How many of them have you met?'

'Not many, unless you count the governesses. Or you.'

She nodded, lifting her eyes to his. He wondered if she expected him to kiss her. 'Don't let anyone tell you that you're not doing your duty,' she said fiercely. 'Because you're helping me right now. Helping me get out.' She took a deep, shuddering breath. 'I'll never forget this.'

Her enthusiasm made it real. He felt a prickling of anxiety, a new wariness as he imagined all they'd need to do. 'Let's get out of here first,' he said. 'Then you can thank me.'

'Tomorrow,' she said. 'I'll pack a bag.'

The next day they met in the kitchen to gather provisions, shoving them into a rough sacking bag Emily had stolen from the servant's quarters. Salted meat, bread, dried fruits; anything that would get them through those first few nights trying to set themselves up in Newcastle. They worked in silence, communicating through gestures, terrified of being discovered.

They went at twilight, as the lamps were being lit, slipped out through the kitchen garden into the trees. On his way outside James slipped a paring knife into his pocket. Sharp enough to slice bread in a pinch, and to cut the throat of anyone stupid enough to try and rob them. He wasn't sure how long they'd get; when they found he was not in his bed there'd be search parties, men on horseback.

There was a coach at nine that night, and with any luck he'd be on it, headed for the city. If not, he had a story ready. He'd been out watching the stars, he had his notebook, he'd fallen in a bog. His clothes weren't dirty enough for that, he knew, but it could be easily fixed.

'Hey,' he whispered. 'Push me over, would you?'

Ahead of him Emily stopped, shot him a bewildered look. 'What?'

'Don't think, just do it.'

He expected more protest. Instead she turned and, in one swift movement, strode towards him and pushed him in the chest with surprising strength. He didn't even have to force himself to fall: he went stumbling backwards, toppling over his own heels, his back coated with thick, sticky mud and half-rotted leaves.

'Thanks,' he said, although it came out a little affronted.

'Come on,' said Emily, as she continued walking. 'Someone will see us.'

He pushed himself to his feet, hurried after her.

The night was cool, the heat of the day almost completely gone, and the mud on his jacket and trousers already felt stiff and heavy.

Emily had disappeared into a gap between the trees, which revealed itself on closer inspection to be a ragged path. In the moonlight it was dappled with the shapes of leaves, although the long limbs of the trees above carved stark bars across their way.

'We don't have to do this,' he heard Emily say. 'We can still turn back.' She was watching him with her arms folded and her head cocked. 'It's fine.'

'I'm going,' he said. Twisting his body away from the house, so that he couldn't see even the faint halo of its lights. 'I need to do this.'

'Whatever you say,' said Emily with a shrug. 'But I understand if – you know – it's not so easy to run away as you thought. Places like this have deep roots.'

The path curved down through the trees at a steep angle. James wore heavy boots, but Emily's feet were clad in a pair of shabby, flat canvas shoes – it was a miracle she'd managed to stay upright so long.

If the mud underfoot bothered her, she didn't show it: she knelt and removed her shoes, holding them both in one hand, the sharp white lines of her feet unexpected and erotic until the mud squelched around them and turned them black.

They walked in silence, Emily ahead of him, the only sounds the slap and crack of their footsteps, the rustling of the trees around – signs of some hidden animal, he hoped, or the wind.

How many times he'd walked these woods by daylight, dimly aware of a strange hum in the soil, the sense this was a place his father could never truly possess. By dark, the woods felt wilder than before, more alive: bristling with a vibrant, unseen presence. More than once he thought he heard something breathing, some massive beast inhaling, and tried to shake it off as childish fear.

But some great sorrow dwelt in these woods, some loss was concealed here. He could feel it on all sides of him. There was a presence in them, like the only survivor after a fire, still walking through a landscape of nightmare, crying nonsense syllables. Some craven mouth still longed desperately for blood, with a thirst that could not be sated. He knew it then, deep in his bones: he was not welcome here.

Then, in the corner of his eye, a flicker of white. Some dim figure in the trees, clothed in rags impossibly bright in the twilight. Out it peered from behind one trunk, vanishing again, like a puppy playing its games. James was wary of those games. The dogs didn't stay playful forever.

Again it darted across his vision, that white shape, not quite human, desperately fast. 'Emily!' he yelled, but she was far from him, off in the darkness further down the hill, and his voice seemed to disappear in the thicket of branches overhead. There were no echoes here. 'Emily!' he called again, and the figure looked up at him, a quick, jerky movement, unavoidably animal. It was frozen behind its tree, watching.

He stared back. 'Listen,' he said quietly. 'You come close and you'll regret it.' Quietly enough that he wasn't sure the figure could hear him — he didn't want to goad it — although he still felt the thrill of adrenaline when he ran his finger across the blade in his pocket.

The figure cocked its head, craned its neck out a little way: long hair, a long, pale face, all spattered in mud. Now it was still he could see what he'd taken for pristine cloth was instead a patchwork of mismatched rags, hastily stitched together and giving the figure an unmistakable look of being dressed in an old rug. He couldn't tell whether it was male or female: whatever softness there was in the features was overtaken by a fierce hunger in the eyes.

'You don't belong here,' he said, feigning an assertiveness he didn't feel. 'Get out.'

The figure narrowed its eyes. Even at this distance the gesture was unmistakably one of displeasure, and James regretted his tone. And then, horribly, it stepped out from behind its tree and began to walk towards him with a strange, jerky motion, like a puppet with tangled strings.

How many times the priest had prepared him for this – told him the devil had no power here. He said the words automatically: 'In the name of Christ, go.'

Its lips twisted into a grotesque parody of a smile, but it didn't stop coming.

'You've no power here,' he shouted, a little hysterical. 'This isn't your land.' But the figure was still coming, forcing him backwards over the mud and leaves, and James was struck by the sudden, terrible sense he'd understood only a fraction of this world. It wasn't God who'd save him, not now: he needed someone closer at hand.

'Emily!' shouted James now, not wanting to turn his back on the approaching figure, yet hardly daring to navigate the buried roots and slick leaves beneath without a lamp to light his feet. 'What in the hell do you want?' he called to the figure, but the figure made no answer, only kept coming, and at the sight of its long hands and sharp, ragged fingernails, whatever was left of James's courage deserted him. He hurled himself down the path, feet scrabbling for purchase, heart pounding, glancing back just once at the dim white shape above him on the path; it was still, apparently weighing up whether he was worth pursuing.

He felt like he'd run for hours when he turned the corner and stumbled over Emily. At the speed he'd been going he was unable to keep himself on the ground, and sailed a considerable distance, cracking his knee on the root of a nearby tree in the process. Emily's expression was furious, but her words were laconic. 'Yew tree,' she said. 'Healing properties.'

He hardly felt the pain he knew must be there. 'There's a man up there,' he said, limping over to her, trying unsuccessfully to pull her to her feet. 'We have to go.'

'What are you talking about?' she said, not moving.

'I saw something. A man, I think. All in white. On the hill.' He pointed, futilely, because all that was visible above was a dim spot of moonlight. 'He's coming.' His chest was heaving, his words effortful and half-formed. 'Come on, Emily!'

He could see the look of alarm that crossed her face, and the effort it took to calm herself down. She swallowed hard. 'It's probably nothing,' she said, although she didn't sound sure.

'People live out here, you know. Vagrants. They're harmless, but they're – they're strange.' She took a deep breath. 'Odds are you saw one of them. Dressed in rags? Slurring their words?' She cocked her head. 'Tell me I'm wrong.'

He felt like an idiot. 'That sounds familiar,' he said, his pride wounded. Already the memory of what he'd seen up there was fading – he couldn't picture it clearly – but he'd been scared out of his wits.

Her lips were pursed, but he thought he could hear a hint of warmth in her tone. 'It's okay. Your mind plays tricks out here at the best of times. Try to ignore them. To not give them a foothold.'

His chest was still heaving, and now it was accompanied by the shameful sense of his own naïvety. He'd felt that way around his father plenty of times – that was his father's specialty. 'So you're saying it's nothing,' he said, not entirely managing to hide his fear.

'No, I'm not saying that,' she countered, her voice firm. 'There's plenty to be worried about here. I'm just not so sure it'll make itself so obvious.'

'But I saw something.' It had felt like a dream, the thing coming for him, its inhuman way of moving, as though every limb had been broken and painfully reset. 'I'm not crazy.'

She held his gaze. 'Okay,' she said a little more warily, glancing up the hill again with a thoughtful look on her face. 'Stick close to me this time. Next time we'll face whatever's out here together.' And, after a pause, '*If* there's anything out here,' she added.

After that he was her shadow: they moved as one through the darkness, slower now, their breathing in unison. With her he felt a safety he couldn't define. Not the safety of the house, closeted, cushioned and confined – but something more daring. He was trusting her with his life.

The path to the village was steeper than he'd imagined. From the house, the hill seemed to undulate gently; up close it dropped away into steep slopes, the path underfoot slippery with rotten leaves and animal scat. He kept his gaze on her alone, trusting her footsteps, not concentrating on the twists and turns.

She walked with grace, as though her steps were ordered, although how he didn't know – the branches overhead had become a thick tunnel, and they might as well have been descending into the bowels of the earth.

The silence was intense: no animals rustled in the leaves now, no foxes cried out in the distance. Only the two of them, descending into the underworld, bound together like Orpheus and Eurydice.

When he saw the sky overhead again it felt like a miracle. He was astounded at the sight of lights below, the village tucked in the hollow at the bottom of the hill.

By the time they passed the houses on the village's outskirts, they'd both been silent for several minutes. He was certain they were being watched. The windows of the cottages on either side were blank, square pools, but in the lightless void behind them he felt as though he could detect movement. Up ahead a few houses were illuminated, their oil lamps casting gauzy squares across the path, although when he and Emily passed there was nobody inside.

'Where is everyone?' he said, lowering his voice on instinct. How incongruous it sounded among these flat, practical buildings. His family might have built this place, but in name only: it was raised by others.

'Drinking, most likely,' she said matter-of-factly. 'The Hare.' She nodded towards the end of the street, where a tall, solidly built house stood with its lights burning. His apprehension must have been more obvious than he'd hoped, as Emily raised her eyebrows. 'We're early. Coach isn't here yet,' she said. 'Either we can wait in the pub, or we can wait in the street.'

'This wasn't the plan,' he muttered. 'Somebody will see us.'

She glared at him. 'You came up with the plan,' she hissed. 'It's on you.'

He sucked on his teeth. 'I don't like this. At all.'

'Nor do I,' she said sharply. 'But ask yourself this: if anyone comes looking for you, where are you going to be more obvious? Inside or outside?'

He glanced over at the door of the pub, the sounds of conversation from inside. The night was dark, clouds scudding across the moon, and God only knew what lurked in the shadows. 'Let's get inside,' he said.

At the door she put her hand on his chest and a finger to her lips. He stared down at it, still startled by her ease with physical contact. 'Remember,' she said. 'Stay quiet.'

'I'll not speak unless I'm spoken to,' he said tersely.

'That's not what I said,' she shot back, but as she did the door was flung open, colliding with her elbow and sending her stumbling backwards. A man peered round it, wearing a rough linen shirt and a dark waistcoat in what looked like moleskin.

'She alright?' he said, addressing James. There was no concern in the man's voice: he asked as if by reflex, perhaps not even expecting a response.

'I'm fine,' muttered Emily tightly, clutching her arm. 'What the hell were you doing?'

'Aye, well,' he said with a shrug, not meeting her eye – his gaze lighting on James again for a moment, with a glimmer of recognition. 'Your parents might have taught you not to listen at doors.' There was the faintest smile on his lips, or maybe it was a sneer, the sign of an argument he thought he'd won.

'You first,' said Emily, nodding to James. Her face was still set in a grimace.

His first thought was how crowded the room was: he'd not imagined there were so many people in the village. They were an odd mixture, the best dressed of them seated at tables next to old men in rags, and James was startled: he'd thought the villagers as a homogenous mass, existing only to work, thinking with one mind.

The room had a surprisingly high ceiling, oil lamps suspended above each table. It felt more like a firelit drawing room than a bar – James felt like he was trespassing. This was something more civilised, more orderly, than he'd been led to believe. He couldn't tell if his father had been naïve, or deliberately misleading. Then again, he wasn't sure when his father last visited the village: he'd spent weeks shut up in that room of his, at least as far as James could tell, and whenever James had peered through the cracks in the wall he'd seen the old man at his desk, poring over his papers or with his head in his hands.

He felt the pressure of Emily's hand on the small of his back, pushing him forward, and let her lead him to the long wooden bar, behind which stood a tall, skeletal man whose brown hair was swept in a neat parting. In different attire he could have been one of his father's old hunting companions: there was the same austere bearing, the same faded nobility.

'Haven't seen you here before,' he said, running his tongue over his teeth. James knew then he'd been recognised, and all without saying a word, but the barman knew to keep his mouth shut for now, at least. God only knew what he'd tell his customers later.

'No,' said Emily, appearing at James's side. 'He's just passing through.'

The barman gave a tiny, barely perceptible shake of his head, fixing Emily with a stare that felt oddly cruel. 'You're back from the big house,' he said, more a statement than a question.

Emily met his gaze with a stare of her own, but behind it James could see a flicker of hesitation, a momentary break in her hardness. 'Just visiting,' she said. 'Can we get a drink?'

The barman nodded, took two pewter tankards from a stack at his side. 'Who's your friend?' he said while he poured their ale. It was a dark, peaty brown, not wholly pleasant.

'He's a mute,' she said in a bored voice, hardly trying to hide the lie. 'Family sent him to the country to recover, for all the good it did him.' She slid a couple of coins across the bar. 'City isn't kind to folk like him.'

The barman turned his sunken, watery eyes onto James, fixing him with that same glassy stare, weighing up Emily's story. He seemed satisfied, sliding the tankard over to James, who nodded in acknowledgement. 'Strange things happen in the countryside,' the barman said, with a low chuckle. 'Mutes finding a voice, blind eyes seeing.' He gave a thin-lipped smile. 'Course, you've got to want it enough.'

James could feel the man's eyes on them as Emily navigated a path through to a corner table. The flickering lights threw strange, sooty shadows on the walls, each of them seeming to shift and distort quite independent of their originator. At the next table along there was the clatter of dice, four grimy-looking men in threadbare jackets playing a game whose rules James couldn't make out. He sat with his back to the bar, shackled to Emily's lie.

'Why did you tell him I was mute?' he hissed, trying to keep his body as still as possible, to hide any sense they were communicating.

'Had to tell him something,' she said, taking a long drag from her tankard and grimacing. 'Would you rather I'd let him ask your name?' She glanced around the bar, her eyes hooded and her scowl deepening. 'Look at this place,' she muttered into her beer. 'There's nothing left here. They're fleeing like rats on a sinking ship. In ten years maybe this village won't even exist.' She snorted. 'We can dream.'

James tried to follow her gaze, but nothing stuck out to him. It was all too new: he had nothing against which to orient himself. 'You think it's that bad?'

'I think people used to hope things would get better,' said Emily bitterly. 'They don't do that anymore.'

'That was never what my father intended,' said James, staring into his own beer. 'He thought he was setting them free, showing them another way.'

'Yeah, well he was wrong,' said Emily, taking another long pull on her beer. 'Maybe he didn't know it at the time, but he was.' She sniffed. 'I'm not saying it was good back then, James, because it wasn't. Still – people knew why they were here.'

'Maybe you ought to slow down on that a bit,' said James, nodding at her tankard.

'Don't you worry about me,' said Emily, with another big swig. 'I can handle my drink perfectly well, thank you.' She swallowed and then set the heavy mug down on the table with a clank. 'They gave him their children, and he held back the void,' she said. 'There's something almost poetic about it.'

'It's monstrous.'

Emily snorted. 'You think there aren't kids starving to death in York as we speak? Not even any purpose to a death like that. In the cities there's children dying just because some factory owner gets greedy, and sees an easy way to maximise his profits.'

He studied her face, bewildered. 'Then why are you running away?'

'Because it's all broken,' she said with a sigh. 'There's no saving this place, not now. Your father saw to that.' She paused, thoughtful, and then seemed to make up her mind; she drained her beer in one swallow. 'Listen,' she said, 'you want to start again, and I think you might even manage it too. So you're my best hope of making it out there.'

'I'm sorry, Emily. I truly am.'

Her smile was a sad one. 'It's not your fault. It's your old man's.'

At that, the grimy man on James's right turned to him with a dawning realisation. 'You're him,' the fellow said, laying a hand on James's arm. 'Harringley's eldest.'

James knew then that he should have told Emily to keep her voice down – he'd felt the risk and brushed it off as anxiety, a mistake he'd not make again soon. 'What's it to you?' he said, trying to muster a confidence that he didn't feel. He shook the man's arm off his coat.

'What's it to us?' said the head of the table, amused. He was a stocky fellow with a mass of greasy curls – Ephraim Miller. James recognised him as the village butcher: he'd been up to the estate, on occasion, bringing his produce. 'What's it to us, he says.'

'As if he doesn't even know,' echoed one of his drinking companions.

'Know what?' said James, trying to sound angry instead of just scared.

'Know what your father did to this place,' said the grimy man, shuffling his chair closer to James's. 'You should have died like the rest.'

'Easy enough to put that right,' muttered Miller, rising from his chair – and as though they'd planned it in advance, his two companions grabbed James's arms and twisted them behind his back. 'Hey!' he yelled, but they were much stronger. 'Somebody – help!' Across the bar, he saw a few faces turning, but none came for him; only Emily followed, chasing Miller as his lackeys dragged James through the bar and into the street.

'I'm begging you,' James heard himself plead, 'let me go. I've done nothing to you.'

In the light from the bar he saw Emily, furious, grabbing at whatever part of James's captors she could reach. 'Let him go, you sons of whores,' she spat, clawing at their faces, their shoulders, their lapels. 'You can't do this to him; he's no use to you now, he's too old—' For a little while they tolerated her blows, but when she managed to catch one of the men in his eye he grabbed her roughly around the arm and shoved her to the ground. She looked briefly affronted and then was up again, pushing herself out of the mud, haranguing him. 'You know his father will have you thrown out of your houses for this – I hope you like living in the streets—'

Miller's lackeys were shoving James down the main street, out beyond the lights of the village into the dark. 'We're not afraid of him, nor you,' said Miller without looking back. 'We've seen real fear.'

'Oh you have, have you?' said Emily, her tone designed to wound. 'You've seen him?' She followed Miller, shaking her head. 'You haven't seen him,' she said. 'If you had you'd know he'd want nothing to do with this. He works in the shadows, not the light.' She stopped, then, hands on her hips, her face a sneer. 'My guess is if he saw what you're doing in his name, you'd be dead before you even knew it.'

And then James saw Ephraim Miller turn, and the knife in his hand. 'You've no idea what we've given up for him,' he said grimly.

Emily stared him down. 'You're not going to use that,' she said, not even glancing at it. 'If you do, you'll be even more fucked than you are now.'

'We have a chance to finish this,' said Miller in a pained tone. His eyes were closed, his chest heaving. 'All of this. Just walk away.'

'Maybe I won't,' said Emily. 'Maybe I'll tear my dress and then march back into that room and cry rape, and see who's willing to turn a blind eye to something like that—'

And that was when Miller dived at her with a cry of rage, stabbing and stabbing and stabbing. James saw Emily fall to the ground, gasping in shock. The night seemed to close around them.

'What is that—?' said one of James's captors, glancing out at the village green. Out in the darkness there was a strange writhing, the shadows seeming to teem as though alive, the air prickling with energy like it might before a lightning storm.

'There's something out there,' muttered Miller, and he was right. There amidst the darkness were figures: black like obsidian, crouched like enormous hounds. They were all angles, and yet when they moved they had a terrible, casual grace. James could see perhaps half a dozen of them, poised and ready to pounce.

In the dim light he could see Miller's henchmen had gone pale. 'What the fuck are those things?' one of the men said, dropping James.

Miller stared out at the things. 'They're – beautiful,' he said. 'The children of the void.' Perhaps he was still thinking that when they rose from their haunches and began to walk towards him, but even without faces James could see the malice in them. On the road next to Miller, he could hear Emily choking back blood.

A moment later and Miller's henchmen were scattering, and yet somehow Miller was still there, staring at the sight – and then came the sound of a rushing wind, sending a swirl of dust blowing across the village green, and there was a figure behind the creatures, tall and spindly as a tree in winter. At once they stopped moving, instead bowing their heads to touch the earth as he lifted his expressionless face to the heavens and the darkness seemed to clothe him, forming itself into a tailcoat, a top hat – and into something that could almost be flesh and bone.

And then there was a voice that seemed to come from the wind, that was at once everywhere and nowhere.

PAY NO ATTENTION TO WHAT THEY DO IN MY NAME, the Tall Man said.

Ephraim Miller was staring ahead of him with his eyes wide. 'Good God,' he muttered. 'I never dreamed I'd get this – this honour. I never, ever believed I'd see your face—'

BE GONE FROM MY SIGHT. I DO NOT KNOW YOU.

'My lord,' said Miller, his head bowed. 'I've brought him to you. The Harringley boy.'

The Tall Man lifted his arm, and for a moment nothing seemed to happen – and then, from out of the darkness, James saw the creatures begin to move. Their limbs made only the faintest of whispers, like a breeze at midnight, and so at first Miller didn't notice. Only at the Tall Man's silence, and James's stare, did he think to turn.

'No,' he said, and in his voice was real dismay. 'No, I did everything you asked.' He was backing off now, as one of the creatures approached, stretching out those strange, angular limbs towards him – and in the moonlight James could see pulsing ripples spreading across Miller's back, as though more limbs might burst from it at any moment. 'Please!' he said, and it was as much a cry to the void as it was to the Tall Man, but there was no mercy in either.

And then, in agony and terror, he fled back to the safety of the village.

The Tall Man was still watching the grim tableau unfolding before him, his sightless eyes gazing down upon James and Emily from a great height. James didn't look at him – he had eyes only for Emily, saw only the ribbons of flesh covering her guts, the blood pooling beneath her.

'She's hurt,' he said, without turning to the Tall Man. 'Really hurt, I think.'

The Tall Man stepped out towards Emily, his footsteps making no sound, and knelt beside her. WILL YOU LET ME HELP? the Tall Man said, and James answered right away.

'Of course. Anything. Anything you want. Just don't let her die.'

But the Tall Man only looked up at him with those blank, sightless eyes, and right then James knew he was not the one being addressed.

MY CHILD, James heard him say in that voice of infinite serenity. WHAT HAVE THEY DONE TO YOU? He ran a hand across Emily's brow and she seemed to stir, as though rising from a deep sleep. Her eyes flickered open and she lifted her head perhaps half an inch. CHILD, the Tall Man said again. YOU NEED NOT FEEL THIS WAY. TAKE MY HAND AND I WILL LEAD YOU WHERE SORROW IS BUT A DISTANT MEMORY.

Emily breathed in, deeper than before, her eyes opening properly now. One side of her face was a striated mass of blood and dirt. 'You know my answer,' she croaked.

The Tall Man nodded, implacable and unfazed.

THEY WILL SUFFER FOR WHAT THEY HAVE DONE.

'They said they were acting in your name,' James said, and Emily's head snapped towards him, the effort making her wince.

'You can see him too?'

'I've seen him for years. I thought you knew.'

Still on the floor, she shook her head, her mouth hanging open. 'Never.'

IF I LEAVE YOU HERE YOU WILL SURELY DIE, he heard the Tall Man say. YOU DON'T DESERVE THAT KIND OF DEATH.

'It's not your choice,' she said. 'If it's my time then so be it.'

When the Tall Man spoke again his tone was the same as ever, but something had changed: there was a new tension to him, a barely disguised anger. YOU ARE BEING FOOLISH, he said.

'Maybe I am,' she said.

'Emily,' James heard himself say. 'Come with me. I can get you back to the house. Get you help.'

NO, said the Tall Man, turning to him. I'M AFRAID THAT IS NOT TRUE AT ALL.

'You've no power over either of us,' James said, with a false confidence he was certain the Tall Man could see through. 'Just what are you planning to do?'

I'M NOT YOUR ENEMY, the Tall Man said.

Right then two dark shapes stepped out from a doorway, a man and a woman, and James knew one of them in an instant, knew him before he stooped to kiss the woman on her neck. Knew his proud bearing, and knew the low murmur of his voice.

His companion was the first to spot the girl lying prone on the floor, and to scream – but when James's father turned to take in the scene, his eyes lighting a moment later on his son, he had no doubt who he was looking at. Even in the gloom James could see his consternation.

When his father opened his mouth it was to bellow. 'Stay away from him,' he roared, his words echoing; it had to be deliberate, an attempt to wake as many people as possible. Then he was next to James, between his son and the Tall Man, talking to the man of shadows. 'I never promised you anything,' he said. 'You've no right.'

The Tall Man only laughed, a hollow sound, eerier for its lack of echoes.

YOU TALK OF RIGHTS AS THOUGH YOU UNDERSTAND THE MEREST FRACTION OF THIS WORLD'S LAWS, the Tall

Man said. YOU HAVE NOT THE FAINTEST UNDERSTANDING OF WHERE THE SPARROW LAYS ITS EGGS, NOR THE FATE OF THE THISTLE CRUSHED UNDERFOOT.

His father's companion, trembling in a doorway, called over to him, her voice shrill and unrefined. 'Who are you talking to?' she cried, but his father didn't answer. Instead he strode across the street, towards where Emily lay on the ground, and knelt next to her, his teeth bared as though he were the one in pain. 'Can you walk?' he said. He kept glancing over towards the Tall Man, suspicious of his motives.

Emily swallowed hard, and tried to sit up. 'I – I'm not sure. Sir,' she said, with a grimace. Her voice had changed: she was talking to the master again now, putting her best foot forward. 'Maybe.'

'You,' his father called, turning to James over his shoulder. 'Help her up.'

'She can't go far,' James said. 'You didn't see what Miller did to her.'

'I said lift her up, for God's sake,' snarled his father. 'We can't stay out here a moment longer.' He was glancing round wildly, searching the shadows, but James could feel in the air that the Tall Man was gone, the shimmer of his presence departed. James knelt and tried to lever his shoulder beneath Emily's arm; he was amazed at how heavy she was.

Emily howled as they hauled her upright, her legs useless beneath her, but somehow between James's strength and his father's they managed to keep her from stumbling. One step, two steps, three. All the while James felt his father's presence next to him. So his father still had desires — James might never have believed it had he not seen it for himself.

Four steps, five, six. He heard the harsh rasp of his father's breathing, felt Emily sag beside him. 'This is madness,' his father said, his tone low, grumbling and familiar. 'I can get her to the inn myself, but it won't be enough. She needs proper medical attention, and I'll be damned if I trust her life to anyone in the village. You'd best run up to the house and get help.'

He stopped then, his father still moving, Emily hanging between them with a low groan. 'He doesn't want her,' James said. 'He wants me.'

There was a flash of anger in his father's tone when he next spoke. 'You're no fool, James,' he said, as if by saying it he could make it true. 'He claims there's no other way. But I know you well enough to know you won't fall for his lies.' He swallowed hard. 'But plenty have,' he said, his jaw set, 'and I have to bear some responsibility for that. If she dies, her blood will be on my hands. So go and fetch some help. And for God's sake, go quickly.'

James nodded, his head spinning. His feet were already in motion when his father called after him once more. 'I can trust you with what happened tonight, yes?'

'You can trust me,' James said without turning, and in that moment he meant it.

Back, then, into the darkness, the only things visible that tight tapestry of branches, the trees closing in on all sides. The night darker than he thought possible. Praying his foot would not stumble, leaving him stranded out there in the trees. He didn't want to think of Emily now, whatever shell of her was propped up on the edge of the village.

There was something in the woods, something that had been there long before any of them, before the house and the family line. Now he thought he could hear it, the echo of his own footsteps, stalking him, matching his pace – impossible to see clearly, of course, to make out anything beyond what the lamplight revealed, but sometimes you didn't need to see clearly. Sometimes the truth was there in the corner of your eye, the movement that happened when you weren't looking directly. There were dark figures there, figures in rags, their bodies angular and distorted, their smiles cracking at the edges.

Enough. He concentrated on his footsteps. Eyes down, ignoring the branches raking his face, the suffocating pressure in his chest. Picking out the next step, the marks of his own footsteps illuminated one by one as he approached them, tracing a path between the thick roots criss-crossing his path. Focussing on his breathing, on forcing out another breath. Letting the sound fill his consciousness.

From somewhere in his mind came a bass note, a swirl of half-recalled phrases, wrenched from context and assembled into the form that provided most comfort. *Lord, protect me. Lord, guide my steps. Though I walk through the valley of the shadow of death… your word is a lamp to my feet and a light to my path.* So the priest had taught him something after all.

Not that it had helped Emily. But now wasn't the time to think of her, to think of who she'd been and what might still remain of her after tonight. Keep walking, he reminded himself. For now that was the only duty he owed.

By the top of the hill he was exhausted, as spent as if he'd been walking for days, the cold seeping into his bones and his head pounding. In the distance the lights of the house were hazy smudges. Being back on the estate felt strangely comforting, although he could not have said exactly when he'd returned to the land that was once his birthright.

Even that was an illusion, of course: one could no more own land than one could own the wind. Still. It was a comforting illusion.

He went back to his prison voluntarily; he went back to his prison on instinct. Ransford led him up to his room, his head spinning, the bile still in his throat. All those years his father claimed to be righteous, and for naught. The hypocrisy turned James's stomach.

He wasn't sure how long his father had been going with whores. Once was an obscenity; anything more was monstrous. Yet when his father entered with shirt open at the neck and his overcoat hastily thrown on top, James neither screamed nor raged. Instead he let the old man speak, though it was more than he deserved.

'I don't know what you think you saw,' his father said, not meeting his eye. 'But you should never have been there, do you understand?'

'Of course,' he said, barely able to look up, his words just a whisper. His father's jaw was clenched and he looked unsure whether to be furious at his own carelessness or his son's impetuousness. He decided on the latter.

'Maybe you think me a fool, James,' he said, with a little sigh. 'But you're in here for your own safety. You saw for yourself what the villagers are like, how they feel towards us.' He shook his head. 'I should have prepared you better. I should never have put you in that position.'

He looked his father straight in the eye. 'I want to see Emily.'

'You should never have been seeing her in the first place,' his father said, his frown deepening. 'Please tell me that's the end of it.' He raised his eyebrows, waiting. 'God forbid there's some bastard child I need worry about.'

'Oh, you want to talk about that now?' James half-yelled, more furious than he could ever remember being. He'd never spoken to his father this way. 'Then let's. You first.'

'It's not the same,' said his father, his anger cold. 'Maybe one day you'll understand.'

James gritted his teeth, appalled still further by his father's hypocrisy. But the old man held all the power in this house: if he wanted to leave James in the dark about Emily, dismiss her to the care of a family member so James never saw her again, his father could do it with a word. James swallowed back his fury, tried to speak calmly. 'Tell me she's alive. Emily.'

'She's alive,' said his father gravely. 'But she's terribly injured.' He put a hand to his head. 'My God, James, the stupidity of what you did tonight. They're savages, those men. The doctors are having to stitch her back together.'

'But she'll be alright.'

'I don't know that,' his father said. 'I'm wary of promises I can't keep.'

James felt his breath tremble in his throat. 'Can I see her?'

His father hesitated for what felt like a long time; it almost seemed a flicker of empathy might break through his hard mask. 'No,' his father said. 'I don't think it's wise for her to come back here, even if by some miracle she survives.'

'That was my choice,' James said. 'I talked her into it.'

'Maybe so,' said his father. 'But that makes you as much of a danger to this family as her.' He closed his eyes and sighed. 'People will talk after tonight,' he said. 'They already tell stories about us. God only knows what they'll make of my own son trying to run away. They'll think you went in search of that – that demon.' He paused, and when he spoke again it was with greater resolve. 'I can't let anything like this happen again.'

James swallowed back nausea. 'Father,' he said. 'No. You need to let me out of here.'

'My boy,' he said, taking a step towards James and speaking with something like tenderness. 'If I could do that, I would. Please believe me.'

'Please,' he heard himself say. 'This is no kind of life.'

His father stared at him for a long time and then, with a tired smile, placed a hand upon his shoulder. 'It's late,' he said. 'Let's talk about this tomorrow.'

He closed his eyes, knowing the battle was lost. 'Of course,' he said. When he opened them again his father was already locking the door.

20

H IS FATHER didn't come the next day, or the next; James's only contact was with the hired help. He ate in his rooms, dragged himself through a book of *The Odyssey*, all the while wondering why he bothered.

When he did encounter his father, the old man wore a pained expression — he could not bear to stay long, would not meet James's eye. He was afraid, James thought, that his son might humiliate him — ask after Emily, or plead with his father to let him go. He needn't have worried. James understood what propriety required of him.

In spare moments he dreamed of speaking with his father as an equal. His father answering not with his usual, commanding voice but in a low, compassionate tone. It had to be possible. He'd seen that man when his father thought no one was watching, seen the emotion welling up in him.

He imagined the old man laying a hand on his arm, asking him what he'd seen, his eyes filling with tears as James recounted why Miller had cut her open.

I'm sorry, he'd say. Let me explain…
No. Even in dreams it was inconceivable.

He spent days drafting the letter. He'd leave it in his father's study, at the heart of the old man's sanctuary. By design it was a mass of contradictions, forceful but humble, reasoned but emotive, deferential but commanding.

> *Father,*
> *You must forgive me. Like the younger brother in the parable, I've spent years blinded to your goodness; but you are good, gracious & merciful. I know you've given me a dozen more chances than I deserve. Now I must ask your mercy once more. I was a fool to run – not understanding why you kept me confined, believing you thought me weak, even dangerous. Now I know otherwise. Now I know what lies out there: I've seen the world you've kept me from.*
> *How much you've given up for me & my brother. I can scarcely conceive of how you raised us without our mother. I've loved you too little, showed you too little of the obedience and respect you are owed.*
> *You've taught me, in this house, to love wisdom & the Lord – whose nature is to have mercy, even when doing so seems the rankest foolishness. Find it in yourself to forgive me.*
> *I ask that as your son & humble servant,*
> *James*

He crept through the walls when his father was at breakfast. On either side of him, the frame of the house, and behind it the low murmurs of conversation, the creak of footsteps.

He didn't dare remain in his father's study more than a minute, wasn't sure what he'd disturb if he picked through the old man's research, what system there was to the chaos. For now, at least, James could deny he'd ever been in the room — claim the servants had left his letter on the desk.

He listened at the door for his father's footsteps as he climbed the stairs after breakfast, waiting for the gradual fading that marked the turning down to his study. Tried to stay calm while he waited for a reply, for the sound of his father's steps drawing closer and a knock at the door. He couldn't settle in his chair, couldn't focus on a book, as everything seemed in perpetual motion — until, after what felt like an eternity, he heard the sound of brisk steps and saw a single folded sheet of paper thrust into the room.

His father's reply was just six words long:

This is for your own good.

When he read it he felt his resistance break with a tangible sensation, like an elastic band snapping. He'd heard that message before, a dozen times, a hundred, but its bluntness, the bald fact of the words on paper, undid him.

For some people, despair came like night falling. Not for him.

He wanted to burn this place to the ground — or if not this place, then his father's hopes for it. He'd failed this family, the old man had made that abundantly clear, and there was nothing left for him here. No future, no blessing, no peace. But there was a way out of here. He removed Emily's key from his pocket, marvelling at its weight in his hand. He thought of how she'd opened the passage: running her hands across the panels until she felt the tiny keyhole. Later she'd put her hands atop his to show him the way, and steered them until he found what he was looking for.

He was alone now, but no matter – she must have known this day would come. He closed his eyes, summoned up the memory of Emily and that first day she pulled back the panels, and placed his hands flat against the wall. It took him a matter of seconds to find what he was looking for, and when he opened his eyes there was a rectangle of pure darkness in front of him, the wood panelling set to one side.

He took a step backwards, the weight of what he was planning heavy upon him – he'd leave this place forever, strike out alone – and he was overcome by practicalities. He'd need clothes, money, food – he couldn't just run, would have to plan—

And then came the sound of the door opening, and before he could think any further he was running into the darkness, running with a sense of elation so strong that it could almost have been terror – he was so close to being out of here, free of this place—

Even as he thought it, as he felt the waves of euphoria crashing over him – he was free, free at last – he felt something dive upon his back, his father leaping onto him, sending him clattering to the floor. His jaw hit the ground first, followed moments later by his arms, and a searing pain bloomed across his whole body, eclipsed only by a mingled humiliation and fury the likes of which he'd never before experienced.

Ignoring the pain in his wrists, he pushed himself over and found himself looking into the face of his father, intense and purposeful, his teeth gritted, his eyes hard.

'You little fool,' his father growled, 'don't you understand a thing?'

And at the disdain in his father's voice James rallied, pushed up towards the old man and caught him off balance, sending him staggering back into one of the high armchairs, the impact causing him to wince. 'I'm doing this for your own good,' his father said tightly, and that was when he picked up his own walking stick, a mahogany cane carved in an uneven series of concentric spirals, and strode towards James—

Somehow James got his arm up in front of his face, and blocked his father's first blow with a forearm. He recalled the pain of it, blinding him, overwhelming his senses, and then before he could turn and run, before he could regain his equilibrium, the blows came again and again, on his shoulders and into his sides, then, finally, on to his head.

He assumed after that his father had stopped, although he'd never know whether someone had stayed his hand – Ransford, maybe, or one of the servants. It hardly mattered. When James woke in his bed the next day, he caught himself wishing the old man had hit him hard enough that he never regained conscious.

After those six weeks, when the pain had faded a little, the Tall Man came to James again.

WHAT DO YOU WANT? he asked that night, and James answered without hesitation.

'I want you to take me away from this place.'

He was no fool. He knew what he was asking. But he couldn't live this way anymore. No friends, no future, no hope. He might as well be dead.

From the shadows he thought he saw the Tall Man smile.

COME WITH ME, he said, and offered his hand.

21

Now he was losing Emily all over again. She vanished into the warren of streets behind the inn, black as the void, and he couldn't have followed her even if he'd wanted to.

But it wasn't fear he saw in her eyes now. It was resolve. She'd not let anyone catch her, because if they did they'd try and shut her up, try and bury the story she had to tell. Nor would she ever let herself die in the gutter of some nameless back street: if she was going to go down, she'd make sure people wondered about it, puzzled over exactly what happened.

He still couldn't believe she'd lasted this long, scratching out a living in this manner. She'd worked as a labourer, a baker, even the tutor to a young girl for a while – but not here, not in the village where they knew her. She came back periodically, every month or two at most, to hear what had happened in her absence, never staying long enough for them to catch her, running if anyone noticed her, all the time whispering in the ears of those who looked like they might have met with some dark figure in the shadows.

'Most of them don't remember,' she'd told James. 'Nothing ever comes of it.' She cocked her head. 'But you – you're different.'

He had to let her go. If she needed him, she'd find him. No matter that he needed her. That wasn't how this worked. He'd a task now. Take the book and get out of here. Make sure the world heard Janey's story. And, for good measure, stop the Tall Man from being able to hide in the shadows ever again.

It was approaching midnight when he sat down on his bed and undid the ribbon around the manuscript, spreading the pages out on the covers before him. Tonight he hardly heard the scratching in the walls: he read in a flurry, flipping through the text with a horrified fascination, testing it against what he knew in his gut.

The pages were crumpled and scrappy, Emily's writing a haphazard scrawl. She must have scribbled down Janey's story at pace, as though fearful of being interrupted. In places James couldn't even decipher it, kept stumbling over the misspellings and the spidery script. But it was true, of that much he was certain. Any reader would see it right away.

When he read in those pages about what his brother had done, he knew – as though by divine revelation – that whatever was in this place went deeper than heredity. It was in the soil itself, leaching away the sanity of the villagers and then making them forget there had ever been another way. He felt its rottenness, eating him from the inside out.

What a fool he'd been to come, to think that by reasoning with his family he could undo all those years of pain. He wasn't strong enough to overcome it alone. But Emily was right: the presence here bred in darkness, sprouting in the hollows of a man's soul, and it wouldn't survive the light. If he told Janey's story, people would come – would begin to talk about this place, to dig up census records and speculate – and the scrutiny would destroy whatever dwelt here. Its power would drain away, and maybe it would starve, or maybe just move on elsewhere, but either way they'd be free.

He wrapped the manuscript carefully and set it inside his bedside table. There'd be no more coaches tonight, but by mid-morning he'd be gone – on his way back to the city, and Gabriel, and an end to all this.

He fell asleep almost immediately, a weight lifted from his chest.

22

H<small>E WAS</small> woken before dawn by a frantic knocking. He opened his door to find the barman, his shirt creased and his waistcoat hanging loose, stubble speckling his cheeks. There was a hollow, glassy look in his eyes.

'Beg your pardon, sir,' said the barman, rubbing a hand across his forehead, 'but something's happened up at the house.'

James was instantly alert. 'What do you mean, something?'

The barman's eyes were down, and he was shaking his head back and forth as though in denial. 'One of the servants came down, sir,' he said, 'asking for Whittell. Something about a missing child.'

'Janey's child.'

'No, sir,' said the barman, with a heavy sigh. 'I'm afraid not. Your brother's child.'

'My God,' murmured James. 'Have you told Whittell yet?'

'No, sir,' said the barman. 'I thought you'd want to know first – being family and all – so you could go to your brother.'

'Of course,' said James, laying a hand on the man's shoulder.

'Now wake the inspector too, would you? They need him up there urgently.' He was already halfway down the corridor, powered by adrenaline and trying not to lose himself in terrible imaginings, when the barman called after him.

'Won't you want to head on up with the inspector, sir?'

James shook his head, spoke without turning. 'There's no time. Edward needs me.'

For a moment he even believed it himself.

Nobody answered the door for him when he rang. He opened it himself. The hall was deserted, an eerie pall hanging over it, and the opening door sounded thunderous among the silence. He hardly dared walk these halls – already he felt like an interloper.

He didn't notice his brother at first: he walked right past the drawing room before he registered that the figure slumped forward in a low armchair was Edward. His brother was unnaturally still, and when James entered the room he looked up slowly, stiffly, as though he'd not shifted his position in hours. When James met his eyes, he saw Edward's gaze was glassy and vacant.

He looked so desperately sad and unwell that for a moment James almost forgot to be angry at him – and then the memory of what he'd done to Janey came back with a tangible force, and James had to hold back his rage.

'Edward,' he said coldly, approaching his brother's chair, 'we need to talk—'

'No – no,' said Edward without looking up, his voice as

tremulous as though he'd spent a whole night outside. 'I can't –
I'm sorry…'

James moved round to the front of his brother's chair,
looking down at him, but still Edward wouldn't meet his eye.
'I know what you did to Janey's son.'

'What does that matter now?' said Edward, his voice choked
with tears. 'She doesn't matter. She never mattered. But he's
gone – my boy is gone.'

'You're a bloody fool, Edward,' he said, taking a breath to
steady his trembling hands. 'But even if you brought the Tall
Man back here somehow, there might still be time.'

Edward was shaking his head, a strangely mechanical gesture.
'You were right all along, James,' he said with a sigh. 'Father
was a fool – and me, I was the worst of fools—'

James raised his voice without even meaning to. 'What does
that mean?' he half-yelled.

'My God,' said Edward, and now tears were streaming down
his face. 'My God…'

From behind James came the sound of footsteps crossing the
hall, and he turned to see Sophia entering the room. Her face
was at once exhausted and expectant, but at the sight of James
her shoulders slumped. He wondered who she'd been expecting.

'He's been like this all morning,' she said matter-of-factly.

'Sophia,' James said. 'I'm so sorry.'

Her smile was half-hearted and automatic – a gesture of
pure habit. 'It happened last night,' she said, looking in James's
direction without actually meeting his eye. 'I went in to see to
him, and he was gone.'

'Gone?'

She nodded. 'Gone,' she said, and then something caught in her throat, and she swallowed hard. She closed her eyes, put a hand to her neck. 'Oh God…'

He wanted to put a hand on her shoulder – anything to help her, to show her he was here with her – but propriety forbade him. That was another thing he'd done away with in the slums. He didn't miss it.

'I swear I heard nothing,' said Sophia, half to herself. 'I'd have killed anyone who laid a finger on him.' There was a shudder in her voice, her emotions threatening to break through despite her best efforts.

Behind them, James could hear his brother quietly weeping. He wondered if Edward had wept for Janey. Somehow he doubted it.

'I know,' said James, keeping his eyes on Sophia to stop his fury boiling over. He'd seen this coming, hadn't he – he'd known this was a risk, they both had – and yet when it happened it was inconceivable, unimaginably awful.

She glanced up at him with watery eyes. 'I always wondered what I would do if anything ever happened to him. I thought I'd die.' She sighed. 'It turns out you just go on.'

He thought of Janey too, dead and cold, her body horribly distorted. He fought back an image of Sophia bleeding out in the drawing room, a shard of broken vase in one stained hand.

'Don't talk like that,' he said firmly. 'We'll find him.' He glanced around. 'Where's my father?'

Sophia took a breath. 'He's upstairs,' she said – and then,

drawing closer to James, she said in an undertone, 'Edward's locked him in. I think he believes your father's involved with this.' Her voice was desperate. 'Surely he can't be. Can he?'

'I don't know what to believe anymore,' said James. How could Edward have been so stupid? He'd no doubt his brother's folly had drawn the Tall Man's eye, but he couldn't believe Edward had been so blind to the risks. He wondered if Sophia felt the same.

Before he could press any further, there came a knock at the front door. Sophia glanced up right away. She took a deep, steadying breath, attempting to force her face into its usual composure, and after a few seconds she crossed into the hall with brisk, composed steps and opened the door without waiting for Ransford.

In strode Whittell, upright and business-like, without even a hint of deference. At the sound of footsteps Edward glanced up, but didn't stand. From the hallway, Whittell shot him a brief, quizzical look, but didn't dwell on Edward's impoliteness. He turned instead to Sophia.

'Ma'am,' he said, acknowledging both Sophia and James with a nod. 'I hear there's a child missing.' He didn't need to say *another child*: that boy's shadow was already there, hanging in the air.

'That's right,' Edward called over, without looking up. 'He vanished last night.'

'Someone took him, you mean,' Whittell said firmly. 'Children don't vanish, sir. At least in my experience.'

In his chair, Edward was already shaking his head –

apparently he'd seen enough of Whittell to make up his mind. 'What use are you, man?' he said scornfully. 'You don't know a bloody thing about this place.'

'Edward!' said Sophia, as if she were rebuking a small child. She turned to Whittell, gave a tiny bow. 'Please,' she said. 'Let me show you my son's room.'

But Whittell was still studying Edward. 'Will your father be joining us?' he said. 'It's awfully strange to see him absent in a time of such grief.'

Edward grimaced. 'My father's not a well man, sir, as you know' he said in a tone of distaste. 'Age isn't kind to any of us, but this shock – it's been a lot for him.'

'I'm sorry to hear that,' said Whittell slowly, 'but all the same…' There was a glint in his eye; perhaps it was simply impatience, but it looked almost as though he was enjoying this. 'I think we need to be clear that a person did this. Someone in this house.'

'With respect, Inspector,' said Sophia with a sigh, 'my father-in-law was locked in his room all last night. There's no way he could have done this.' James thought he could hear a note of disappointment in her voice. 'Unless you have some other evidence of his involvement?'

'Not at all,' said Whittell genially. 'But surely you can see it seems mightily strange that he's not here with the rest of you, at a time like this.'

Edward threw up his hands in exasperation. 'Go and find him then, if you must,' he said. 'Although you won't get any sense out of him, I assure you. Any of our servants will swear he's not himself. He's confused, prone to blackouts. He can barely remember what he did yesterday.'

Now Whittell bristled with irritation. 'Where is your father, sir?'

'He's still locked away upstairs,' said Edward. 'I don't want him near me.'

'You needn't see him again, sir,' said Whittell, cocking his head. 'But I'm afraid to say that I must. It's my duty. And I won't – nay, can't – let you refuse me.'

'What exactly are you looking for, Inspector?' said Sophia.

'You say your father's ill,' said Whittell to Edward. 'Has he been violent? Has he made threats towards the child?' Now he turned to Sophia, exasperated: 'Evidence, ma'am, that's what I'm looking for. In my experience, even the mad don't commit acts of violence without a reason. No matter how unhinged their justification might be.'

'Well, he's certainly not going anywhere,' muttered Edward. 'You might as well go and see my son's room first, for all the good it'll do you.'

'Very well,' said Whittell, his gaze lingering on Edward just a moment longer than was strictly necessary. 'We can do that first. But I won't leave here without seeing your father, you hear?'

James saw Edward bristle at Whittell's tone, but he could hardly rebuke him – not after he'd treated the man so shabbily. He didn't follow Sophia as she led Whittell upstairs, and for a moment James considered staying with his brother too, grilling him on what he'd done. Perhaps he might have, were it not for the look of suspicion that Whittell shot him before leaving the room. Whittell had trusted him this far, but his faith could easily curdle.

The child's room had the air of a place not long departed – the toys and rocking chair still warm, the dust not yet settled on anything. On a low table by the crib sat a stack of books that the nursemaid must have picked out to read the previous night.

Sophia had arranged this room, that much was clear. It was bright and modern, a far cry from the heavy panelling elsewhere in the house, and there were no shadows anywhere. Whittell took it all in without emotion, fixing his meticulous attention on everything in turn, searching for anything out of place.

When Whittell spoke he addressed Sophia, without turning to acknowledge James. 'Only yourselves and the servants have access to this room?'

'That's right,' said Sophia.

Whittell ran his tongue over his teeth. 'How could your father-in-law have gained entry?'

Sophia shook her head sadly. 'He's the head of this house, Inspector. I can't suppose any of the servants would dare deny him a key to his own property if he asked.'

'But then surely they'd know what happened,' muttered Whittell after a moment, rubbing his chin. 'Someone here would know.'

He began to walk slowly around the room, his footsteps tracing a pattern James couldn't discern: he seemed to turn at random. He stooped, ran his hands along the walls, knelt to the skirting board. The frown on Whittell's face was eloquent: there was nothing.

After several silent minutes, Whittell gave a faint, irritable sigh. 'So there was nothing unusual last night,' he said to Sophia, 'nothing out of the ordinary?'

'No, Inspector,' said Sophia vaguely. 'Nothing at all.'

Whittell was silent again, rubbing together his thumb and forefinger, and then he seemed to decide on something. Turning on his heel, he spun to face James. 'And you, sir,' he said, raising his eyebrows. 'Tell me again exactly how you came to be in the house this week?'

For a second James almost felt betrayed: surely he'd given Whittell enough that he didn't deserve this treatment. 'This has nothing to do with me,' he said.

'I never claimed it did, sir,' said Whittell, his eyes narrowing. 'Only that I've determined you're not a resident here, that you've recently arrived from the city – and at a time like this, that in itself seems rather unusual, don't you agree?'

James felt an irrational panic stirring in his chest. 'I – I received a letter,' he stammered.

'Saying?'

He had to stay calm, not let Whittell rile him. He'd done nothing wrong.

'It's as Edward told you,' he said, keeping the tremor out of his voice. '*Father's ill, he's not himself, he's calling for you. Come soon.*'

'Hm. You'll recall I received a letter too, in a lady's hand. Almost as though someone were trying to draw attention to what was going on here. As if they wanted someone to intervene.' Whittell's eyes were still narrowed, his tone calm and collected, although when he spoke James saw him glance over at Sophia to check her reaction. 'Why might your father have been calling for you, do you think?'

'I suppose you'd have to ask him that,' said James, a little defensively.

'Oh, I fully intend to,' said Whittell with a grim smile. 'But I'm interested to see whether his view tallies with your own.'

'Come on, Inspector,' said James. 'You know I didn't do this.'

'I know no such thing,' said Whittell with a hint of steel. 'And, you see, this is my job. To pursue every avenue, every possibility, until, by a process of careful deduction, I reach the truth.'

'Every avenue?' said James.

Whittell actually groaned. 'I hope you're not going to trot out that confounded superstition again, sir.'

'You mean the Tall Man,' said Sophia, and James stared at her, amazed.

'That's right, ma'am,' said Whittell wearily. 'I've heard enough about the fellow to believe this whole village unhinged. But I'm yet to be convinced.'

Sophia gave a tiny cough; tiny, but forceful. Whittell motioned for her to speak. 'You'll have to forgive me speculating,' she said quietly. 'You don't think one of the servants – acting on his authority – could have taken him?' She shuddered. 'Could they have snatched him away because of his status, his name?'

'That's not how it works,' said James, without thinking, and everyone was silent.

Whittell was the first to break it. 'I beg your pardon?' he said, sounding appalled, his reserve momentarily forgotten. James had gone too far this time: there was no turning back now.

'You heard me, Inspector,' he said, more assertive now. 'I've seen the Tall Man. He wouldn't send an envoy. He'd come himself.'

'Good grief, man,' said Whittell, his face reddening, 'get out of here.' He jerked his head towards Sophia. 'Stop filling this woman's head with your tawdry nonsense.'

'It's not nonsense,' Sophia burst out. 'If I thought it was, I'd never have written to you—' But James hardly heard her. He was staring Whittell down, unfazed by his scepticism and determined to be heard.

'And what if I could show you?' he said. 'What if there were evidence?'

'There's no such thing,' Whittell spat.

'So much for pursuing every avenue.'

Whittell's face was set in a grimace, his hands clenched into fists at his side. 'I'm not sure I like your tone, sir,' he said.

James reached into his breast pocket and Whittell flinched, as though planning to leap in front of Sophia and protect her. With a single, slow movement, James removed the metal key from where it had sat so long next to his heart.

'You wanted answers, Inspector,' he said, and strode across the room, finding the keyhole with his fingers without even needing to look. With a single turn of the key, the wall panel clicked backwards, and James slid it open to reveal that familiar rectangle of darkness. 'I'll take you to him,' said James. 'I might be the only one who can.'

23

SIX WEEKS after James's father broke his leg, the Tall Man asked him, WHAT DO YOU WANT? and James answered, 'I want you to take me away from this place.'

That night, in the shadows, he thought he saw the Tall Man smile. COME WITH ME, he said, and rose from the darkness, seeming to attain form, to become taller, more defined, offering his hand to James.

The long, thin fingers felt like they were coated in dirt, but they bore no calluses: it was the hand of an unlikely labourer, a gentleman not used to manual work. James hesitated for only a moment before letting the Tall Man pull him from his bed and to his feet.

He wasn't sure how the Tall Man noiselessly opened the passage in the wall with no key, or how the darkness of that passage seemed somehow deeper than all that surrounded it. Couldn't understand why his footsteps made no echoes, or why the familiar cold of the tunnels seemed absent, replaced by a throbbing warmth like he was inside the veins of some great body. He found he no longer cared, no longer tried to trace the route along which the Tall Man led him as it corkscrewed further and further away from the house, its stone giving way to soil and roots.

There was a peace in this: to submit to someone who was not his father, to give himself wholly in trust to a fellow who, by that time, he'd come to know as a steady presence. He heard again his father's warnings – the Tall Man was a liar, a trickster who promised a world he couldn't deliver – and found he no longer cared. He'd seen the roots of his father's rhetoric in his composition books: it was dried up now, belonging to a different world and a different time.

God only knew he'd tried to be the man his father wanted him to be.

YOU'RE SURE YOU WANT TO DO THIS, the Tall Man said.

'I'd not be here otherwise,' he answered.

I WANT YOU TO THINK.

'I am. I have. I've made my choice.'

HMM.

Was it then he felt the first creeping tendrils of fear, began to realise what he'd done? He saw all this clearly once more: he was surrounded by darkness on all sides, his trousers nicked and torn, spattered with mud.

He felt the house above him, but couldn't orientate himself, and felt a terrible, choking dread like a man drowning. He'd believed himself able to escape, but now he saw this all for what it was: not courage but capitulation. To the Tall Man he said nothing, but the Tall Man knew – James was certain of that.

When the tunnels finally began to gleam with reflected candlelight, marking out a stairway curving down into the earth, James should have felt overjoyed. Purified.

How he wished he could have felt it.

WE'RE HERE, said the Tall Man, beginning his descent.

James said nothing. He was acutely aware of his own smallness, and felt a kind of terror at all he'd left behind: the only world he'd ever truly known.

'Tell me about it again,' he said.

The Tall Man turned. There was no anger in his expression, but James felt the pressure of his gaze, those blank, searching eyes. IN THE NEW WORLD YOU'LL BE A KING, he said, LIKE NO KING YOU'VE EVER KNOWN. OWNING NOTHING, BUT POSSESSING EVERYTHING. LIVING NOWHERE, BUT MAKING THE WHOLE WORLD YOUR HOME. DO YOU UNDERSTAND WHAT I'M OFFERING YOU?

What had made such sense in the house now seemed a jumble of incoherent thoughts. There was nothing to it; it was without foundations, nothing he could hold in his hand.

'I want to see,' he said.

COME, said the Tall Man, offering his hand again to help James down the steps. On one side of the tunnel the roots of a huge tree had worked their way down like great gnarled pillars, had knotted and split in the process. Here, beneath the earth, the silence was total: there was no shuffling sound of movement, no dripping water.

At the bottom of the stairs was a raised dais, upon which was a small basin. It had a strangely organic appearance to it, as though it were carved out of the earth itself, but it had been polished to a high sheen. Across it danced the reflection of candles set in hollows in the walls.

YOU HAVE SEEN THIS PLACE IN DREAMS, said the Tall Man from behind him, and when he said it James knew it to be true.

'This is where it happened? Where you – you – killed them?'

The Tall Man paused a moment, but it was not a hesitation; it felt almost as though he was offended by James's suggestion. I TOLD YOU THEY BECAME LIKE KINGS, he said. LET ME SHOW YOU.

And the Tall Man spoke syllables that were as old as the world in a voice lower than a tremor – ancient sounds that James felt within his marrow – and the walls began to uncurl themselves.

The figures were huge and black and angular, perhaps ten or eleven feet tall. Their limbs grotesquely elongated, their joints somehow misaligned, and their faces blank masks. When they moved towards James they made a low rustling sound like scraps of paper blowing in a breeze, a sound that could have been soothing in isolation had it not seemed to surround him. They turned towards the Tall Man and knelt in something like a bow – and there were dozens of them, perhaps hundreds, more peeling off from the darkness even as James watched.

THEY HAVE TAKEN THE VOID INTO THEMSELVES, said the Tall Man. THEY GREW UP IN DARKNESS, AND IT DWELLS WITHIN THEM NOW. IN THIS, THEY HAVE SAVED THE WORLD.

There was a hideous, numb dread in the pit of James's stomach.

DO YOU SEE, NOW, THE FORCE OF THIS PLACE? ITS POWER?

Still James could not speak, could not run.

I CANNOT HOLD THIS BACK, said the Tall Man. THAT IS NOT WITHIN MY POWER. He was silent a moment. DO YOU SEE NOW THE NATURE OF YOUR FATHER'S ERROR? THE BLIGHT HE BROUGHT UPON THIS LAND?

'There must be another way,' James heard himself mutter.

THERE IS NOT. THE VOID IS INSATIABLE. IT IS WITHOUT COMPASSION.

'I can't,' James said, already trying to will his feet to turn and carry him out of this place. 'I won't do this. This is – it's monstrous.'

The Tall Man hesitated only a moment. VERY WELL, he said then. BUT YOU WILL NEVER LEAVE THIS PLACE.

And then the Tall Man did something James hadn't predicted. He stepped forward and took James by the wrist. PLEASE, he said, pulling James towards him with a startling strength, as though he'd wrestle him down into the pit. YOU MUST UNDERSTAND THE IMPORTANCE OF YOUR SACRIFICE.

James tried to pull back, but the Tall Man's grip was strong, and he found himself stumbling in the dirt, falling to the ground while the Tall Man remained rooted. 'You said I had a choice!' he yelled.

YOU HAVE MADE THAT CHOICE ALREADY, said the Tall Man, beginning to drag James across the earth.

'No,' said James. 'No, I refuse.' Digging his feet into the ground, scrabbling for purchase, occasionally catching somewhere but succeeding only in hurting himself. 'Please!' he heard himself shout again, as the Tall Man pulled him deeper underground, his hands flailing around for a handhold, until at last they found one: a long, tough root dangling by James's side. That was all it took to pull the Tall Man up short, and what James needed to wedge the rest of his body into the dirt, bracing himself against the Tall Man's efforts.

The light at the tunnel's base was stronger now, rippling like sunshine on a river's surface, and from somewhere James heard the distant sound of laughter without malice. It was beautiful, somehow, and he felt a sudden rush of melancholy for a life he'd never known.

The Tall Man turned, the candlelight flickering over his face, and when James looked at the Tall Man's hands they were cracked at the joints, flakes falling away from them like ashes. COME WITH ME, he said, his tone still cold even as his words became more and more agitated. I BEG YOU.

And then he reached down for James, and James bit him hard, puncturing the skin – except it wasn't skin, it was something like thick paper, and what his teeth collided with was not muscle and bone but a different material altogether, with the loamy taste of soil and the hardness of polished wood, at once familiar and utterly inhuman. The Tall Man let out a howl of pain and released his grip, just a fraction, and it was enough: James was on the ground, and then he was running, away from the light and back into an unfamiliar darkness.

∽

He had no guide now. Whatever route he'd taken with the Tall Man was a mystery. These tunnels were far from the house, their construction organic rather than rigid; there was no muffled sound of conversation on the other side of a wall, nothing but James's footsteps and the sound of his breathing. Somewhere at his back he felt the Tall Man, but he was certain he was not being followed – it felt only as though the Tall Man was watching him with eyes able to penetrate the earth, an infinite sadness in them.

There was a chill in his bones again now, his shins painful from where they'd collided with the walls; his head was throbbing, his throat parched, his only solace being that if he died he would at least die free. Every step was a fight. Every step an effort. He was fighting to return to a place he didn't even want to be – imagining his father on the other side, arms folded, wearing a look of utter disdain at this ragged, dishevelled young man he'd once called his son.

He was not sure how long he'd been walking when he saw the light: a different light to the one he'd seen far beneath the earth, dim and grey, without even a hint of luminescence. At first he thought he'd imagined it, dreamed up an escape – but he groped his way towards it nonetheless, like desperate men the world over, and found himself rewarded with the sight of a tangled thicket of branches and thorns.

Before him sat the ruins of an ancient fire, and on the rock walls were scratched hundreds of chalk symbols. He'd been here before, a child stumbling across a vagrant's cave. Even now it felt like a dream, but he'd never been so glad to see the woods.

The path ahead of him was overgrown with thorn and briar, snagging him, blocking his path, sticking in his arms, legs, torso; it would not yield to him as it had as a boy.

He'd never understood this world. He was not sure he ever would.

There was nothing left for him at the house, he knew that. It held nothing for him. There was only his father, his father's world, and if he didn't want the Tall Man, nor did he want what the old man was offering him: prestige, a name, a boundless store of wealth. It was too high a cost; already he felt himself shaking off the weight of that name. He'd not be that man. That man had died out in the darkness.

He'd known what he was running from; maybe he'd just never known what he was running towards. It was not the Tall Man, he knew that much. James had seen that strange light glowing far beneath the earth, those symbols carved into the walls; he'd felt the heady strangeness of that place, but it was not the kind of salvation he needed.

What little he'd understood about this world he'd learned from Emily, and she was gone now too. How ludicrous his father would think him now, streaked in blood, every item of his clothing tattered and ripped. How little his father knew about his son, about this world, about anything.

He'd lost all sense of direction in the woods. He no longer knew which way was home. But there was a patch of lesser resistance here: a path which yielded to his touch, that didn't fight back. Pitch black, suffocating, pointed on all sides, he found himself channelled, moving again, more gently and tentatively than before. Testing the thorns against his flesh, learning when to halt and when to move. Ignoring the pain that stabbed into him with every step.

It was the strangest kind of freedom he'd ever known, but it was freedom, nonetheless.

When he emerged from the trees it was mid-afternoon, the sun setting over the village. He couldn't have travelled more than a mile, but by his reckoning the journey had taken nearly six hours, carving deep scratches into the leather of his shoes and the skin of his chest and arms.

He did not look back up the hill towards the house. He'd not have been able to see it even if he had: the woods were at his back, blocking all view. But his gaze was fixed firmly forward. Towards the village, the main street, and the carriage that would take him out of this place, never to return.

24

JAMES SAW Whittell flinch when he rolled back the panel and revealed the tunnels beyond. It wasn't hard to see why: the darkness was total, the corridor stretching off into eternity.

'This place you're taking me,' Whittell said, peering into the impenetrable gloom. 'It's some sort of secret room?'

'No,' said James. 'It's on the estate. I think.'

'It's not part of the house?' Whittell sounded disappointed, and it wasn't hard to see why: if they were part of the house, they'd be on the blueprints, and blueprints meant evidence.

'It's deeper than that,' said James. 'Down in the earth.'

Whittell stopped then. 'You're kidding,' he said. 'So all those years, people could have been coming and going into this house, unseen?'

'You don't know houses like this, Inspector.'

'You'd be surprised,' Whittell said, sounding faintly bitter. He was still as calm and collected as ever, but behind his furrowed brow James thought he detected a deeper anxiety. 'And where do these tunnels come out?' Whittell said after a moment. 'If there's an exit, that means there's an entrance somewhere.'

James studied Whittell's hard, solemn face. Even now the inspector thought this was the work of a villager, a vagrant. He'd never talk like this if he'd seen the Tall Man for himself, seen the shadows resolve themselves into a darkness deeper than dark.

Whittell caught him watching, held his hands up as though in surrender. 'I don't mean to be dismissive,' he said, 'but you really do have to consider every option. What if you've imagined it all, and there's nothing magical here? Merely a set of servants' passages?' He stopped, as though startled by his own harshness. 'Forgive me,' he said, 'because I know this is hard – but isn't it possible that you might have been mistaken?'

James didn't acknowledge him. Every ounce of his strength was focussed on maintaining his resolve. He wanted to run back to the comfortable life he'd built a hundred miles from here – not to step back into that beckoning darkness. But if he ran, nothing would ever change.

'I'm asking you to trust me, Inspector,' he said quietly. 'If you want to know the truth, this is how to get there.' Whittell didn't argue back, and James supposed that was a good sign. 'Now I'm going to ask you to stay close,' he said. 'I don't want us to get separated.' Whittell laid his hand gently on James's back, and James felt the man's fingers tighten on his shoulder, his presence retaining just the trace of a threat.

'This is madness,' he heard Whittell mutter under his breath. 'Madness.'

There was no need to tell Whittell to stay close. He dogged James's heels, his oil lantern crashing against James's hip, the low rasp of his breath a constant presence. He kept up an occasional stream of conversation, too, as though to reassure himself James was still there – or maybe to keep him amenable, as protection against being abandoned down here.

'You know your way around all of this?' Whittell said after they'd walked for perhaps ten minutes, down endless twisting corridors. In his voice was something like awe.

'That's right,' said James, although he wasn't sure how. This time he knew the way even without the Tall Man leading him. Knew when they were leaving the confines of the house, felt the timber frames giving way to tunnels curving down into the earth. Maybe some part of him had always known how to get back here.

'How?'

'I've had a lot of time to explore.'

Whittell thought a moment. 'Who else knows about these tunnels?'

'Just me and Edward.' He could feel Whittell staring at him even in the darkness. 'There was somebody else once,' he said. 'One of the servants.'

'And they can still come and go as they please?'

'No,' he said. 'No, I can't imagine she'd ever come back.'

He couldn't say how long they'd walked for before they saw the first glistening reflections of candlelight. He'd felt it, though, long before it appeared – that swelling warmth in the earth, the stillness on all sides. 'We're close,' he murmured to Whittell. 'No need for the lantern now.'

'I certainly hope so,' came Whittell's gruff reply as he killed the flame.

When he saw those rippling waves of candlelight across the walls, James felt a thrill within his breast. He'd found this place by himself, followed the thread of his memories back to the Tall Man. In the dirt at his feet were the boot marks from the last time he'd come here; there were no traces of the Tall Man's footsteps, of course.

Even Whittell looked startled at the top of that stairwell, dazzled by the strange quality of the light. 'My God,' he said. 'You were telling the truth.'

James ignored the slight: he still felt that swell of pride in his breast. 'Can't you feel it?' he said. 'It's extraordinary.'

Whittell snorted, a tiny noise of doubt. 'You want to tell me what I'm going to find down there?' he said. 'Or shall I find out for myself?'

'It's – it's strangely beautiful.' James found himself paralysed, his feet once more unwilling to move, and he hated himself for it. 'There aren't the words.' He sighed. 'See for yourself, Inspector,' he said, resigned. 'You've come this far.'

With a single curt nod, Whittell set off down the steps, leaving James where he stood. How many nights he'd dreamed of returning to this place, but today the flickering candlelight revealed a detail his mind had blotted out: a floor made of bones, thousands and thousands of tiny bones, skulls and ribs and legs, stretching down to an unfathomable depth.

His breath caught in his throat, his whole body beginning to shake with a sensation like drowning, when he heard Whittell exclaim, 'Dear God.'

Under the shock, his voice was infused with wonder. For there, in the centre of the room, laying in a black font atop a raised dais, was Edward's son – stark and pink amongst all that darkness, sleeping peacefully amidst the accumulated wreckage of his family's past. 'He's still alive,' muttered Whittell, and before James could stop him, he was bounding down the steps, his feet crunching across the bones, his arms outstretched to scoop up the child.

He didn't see the shapes peel themselves out of the shadows, impossibly tall and black like jade, stalking towards where the child lay. There were two of them – and then three, four, five – and in seconds it seemed like the chamber itself was made of glistening, angular figures.

They reached the dais before Whittell, and the first swept him across the room with a single swipe of its spindly arm. He went flying into the wall, colliding with the earth with an almighty thud that sent dirt tumbling onto white bone. The second creature swooped down upon the child, scooping it up into a tight embrace that seemed almost maternal – it clutched Edward's son to its breast, shielding its head from the unfolding chaos.

The child was awake now, squalling and crying in the creature's arms, and there was no sign of Whittell stirring in the corner where he lay.

James hurled himself towards the second creature, but its companions encircled it. He lifted his cane, aiming at the nearest creature's upraised arm, and put his full weight behind the blow – but when it landed it felt like colliding with hard wood, the shock of it reverberating up his arm. The creature gave no sign that it had felt a thing.

They were massed in front of the child now, Edward's son visible only in glimpses, as though through a tangle of overgrown branches. Again James took aim at them, swinging the cane into what he imagined must be the nearest creature's midriff, but as the blow landed he knew there was no humanity in it, no pain, just a sheer and powerful darkness. A second later the thing grasped James's cane, twisted it in his hand – and he clung on with all his force to this most beautiful of objects, this sign of a life he'd fought for with all his might, but the lacquered wood was beginning to creak and cracks were appearing on its surface—

James stepped backwards, wrenching the cane from out of the creature's grasp, his eyes lighting for just a moment on the lattice of cracked varnish before the light in the pit shifted. Whittell had stirred, was getting unsteadily to his feet, the lantern in his hand swinging crazily. He fumbled with the lantern's door, trying to reach the oil well, then tipped the lamp straight upright, apparently trying to set this place ablaze.

Except what oil Whittell could loose from the lantern was minimal – its collar was high, and any liquid that escaped from it came out in a trickle rather than a gush. And then, before James could yell, Whittell gave a bellow of frustration, took the lantern in both hands and swung it hard towards the creatures, where it shattered immediately. He heard Whittell curse, and then without warning the creatures were coming, the whole room a swarm of angular bodies, and James found himself running for the exit. The floor shifting beneath his feet, his whole world filled with the squalling of the infant and the crunch of footsteps and the creatures' strange, inhuman rustling, like dead leaves blowing across an empty promenade.

Then, miraculously, James felt a hand – a human hand – collide with his back. 'Thank God,' Whittell said. 'Thank God.' His voice was panicked, his breaths ragged.

'We have to go,' James said, hauling him up the stairs. That strange rustling was behind them, getting closer and closer, and it was all too easy to imagine being wrenched backwards and buried down here forever.

'No,' Whittell said, his breath still coming in gasps. James heard him rummaging in his jacket. 'Let me find my tinderbox.'

'No?' said James, stunned.

'No.' The tinderbox rattled as Whittell removed it from his pocket. 'That child is still alive, James. We can get him back.' He fumbled with the tinderbox again and then cursed loudly as it fell to the floor. 'We can still save him.'

But even as he said it, James heard the child's crying come to an abrupt stop. A gasp, and a wet, choking sound, and then a hideous silence.

'No,' said James. 'No, we can't.'

'I won't accept that.' James felt Whittell drop to his knees, scrabbling in the dirt for the tinderbox. But the creatures were coming – James could feel the shimmer of movement in the air, of limbs straining towards them. He didn't hesitate. Grabbing wildly towards where he thought Whittell must be, his fingers lighted on the inspector's collar, and he almost wept with furious joy. He threw his arms around the man, hauling him upright.

'We have got to get out of here right now,' he yelled. 'Tell me you understand that.'

James felt Whittell resist then, felt him pull back, but they were already moving, fumbling through the darkness, one hand on the wall to steady them. He had no idea where they were going, no idea of the way out; he only walked, expecting with every step to be pulled back into the darkness, torn apart, or else wrenched into some monstrous new shape…

When Whittell finally begged for James to stop, they were far from the light. All around them was the chill and dark earth, muffling their footsteps as they hurried through the tunnel. There was nothing following them now – they'd be able to hear it.

Whittell's breath was coming in ragged gasps. He sounded like he might be sobbing. 'We have to go back,' he said. 'There's still hope.'

'There's not,' James said grimly, not even turning. 'That child is gone.'

'How the devil can you be so cold? Don't you care, man?' Whittell half-yelled, and to his surprise James found he was shouting too.

'Of course I care!' he said. 'Of course I do! Don't you see what this means? Don't you see what this says about my family, my bloodline, everything I grew up with?' He took a breath, anger coursing through him. 'That's why I want to bring this down. But we have to be alive to do it, Whittell. What use is it for us to die down there in the darkness with that little boy?'

Whittell sounded somewhat mollified. 'You'll show my colleagues the way down there?' he said, more quietly. 'Even if it destroys your brother's legacy?'

'I think he destroyed this family's legacy a long time ago, Inspector.'

25

WHITTELL WAS silent as James led him back through the tunnels, but it was a brooding, purposeful silence. Some men might have crumbled after what they'd seen down there, tumbling into the void, but James could almost feel Whittell piecing it all together now.

He wondered if they'd let him see Gabriel again, if his co-operation here would count for anything. He doubted it. They'd see him as complicit, and perhaps they'd be right. All these years he'd known about what was happening here and he'd done nothing, said nothing. He'd thought himself brave, to walk away from his inheritance and start his life anew – now he felt like the worst of cowards.

The door back to the house was lit by a corona of light, and when they got close James became aware of the low murmur of activity beyond the darkness. Servants preparing food, changing bed linens – the dark was different here, without the chilly isolation they'd felt as they travelled to the pit. When he finally saw the doorway, Whittell put a steadying hand against the wall, his breaths coming in deep gasps. 'Thank God,' James heard him mutter. 'Thank God.'

'You're sure it has to be now, Inspector?'

'It has to be now, sir. I won't risk losing them. Not after what I've seen.'

James hesitated. He could feel Whittell's anger radiating off the man in the darkness, and rage made people careless. 'You could fetch your colleagues – dig up everything you need.'

'I dare say they wouldn't believe me if I told them,' he said. 'I won't let them bury this.' He sighed. 'Your father and your brother – they're both guilty, sir. Surely you can see that. All those years your father could have set this right, could have told somebody.'

'That's not how things work around here.'

'I'll have them both in handcuffs by the end of the day,' said Whittell briskly. 'We can sort out the details later.' He fumbled on the wall for the release mechanism, listening for the click as the panel released and then sliding it open. After the dark of the tunnels, the midday sun shining through the windows was blinding, and as he stepped out James saw the inspector wince. He recovered quickly, and then he was back to giving orders. 'Ask Ransford to get your father and brother into the drawing room,' he said without turning. 'I'll address them there.'

As though he expects either of them to come quietly, James thought. *After all he's seen.*

As it transpired there was no need to call for Ransford: from round the corner, apparently drawn by the sound of the panel opening, came James's father. His hair was a dishevelled mess and he shuffled along the corridor in a set of navy pyjamas – it was the most unkempt James had ever seen his father.

The old man didn't look Whittell in the eye, muttering instead to himself with an air of preoccupied irritation. His right hand rummaged endlessly in his pocket, and for a moment James wondered if his father was fondling his own genitals. 'No, no,' he rambled, 'no need for Ransford. I'm right here.' He shook his head back and forth. 'And your name is?'

Whittell looked at him quizzically. 'I'm Inspector Herbert Whittell, sir, with the police.' James's father was still wandering past Whittell, heading deeper into the bowels of the house, and Whittell had to physically block his way to stop him.

James's father lifted his eyes to Whittell for just a moment: they looked as rheumy and tired as a bloodhound's. 'Oh yes?' he said. 'Very well, very well.'

But Whittell was having none of it. Before the old man could walk on again, Whittell stopped him with a statement he couldn't ignore. 'Your grandson is dead, sir,' he said firmly. 'And what's more, I think you know it.'

'My – my grandson?' said James's father, his brow furrowed.

'Buried in the pit beneath your estate, along with lord only knows how many others. Sacrificed to some ungodly thing.' Whittell's voice was terse, and it was clear he was fighting back his anger. 'All these years you knew,' he said, his voice rising. 'How did you bear it? How did you keep from tearing this place down to its very foundations?'

James's father turned to him then, a dim sense of being

wronged beginning to prickle at him. 'Do you know this – this man?' he said, his mouth open slightly. 'Is he quite mad?'

Whittell laughed, a harsh bark that felt at odds with the quiet of the house. 'That's awfully convenient,' he said. 'But I'm afraid it won't wash.'

'You're an insolent fellow, sir,' said James's father, scowling. His hand was out of his pocket now, his finger pointed in Whittell's face. 'I don't like insolence.'

'Have you not heard a word I've said, man?' said Whittell, taking a step towards him. James wondered if Whittell might actually throttle his father; he looked angry enough.

The old man called out without turning, 'Ransford.' His voice was hoarse, and surprisingly quiet; it was lost amongst that vast house. For a few seconds, both he and Whittell waited, listening for the sound of footsteps, but none came. He called again then, louder. 'RANSFORD!'

But there was no sign of the butler. James's father shook his head again, vigorously this time, as though trying to shake his memories loose. 'Stupid man,' he muttered eventually. There was a new light in his eyes now, a greater sharpness – perhaps irritation had brought him back to himself. 'I didn't kill my grandson,' he said confidently. 'I know that much.'

'You're certain?' said Whittell, his tone cynical, his head cocked.

'Of course I'm certain,' said James's father irascibly. 'My whole life I've opposed him, my whole life—' He put a hand to his chest, the words catching in his throat. His voice was quavering, barely even a whisper. 'If you only knew how much it had cost to do it.' He paused, took a long breath, but when he spoke again the tremor in his voice was not from age but from anger. 'And you have the temerity to come into this house and accuse me——'

'Whittell,' said James, staring at his father and knowing then that no madness could have ever shifted the old man's stubborn resolve, 'he's telling the truth.'

'Dear God,' exclaimed James's father in apparent despair, slumping forward, his hands flowing through his long, straggly hair. 'Dear God, so he managed it at last...'

And then a voice echoed out into the hallway, arrogant and irritable. 'What are you yelling about now, you mad old fool?' called Edward, and then James heard a sigh, and the scrape of a chair from within the dining room. 'Can't you even let us eat in peace?' he said, emerging into the hall.

At the sight of James and Whittell, he stopped dead. 'Oh,' he said curtly. 'It's you.' He peered at them both and grimaced. 'Where have you been? You're filthy.'

'Stop there,' said Whittell. 'Don't take another step.'

Edward continued walking, crossing the hall to where James stood. His father had taken a step backward, as though to hide himself from view. 'I should have known not to trust you,' said Edward grimly, shaking his head. 'I thought you understood the importance of this family. What happens without us here.'

'Your own son, Edward,' said James, his jaw clenched. 'How did it come to this?'

James's father was still backing away, towards the wall, as

though hoping to ensure nobody could sneak up on him – but Edward paid him no mind.

'You couldn't tell, James?' he said. 'From his study?' He thought for a moment and then answered his own question. 'No, I suppose you didn't think to look at the accounts.' He swallowed hard, as though remembering what he'd seen upstairs left him feeling personally ashamed. 'We're ruined,' he said heavily. 'There's nothing left.' His laugh bordered on hysteria. 'There hasn't been anything for years.' Now he turned on their father, glaring over to where the old man had pressed himself up against the wall. 'All that time he's been waiving the rents, or paying out widows' pensions, he's been hollowing out our foundations. Once upon a time we had the Tall Man's protection, but he threw that away long ago.' He raised his voice, and his fury was undeniable. 'Isn't that right, you old bastard?'

James's father was white, and in his trembling hands he held a pocket knife. 'Get him away from me,' he muttered, 'he's a demon.'

Edward was at his father in two steps, grabbing him by the lapels and slamming his head against the wood panelling. The knife skittered away from him across the floor. 'I did what needed to be done to secure that protection,' Edward spat. 'I did what needed to be done to ensure this family survives.' He released his grip, thrusting the old man from him as though in disgust. 'That's more than he ever did,' he said to James. Their father had slumped to the ground, groaning faintly. His head was thrown back, his eyes vacant.

'So you thought you could – what – bargain with him?' James said. 'With the Tall Man?' He felt like he was trapped in a room with a rabid dog; he hardly dared look away from Edward, for fear of what his brother might do next.

'Yes!' Edward half-shouted. 'You said it yourself, James, he's saved this family more than once. All those people who tried to stand against us and he's worn them down, whispered in their ears, driven them over the edge.' Edward ran his hands through his hair. 'He doesn't have to be a curse,' he said, his voice strained. 'For us, he can be a blessing.'

Next to him, James could see Whittell reaching into his jacket pocket for his heavy iron handcuffs. His eyes didn't leave Edward. 'One way or another, sir,' he said to Edward, 'you're leaving this place with me. You can still leave with your dignity intact.'

'Really, Inspector?' said Edward, rolling his eyes. 'You're going to tackle me to the ground?' His tone was withering. 'You'd never do something that stupid if you knew the consequences.' But Edward was nevertheless watching Whittell carefully, and took a step to the side as Whittell positioned the handcuffs across his knuckles.

'I won't say it again,' said Whittell, moving towards Edward. 'This is your last chance to leave this place with honour.'

Then, from behind Edward, there came a scream. 'Edward, what is this?' shouted Sophia from the door of the dining room, and for perhaps a second Whittell glanced up at her. It was all Edward needed: he dipped down and lunged at the inspector, and as he did so James saw the knife in his hand. At the flash of steel, Whittell jumped backwards too, stepping away from Edward as though he were a dangerous animal.

There was a ringing sound in the back of James's head and for a moment he couldn't place it – only when he saw the doorbell swaying back and forth did he understand. Edward saw it too, and James suspected he was wondering where Ransford was. Whittell seized his chance and leapt at Edward, swinging his iron-clad fist towards his face. But Edward was ready, and sent him reeling backwards with a vicious shove.

Whittell was cornered now, his only escape into the dining room. James could see in his eyes he hadn't realised. 'Whittell,' he yelled. 'Don't let him box you in.'

And maybe it was anger at his brother's betrayal – or maybe Whittell simply thought too long, and too hard, about tactics – but something gave Edward the upper hand. He charged forward into the dining room, his face wild, driving Whittell backwards against the table.

Sophia dived out of his way, screaming – and then all was cacophony, her cries mingling with Whittell's yells and the frantic ringing of the doorbell—

'I'm not a monster, Inspector,' said Edward, his arm against Whittell's throat, pressing him backwards at the waist.

'I think we differ on that point,' said Whittell in a hoarse croak, and then drove his fist into Edward's guts, sending him reeling. Behind them James could see Sophia making her way around the table, fumbling uselessly with the handle on the patio doors and finding no escape.

There was no getting past Edward. Whittell made the most

of his momentary advantage, leaping onto the dining table and sending what looked like a whole roast duck tumbling to the floor – but seconds later Edward was after him, his breathing hoarse and ragged.

Now Edward was on the table too, his shoulder lowered, hurling himself at Whittell – and then, as Whittell landed and spun to face Edward, Edward charged straight at him, driving him back into the wall. Whittell let out a stifled groan, a wheezing gasp, and before he could rally Edward had drawn back the blade and plunged it into Whittell's chest.

'No!' James yelled, but Edward was in a frenzy, withdrawing the blade and slashing sideways at Whittell's guts, again and again, turning them into a mass of wet flesh. Then he was at Whittell's neck, the knife sticking on bone or tendon, forcing Edward to wrench it free with a crack – but surely Whittell was dead by now, his body disintegrating beneath the blows.

James could see his father staring aghast at Whittell's corpse. His mouth opened and closed, mouthing silent words – prayers or profanities, James couldn't tell.

He stared at the dead thing on the floor too, Whittell's features only dimly visible beneath the mess of ragged flesh. Edward was steeped in gore, barely recognisable himself, his hands on his knees and panting heavily from the effort of the attack. He wiped blood from his eyes and looked over at Sophia, who was staring aghast at her husband. Her dress was splattered with crimson and she seemed unable to move.

Edward's jaw was set, his eyes hard. 'He'd have destroyed

this family, Sophia,' he said, looking over at his wife. 'There's
no other way.'

'You destroyed this family,' howled James, his voice full of
despair. In the hall the doorbell was still ringing, and now it was
accompanied by a frantic knocking. 'You were the strongest of
us, Edward, the best of us,' he heard himself cry. 'How did he
get to you?'

Above Whittell's corpse, Edward was swaying slightly.
'Father failed us, James,' he said. 'All those years our family
helped contain the void, and then Father let it loose.' He sniffed.
'It was time to put his error right. To make the Harringleys
into a blessing again.' His eyes were dreamy, unfocussed. 'And
so I gave him what he asked,' he said in a whisper.

Sophia was backing away from him in horror, but there was
nowhere to go. 'No. NO—'

'Don't you understand?' shouted James, his voice hoarse.
'He'll never be satisfied. He'll never stop—'

Edward didn't even glance at him. He was making his way
around the table towards Sophia. He spoke to her in a tone
that, under different circumstances, might have been tender.
'Don't you understand – this is what we're here to do – to hold
back the dark—'

'Don't take another step,' she snarled, backing away.

'Sophia,' he said. The compassion had drained from Edward's
voice now, replaced by something like alarm.

'Say it!' Sophia screamed, her voice echoing in the hall,
cracked and distorted. 'I want to hear you say you didn't kill
our child!' She closed her eyes, looking as though she might

vomit; she ran a shaking hand through her hair, and began murmuring 'no, no', and then something snapped. She glanced up at her husband, a frenzied rage in her eyes, and once more her howl of 'NO!' flowed through the house, seeping into its every panel, saturating it with grief.

And then she was throwing herself at Edward, and he was staggering, falling backward onto the floor – and then Sophia was on top of him, clawing at his face, his eyes. She wrenched at his clothes, keening, as if she wanted to unmask him, or perhaps tear him apart. It almost looked like she might succeed, the strength in her petite form so unexpected that Edward seemed overcome: James saw the panic in his eyes.

'James,' she howled, her voice echoing in the hall. 'Get help!'

James tore out from the dining room into the hall, shouting for help, and flung open the door. There, standing against the morning sun, stood Gabriel, his arm upraised and his face anguished. 'Oh thank God,' said Gabriel, a hand to his forehead, and James's initial joy was swiftly followed by a blinding terror.

'What?' he said, stunned. 'Gabriel, what – what is this?' He was dizzy with fear. 'You can't be – mustn't be—' He blinked hard. 'You should never have come.'

Gabriel looked past James into the house, where Whittell's mangled body was just visible, and where next to it a blood-streaked Sophia was straddling her prostrate husband.

'What in God's name has happened here?' Gabriel murmured, and before James could answer Sophia was up and running across the hall, screaming for help.

And then James was shoving Gabriel out of the door, shouting at him to get her to safety, to get her back to the village and take shelter in the inn – and then Gabriel was turning on his heel, grabbing Sophia by the shoulder and hauling her down the front steps—

And James turned to see Edward coming, charging after his wife like some great slathering beast, his knife still clutched in his hand—

And he felt himself grip the cane – and felt himself bring it upwards with all his force, colliding with his brother's jaw – and then Edward was flying backwards into the wall, the lower half of his face all of a sudden terribly misshapen...

Gabriel and Sophia were still running down that long driveway when James stepped out of the house. For a moment he watched them go – knowing they would be better off far from here, somewhere none of this house's poison could ever reach them.

But as James watched, Gabriel glanced back over his shoulder, and then stopped. He cocked his head, as though trying to make out whether it was really James he was looking at, and his expression twisted into a quizzical one.

He heard Gabriel call something to him, but he couldn't make it out. He took one step out of the house's shadow, and then another – trying to discern Gabriel's voice amidst the thundering in his ears. Gabriel called again, and James shook his head.

Now Gabriel was standing in front of him, putting a hand on his shoulder and leaning close. In his eyes was an infinite tenderness. 'Is it over?' he said.

'I'm not sure it'll ever be over,' James said, and the smile Gabriel gave him was wintery.

Behind Gabriel, James could see Sophia staring up at the house, her shoulders slumped.

'So this is your family,' said Gabriel quietly.

James shook his head. 'Not anymore.'

26

EDWARD'S PRONE form lay against the wall. It hardly looked human – it was a ragged, shapeless mass of clothing, a marionette with its strings cut.

'Is he dead?' said Gabriel, peering at it. Neither of them wanted to go inside.

'I hope so.'

'What he did was terrible, James,' said Gabriel. 'There's no words.'

James didn't answer right away – he was thinking back to how Edward had been when he first arrived, how he'd appeared in his letter. Maybe his virtue had all been lies; maybe it had always been lies. But he wasn't so sure. 'He was the best of us once, Gabriel,' he said finally. 'And the Tall Man still got to him.'

He could feel Gabriel's eyes on him – as though Gabriel could read his mind. 'You're not like him,' he said quietly. 'You got out.'

James felt suddenly, bitterly tired. 'He did it because he was afraid,' he said. 'He couldn't see any other way. And what's more I think Sophia knew it too, in a way she couldn't name.

That's why she wrote to me, and to Whittell. She was trying to save him.'

'There has to be another way,' Gabriel said hotly. 'This can't be it.'

'You've seen the void,' said James. 'It's coming. There's nothing to hold it back.' *It's already come*, he thought. *It's too late.*

Gabriel was silent, lost in thought. 'We have to tell people,' he said after a pause. 'Warn them.'

'They'll never believe it.'

'How are they going to explain what happened here?'

'It'll disappear,' said James, and as he said it he knew it was true. 'Ransford will cover it up, and then the rest of the country will go back to ignoring this corner of the world like it has for the past four hundred years.'

In Gabriel's voice he heard that deep optimism that even now felt like a miracle. 'Somebody will come looking for Whittell,' he said, and he almost sounded as if he believed something so paltry might make a difference.

'Maybe,' said James, flatly. 'But that doesn't mean they'll find him. And it doesn't mean they'll understand what happened if they do.'

Gabriel was silent again then, for a long time. The only sound in the room was Edward's ragged breathing. When James looked up, he saw Gabriel staring at him, his brow furrowed. 'We'll make people listen,' he said, laying a hand on James's shoulder. 'You can't carry this alone. I won't let you.'

'You're a good man,' said James, his voice catching in his throat. At least he wouldn't have to face this alone. He sighed.

'But there's one more thing we have to do.'

'Anything,' said Gabriel.

'We have to go back in. I want to make sure Edward pays for what he did.'

They stood before that rectangle of darkness, and James felt Gabriel resist. It was a tiny gesture, like a dog slowing its footsteps at the end of a walk, but James noticed. He was thinking of the Tall Man, and what they'd seen in that strange corner of Newcastle.

'I don't like this, James,' he said. 'Not if – if *he's* in there.'

James sighed. 'He doesn't need me now,' he said. 'He's got Edward.'

Edward was flung over Gabriel's shoulder, his eyes still closed and his jaw hanging loosely open like a ventriloquist's dummy in need of repair. His face was white and he'd made no sign of stirring – but all the same James dreaded seeing those eyes open unexpectedly, exposing his brother's blank gaze.

Gabriel looked as though he couldn't persuade his feet to move. 'I can go in alone if you need me to,' James said. 'You don't need to worry about me.'

'No,' said Gabriel firmly. 'I told you I wouldn't let you do this alone.'

'Come on then,' said James, stepping into the darkness. 'You need to see this.'

He walked until he was sure they were far from the house – until the distant murmur of conversation had faded, and all that was left was chill isolation. He could hear Gabriel's footsteps behind him, and in that sound James felt the absoluteness of Gabriel's trust. Perhaps he'd thought he was walking to his own death, but if so, he'd die with James.

Finally, when he was certain they were deep enough, he told Gabriel to stop. 'You can put him down now,' he said. 'This is where he belongs.' They'd walked for what felt like miles by then, the tunnels twisting into impossible shapes, an endless spiral burrowing down into the earth.

'You're sure about this?' Gabriel said. James could hear the shuffling sound of Edward being lowered down to the ground. His mental image of Edward's terrible, distorted face was dreadful – he almost wished he could see his brother one last time. Gabriel shuddered. 'God, if I woke up here,' he said, 'I think I'd lose my mind.'

James heard the bitterness in his own voice. 'I think that happened already.'

Gabriel took a long breath. 'If it were up to me, I'd burn it to the ground,' he said quietly.

James could imagine that vividly: the house like a beacon on the hill, drawing the villagers like flickering shadows. He could almost see the lines of servants with their buckets of water, beating back at the flames, howling when the upper floors collapsed, or when the flames caught the wallpaper and climbed ever and ever higher.

'What good would it do?' he heard himself say.

'You'd be free of it,' Gabriel said. 'Once and for all.'

He could hear the tenderness in Gabriel's voice, the compassion there, but Gabriel didn't understand. He couldn't.

'No, I wouldn't,' he said, reaching for Gabriel's hand in the dark. 'It's in the soil, Gabriel. It's in my blood.'

Gabriel took his hand and squeezed it, the two of them silent. James could feel a seed of terror in Gabriel, trying to take root, despite his best efforts. 'You're saying you could end up like him?'

'I'm already like him,' James said.

'No,' said Gabriel, his voice choked. 'I won't believe it.'

James held his hand tighter, even as Gabriel tried to pull away. 'I'm better at fighting it than he was,' he said. 'I learned that from my father.'

Gabriel was silent again then, as though not wanting to move on, wanting to thrash out every terrible detail of this family's history. But he sighed, let it go, let the conversation take its course. 'Do you think he'll recover?' he said. 'Your father.'

'I wouldn't bet against it,' said James. 'He's strong.'

Gabriel paused, his voice a little choked. 'I can't believe how close I came to losing you.'

James lifted his hand from Gabriel's, sought out his chest. He pressed a palm on Gabriel's breast. 'I can't believe how close I came to losing myself.'

'Promise me something,' said Gabriel.

'Go on,' said James, a little apprehensive in spite of himself.

'Never come back here.'

He almost pulled away then, had to fight his instincts: he was sure Gabriel must have noticed his hesitation. 'It's my home, Gabriel,' he said, hoping he sounded resigned instead of angry. 'It'll always be.'

'I thought I was your home.'

James sighed. 'That's different.'

He felt Gabriel pull away from him. 'I can't believe this is real. That it all happened down here,' said Gabriel, and James heard an eerie curiosity in his voice – thought for a moment that Gabriel might even ask to see that pile of bones deep beneath the earth – but then he spoke again. 'I don't want to spend another second in this place,' he said.

And so they made their way back into the light.

When they emerged from the walls the house had a familiar hush to it, as if it muffled the outside world. There must have been servants downstairs, whispering about what had happened – but they knew to keep themselves quiet.

All he wanted was to be free of this place. Gabriel was already heading for the main stairs, and James might have followed had his father's door not been open.

'Just a second,' he said quietly to Gabriel, his voice still uncomfortably loud in the hush. He was at his father's door in half a dozen steps, and when he peered round he saw his father sat up in bed, pale and apparently dozing. Across his lap sat a long mahogany tray, on which was placed an open book.

Even at a distance, James could see the bloom of red and purple bruises on his father's crown.

Ransford rose from his seat at James's father's bedside when James came in, gave a slight bow. 'No need to stand on ceremony for me, Ransford,' James said, and the butler nodded, giving James a vague half-smile. 'How is he?'

Ransford looked pensive. 'Your father is somewhat – bewildered, sir.'

'Bewildered?'

A moment's hesitation. 'Groggy. Unfocussed.'

'What does that mean?' said James, peering past the butler. He realised now there was something in the old man's hand, and James could make out the faintest scratching sound.

Scratch, scratch, scratch.

Ransford was blocking the door now, his tall frame seeming to fill all the space. James could hardly see his father now, had to crane his neck to make him out.

'I'm sure it's no cause for alarm, sir,' said Ransford, with an air of quiet assurance that James wasn't sure he'd earned. 'Given the circumstances. Naturally I've summoned the doctor.'

'Can I see him?'

'Of course, sir,' said Ransford, stepping backward.

Now James could see him properly. The old man's normally ruddy face was hollowed out, every jowl and line blasted into high contrast against that stark background. Worse still were his eyes, which seemed entirely unable to focus: one pupil in his eye was blown, a huge black void, and his face was askew.

'Father,' said James. 'Can you hear me?'

His father lifted his head and gave a kind of strangled groan; it wasn't clear who he thought he was seeing. James took a couple of steps closer, still wary. In all these years he'd never seen his father in bed before; he felt the full weight of his transgression. There was the smell of urine from somewhere, but James couldn't see the bedpan. Some part of him still feared his father's fury, knew how much this had to be hurting the old man.

'I shouldn't be here,' said James, taking another step towards the bed. Now he was closer, he could see his father's hand moving across the wooden tray in regular, frantic motions, apparently quite unconsciously.

Scratch, scratch, scratch.

'What is that?' he said, leaning over the bed, and then he saw it. Clenched in his father's right hand, his fingers closed around its bloodied blade, was his father's tiny letter opener. Carved into the wood was a mass of deep scratches, one atop another, spiralling downwards into a ragged black hole. James recoiled, acting on instinct; he should have taken the blade calmly from his father, tended to his damaged hand, but in that moment he couldn't shake the horror and futility of his gesture.

'My God, Ransford, look at him!' James said, steeling himself, leaning across his father's body to prise the letter opener from his hand. Then, with a remarkable grip, the old man raised himself from the bed – only a couple of inches, but it must have cost him a huge amount of effort – and clamped his hand around James's arm.

'Help me,' he snarled, his eyes wild, his teeth bared. 'Please.'

He turned to Ransford. 'You can't leave him like this,' he said desperately.

Ransford's smile was tight-lipped. 'We're doing all we can for your father, sir,' he said, with a faint bow. 'But as you can see, he's most unwell.'

Through the door James could see Gabriel standing at the top of the stairs. There was no life for them here – but this was no way for his father to end his days.

'We have to take him with us,' he said to Gabriel. 'We can't leave him here.'

'He doesn't want to go,' said Ransford tersely, and James looked up at him in astonishment. Ransford's face was grim, his gaze impassive. 'You can check his will, sir, if you must,' he went on, in a level tone that seemed to mask a considerable anger. 'He was quite certain that, in the event of his being incapacitated, he wished to end his days in this house – and be buried in the village.'

'That's not his choice to make,' said James. 'Look at him.'

Ransford took a long breath. 'It's not my place to give counsel, sir,' he said, 'simply to let you know your father's wishes.' He held James's eye. 'He was committed to showing the people of this village there was a better way to live. I believe he thought a similar principle applied to his death.'

'Gabriel,' said James, turning to him. 'Surely you can see I'm right?'

Gabriel's hand was pressed to his forehead, his eyes wet. 'Ransford's right, James,' he said, hardly meeting James's eye. 'You have to let him go.' He'd not even set foot in the room, as though fearful of being contaminated somehow.

James closed his eyes. 'I owe him this,' he said.

'No,' said Gabriel quietly. 'He gave his life to this place. Let him die here.'

James crossed the room, his father's eyes following him the whole way, laid a hand on his father's shoulder. 'I'm sorry, old man,' he said, and he meant it. 'You deserved better than this.' He paused then, made the mistake of thinking about Edward, Sophia, their child, and the weight of it all threatened to overpower him. 'We all did,' he said.

And then, before he could let himself hesitate, he walked away.

He glanced back at his father's window as they made their way down the driveway, and for a moment he convinced himself the old man was there, watching him, but it was just a shadow.

There was nothing left for him here but ghosts.

Gabriel took his hand. 'One day soon this will all be a distant memory,' he said.

How James wished that was true.

Epilogue

FOR A long time after leaving the house he dreamed of Edward, in the way one dreamed of the lost: forever walking away, turning from him. In those dreams he'd tried to stop him, to hold on to him, for what was a dream but an attempt at resurrection, a figment of something already fading from you? But even in dreams he wasn't strong enough; he couldn't persuade his brother. Edward was walking into the forest, he was ascending the long stairs in the hall and dissolving into the light, he was standing at the Tall Man's side beneath a bower of bare branches.

Their pamphlet came out less than two months after they'd fled the house. It was a shabby thing, indifferently printed in a small run, but it did what Emily had asked – it told Janey's story. Within a few days someone from the newspapers had got hold of it, and made the connection to Harringley Manor. A few days later, it sold out another print run, and then another.

James saw the relief on Gabriel's face when he opened the

letter from their publisher. 'It's over,' he said. 'He can't hide anymore.'

And he was right. It happened just like Emily said it would. The village was flooded with visitors – they poured northwards, searching for a network of subterranean tunnels beneath the moors, a pit of human bones. Maybe some of them even found what they were looking for, although somehow James doubted it.

It wasn't over, though. Every morning when he picked up the paper and stopped to read it in the dim light of William's fire, there was another story. An engineer discovered a subterranean city below Hull, an impossible mirror of the city above. On the Alnwick coast, a fisherman ventured into a network of caves and emerged to find a black and glassy ocean on the other side. In Whitby, a brace of goats were born deformed – their hips, shoulders or heads multiplied once, twice, even a dozen times. They were destroyed, but not before James saw the photos.

Before long children started disappearing too. At first they were being taken from the slums, and the papers paid little attention: a tawdry story here and there, the whispers of a darkness stalking the streets. Then the tragedies hit the society pages. That was when Sophia came to find James, knocking on his door late at night with a newspaper in hand.

They'd hid her in plain sight. Gabriel had a friend, a forger, who'd drafted the papers; the biggest challenge was combing the society pages to find a suitable place for Sophia to re-emerge.

There were endless second cousins or wards who'd never been seen in the city – they were running plantations or drinking themselves to death in Parisian brothels – it was no great thing to take on their identity, to step through a door bearing their name.

'Have you seen this?' she said when she was inside, thrusting the page at him. Her face was ashen, and she looked like she'd aged ten years since he'd last seen her. For a brief moment, he felt an unexpected thrill – he'd wondered if he was seeing the Tall Man where there was nothing to see – followed quickly by a numb terror.

'It's him,' James said simply. 'It must be.'

'No,' she said, her voice anguished. 'No, James, it's not.' She put a hand to her temple. 'My God, don't you see what we've done? We've sent them right to him.'

He felt cold fingers grip his heart. 'No,' he said. 'No – they can't be—'

'Janey gave them everything they needed,' she said, her eyes hollow. 'They're doing it to hold back the void.'

'They couldn't – they can't be—' He closed his eyes in dismay. 'How could they read what she wrote and see anything but evil?'

'Maybe they didn't see evil,' she said bitterly. 'Maybe they saw duty. Like Edward did.'

He didn't tell Gabriel at first. He remembered what Gabriel had said the night he'd first encountered the void: *why do you have to bear the weight of this?*

James still wasn't sure he knew the answer to that. He'd run from what was asked of him, refused twice to be a sacrifice freely given. Now someone else had to die instead – someone braver, wiser, more courageous. None of it was fair.

He'd think of his brother that night, in the room he shared with Gabriel, and all Edward had sacrificed. For a moment he'd wonder if the shadows would curl themselves into the shape of a man, offering him the chance to lay down his life.

But this was the world he'd chosen. There was no way back now.

He'd press himself up close against Gabriel then, and try to sleep. And, by the time daylight would come, he might even manage to convince himself he'd made the right choice.

Acknowledgements

Writing a book takes an incredibly long time – far, far longer than I ever realised. *Blight* would never have seen the light of day without the help of a list of people to whom I'll forever be indebted. So, in no particular order:

Thanks to Jordan Lees, who saw something he liked all those years ago when he read my first, mad Ukrainian-war-meets-folk-horror novel and reached out to see if I was seeking representation. I couldn't have asked for more from an agent. Your job seems to be at least four roles in one: part counsellor, part editor, part advocate and part cheerleader (somebody call HR), and I've needed every one of them over the past few years. I can't begin to tell you how thankful I am for your consistent support, encouragement and wisdom. Sorry I've not yet made you millions, but there's time yet.

To Sophie Robinson, my editor at Titan Books, for taking a chance on me. When I first submitted *Blight,* I thought it was in pretty good shape, but your judicious edits have shaped it into something that's better than I could have imagined. I'm grateful for your tenacity, your patience and your insight – thanks for the work that you've put in to get it to this point. (The next book will have fewer em-dashes, I promise.)

To Hayley Shepherd, whose copy-editing skills are second to none. I honestly don't know how you managed to catch all the continuity and geography errors in this book, and I suspect it's probably some kind of witchcraft. Whatever the case, I am in awe of you, and profoundly grateful for the work you did to bash this manuscript back into shape after it had been battered by several rounds of structural edits.

To Julia Lloyd, *Blight's* cover designer, who produced a cover that's better than I could ever have hoped for. From the moment I sold this book, I had a vision in my head of what this book was going to look like – I think most writers probably do – and what eventually materialised is entirely different from that vision. It's also better by several orders of magnitude.

Much of my writing was honed by my experience on the Bath Spa Creative Writing MA, to which I'm indebted to my tutors – among them Richard Kerridge, Gavin Cologne-Brookes, Ian Ross and the late Fay Weldon. But I'm also indebted to the friends I made on that course, who've honed this book, including reading through at least one spectacularly ropey draft, and helped prop me up when I thought I might never finish. Sian, Camilla, Sarah, Liz, Martin, Miranda, Nicola, Toni – you'll never know how much I've appreciated it.

I'd never have been able to do that course without the kind support of my family and extended family, and so I'm forever thankful for their generosity. In particular, I remain awestruck by my parents, whose example is one I'll spend the rest of my life trying to emulate. Perhaps what I'm trying to say is – *Dad, don't worry, this book isn't about you.*

Luke – it's about fifteen years after we first attempted to be a low-budget version of the Inklings in the Eagle and Child, but it finally happened. And you were right. I should have started writing genre fiction years ago. I can't begin to tell you how grateful I am for your ongoing support, both in writing and in life, and the example you've set in getting the words on the page. I also can't believe how exhausting it is to write a book. Nobody ever tells you this.

And finally, to Mel, Ellen and Bounderby, a better family than the Harringleys. Thank you for being a beacon of light after all the time I've spent in the darkness of this book. Ellen – if you're reading this before you're fifteen, you're too young. Bounderby – I'll be finished typing in a minute, I promise. And Mel – sorry for all the nights I left you to watch TV alone while I edited this thing for the four hundredth time. I couldn't have done this without you, and I'm forever grateful to you for letting me pursue this ludicrous hobby. Thanks so much.

About the Author

Tom Carlisle is interested in horror centred on folklore and religious belief. In 2017 he graduated with distinction from Bath Spa's Creative Writing MA, also winning the Bath Spa Writer's Award for outstanding writing. Originally from the north of England, he now lives in Bristol with his family. *Blight* is his debut novel.

The Others of Edenwell
Verity M. Holloway

"Tender, unsettling, and oddly beautiful,
this book is a real heartbreaker."
SFX

Norfolk, 1917.

Unable to join the army due to a heart condition, Freddie lives and
works with his father in the grounds of the Edenwell Hydropathic,
a wellness retreat in the Norfolk brecks. Preferring the company
of birds – who talk to him as one of their own – over the eccentric
characters who live in the spa, bathing in its healing waters, Freddie
overhears their premonitions of murder.

Eustace Moncrieff is a troublemaker, desperate to go to war and
leave behind his wealthy family. Shipped to Edenwell by his mother
to keep him safe from the horrors of the trenches, he strikes up
a friendship with Freddie at the behest of Doctor Chalice, the
American owner of the Hydropathic.

As the two friends grow closer and grapple with their demons,
they discover a body, and something terrifying stalking the woods.
The dark halls of the spa are breached, haunted by the woodland
beast, and the boys soon realise that they may be the only things
standing between this monster and the whole of Edenwell.

TITANBOOKS.COM

For more fantastic fiction, author events,
exclusive excerpts, competitions, limited editions and more

VISIT OUR WEBSITE
titanbooks.com

LIKE US ON FACEBOOK
facebook.com/titanbooks

FOLLOW US ON TWITTER AND INSTAGRAM
@TitanBooks

EMAIL US
readerfeedback@titanemail.com